DATE DUE

JAN 1 9 2008	JUL 0 8 2008
5-2	AUG 1 3 2008
	AUG 2 0 2008
FEB 0 1 2008	SEP 0 8 2008
FEB 0 8 2008	
FEB 2 3 2008	
MAR 0 1 2008	
MAR 2 2 2008	
APR 0 8 2008	
APR 1 9 2008	
5-22-08	
JUN 1 1 2008	
JUN 2 2 2008	

False
Witness

False Witness

AIMÉE AND DAVID THURLO

St. Martin's Minotaur ⚹ New York

FALSE WITNESS. Copyright © 2007 by Aimée and David Thurlo. All rights reserved. Printed in the United States of America. No part of this book may be used or reproduced in any matter whatsoever without written permission except in the case of brief quotations embodied in critical articles or reviews. For information, address St. Martin's Press, 175 Fifth Avenue, New York, N.Y. 10010.

www.minotaurbooks.com

Library of Congress Cataloging-in-Publication Data

Thurlo, Aimée
    False witness / Aimée and David Thurlo.—1st ed.
        p. cm.
    ISBN-13: 978-0-312-32212-0
    ISBN-10: 0-312-32212-7
    1. Nuns—Fiction. 2. Missing persons—Fiction. 3. Catholics—Fiction. 4. New Mexico—Fiction. 5. Monasteries—Fiction. I. Thurlo, David. II. Title.

PS3570.H82F35 2007
813'.54—dc22

                                                                    2007016655

First Edition: October 2007

10 9 8 7 6 5 4 3 2

To Keith. Thanks for believing in us and our Sister Agatha.

And to my sister Silvia Rodriguez and all the Sacred Heart gagas for making me an honorary member.

Acknowledgments

With special thanks to Michael Rissman and Jim Williams for sharing their computer expertise with us. If we made any mistakes, guys, it's our fault, not yours.

And to Diane and Phillip Uzdawinis, who are always on call and ready to help. We couldn't do it without you!

I

T WAS A BEAUTIFUL, SUNNY NEW MEXICO MORNING, and Sister Agatha unlocked the parlor doors in preparation for the new day. Standing on the front step, she gazed back at Our Lady of Hope Monastery. Though it was scarcely grand, she liked to think of the reconverted adobe farmhouse with its new bell tower as God's fortress in a world increasingly determined to forget Him.

Inside, the sisters lived and prayed in quiet seclusion. That blessed stillness, almost always absent on the outside, defined their monastery and became an ever-present companion that drew them closer to the One they served.

Contrary to what some people believed, the locks on the doors and the grille that separated the cloistered sisters from the world weren't there to keep anyone in. They were a line of defense meant to keep the secular world out.

Soon Sister Bernarda, who'd asked for a few moments

alone in chapel again this morning, came into the parlor. Sister Agatha hurried inside, worried about her. She could tell Sister Bernarda had been crying.

"Are you all right?" Sister Agatha asked gently.

"Of course," she answered briskly. "I'm ready to take over as portress. You have other pressing business."

As soon as Sister Bernarda took a seat behind the old oak desk, the phone rang. Externs like Sister Bernarda, Sister Agatha, and Sister de Lourdes were not bound by a vow of enclosure. They were a vital link between the monastery and the world.

Knowing her fellow extern was not ready to talk about whatever was troubling her, Sister Agatha left her to her work and hurried down the hall. When she arrived at the scriptorium, Sister de Lourdes was working at the server—the main computer.

"I'm glad you're here," Sister de Lourdes said with a grim smile. "I've done everything I know to get the computer to work right, but the hacker really messed things up for us this time."

"You'd mentioned that last night at recreation, but then the bells for Compline rang and the Great Silence began," Sister Agatha said. She'd been dying of curiosity since then, but the Great Silence couldn't be broken except in a grave emergency. "You'd said something about letters?"

Sister de Lourdes nodded. "We've received two very disturbing e-mails—one yesterday, another just a few minutes ago. They're both signed by someone named Wilder."

"First or last name?"

"I'm not sure," Sister de Lourdes answered, handing her a copy of each. "But the messages both originate locally, according to the ISP address."

Sister Agatha read the short notes. The first said, "War means casualties. I can deal. Can you?" The next was just as cryptic. "I'm watching you!" Below the signature of that second note was an emoticon stick figure depicting someone looking over a wall.

"He's certainly no poet . . . or artist," Sister Agatha said. "But the viruses he keeps sending are going to create major problems for us with NexCen Corporation. We've got to put a stop to this. Our work for them is about the only thing that's keeping our monastery from going completely broke right now."

"Each virus has been worse than the last," Sister de Lourdes said. "He's stepping up the game."

"We can't disappoint NexCen. There are very few jobs like this one that won't interfere with our schedule of work and prayer. Taking computer orders is something we can do at our own time. But if we keep having problems we can't fix ourselves, NexCen will think we're unreliable and turn the work to someone else."

"God won't let us lose this job. The monastery needs rewiring, and we're in a financial hole. At least the dedicated lines protect the computers. If only we could get rid of this hacker!" Sister de Lourdes said. "The NexCen representative is coming over soon—a woman. She's been given permission to come into the scriptorium to check the software and computers so we can be up and running again soon. I'll see if there's anything she could teach me so we won't have to keep calling them."

"When's she supposed to be here?" Sister Agatha asked.

"She should be arriving anytime." Hearing the clapper, a manual device that resembled castanets, Sister de Lourdes smiled. "Sister Bernarda's calling, so I bet our guest has arrived."

"I'll go," Sister Agatha said.

As she entered the parlor, Sister Agatha nodded to Sister Bernarda, who promptly introduced her to their visitor. "Sister Agatha, this is Merilee Brown, NexCen's senior computer technician."

"I prefer 'head geek,'" Merilee said with an easy smile.

The young woman, a brunette barely in her twenties, was wearing jeans and a loose-fitting green cotton sweater. She wore little or no makeup, and her hair hung loosely in a pageboy style that brushed the top of her shoulders.

"I'll escort you to our scriptorium," Sister Agatha said. "Please remain silent while we're walking through the cloister. Once we're inside the scriptorium and the door is closed, you can speak freely."

Merilee gave Sister Agatha an uneasy, wide-eyed look and nodded. "Okay. Got it."

Sister Agatha gave her a sympathetic smile. "Silence makes continual prayer easier."

Merilee nodded somberly. "I understand."

Sister Agatha led the way and, after they'd both entered the scriptorium, closed the door. "May I get you something to drink? We have coffee, but I personally recommend the tea. It's our own special blend."

Merilee shook her head, her gaze already on the computer screen. "Thanks, but no, I'm eager to get started. Your problem intrigued me."

Sister de Lourdes introduced herself. "The second I hit a key, I got a blue screen and a message in a gray box telling me to hit alt, control, and delete all at once, and restart. But when I did that, it just repeated the cycle all over again."

"Let me give it a try," Merilee said.

Sister Agatha and Sister de Lourdes watched as she repeated the process, then sat back and stared at the blue screen and error message. "Either your startup files are corrupted or you've got a virus. I can get around this with a special boot disk, but debugging might take some time," she said slowly, reaching into a small briefcase and bringing out a set of CDs. "If that doesn't work, I may have to reinstall all the software, including your operating system. That means you're going to lose everything that's stored on your hard drive, so I suggest you back up all of your data files once I find a way around this error message."

Once Merilee got into the system with the emergency boot disk, the two nuns worked quickly and efficiently, selecting every data file and then saving it to a separate DVD. Within a half hour they were done. Then, just as Merilee took their place at the keyboard, the lights in the room began to flicker.

"Do you have battery backups in place?" Merilee asked, her gaze never leaving the screen.

"Yes," Sister Agatha said. "Power to the computers is maintained even if we have a blackout." Just as she spoke, the lights came back up. "Ah there, it's all back to normal," she said with a lot more confidence than she actually felt.

As Merilee began to work, Sister Agatha left her in Sister de Lourdes' care and hurried down the hall. She had a meeting with Reverend Mother this morning. On her way she saw Sister Bernarda in the hallway inspecting the wall outlets.

"Did the lights flicker in the parlor, too?" Sister Agatha asked, quickly joining her.

"Yes," Sister Bernarda answered. "This goes to prove what the electrician said—our main electrical panel is overloaded. I decided to check for overheated outlets."

"I'd intended on asking NexCen for an advance. But with all the problems we're having making our deadlines because of this hacker, now's just not a good time," Sister Agatha said. "I left Sister de Lourdes with Merilee, and I'm on my way to talk to Reverend Mother. Are you okay here?"

"Yes, but would you give Mother a message for me?" Seeing Sister Agatha nod, she continued. "My father was an electrician, and I learned quite a bit from him. I could do the rewiring at the outlets and the light fixtures myself, adding the pigtails and connectors needed to connect aluminum to copper. A licensed electrician would still have to sign off on my work, but maybe Bobby Fiorino will give us a reduced rate if I do the bulk of the work," she said. "Ask Reverend Mother what she thinks."

"I will."

Sister Agatha hurried down the hall to Reverend Mother's office, then knocked on the open door. "Praised be Jesus Christ," Sister Agatha said.

"Now and forever," Reverend Mother answered. "Come in, child." Reverend Mother called all of the sisters "child" according to their monastic custom. As prioress, she considered them all her spiritual children.

Sister Agatha sat down on the wooden chair across from the desk.

"The lights have been flickering again," Reverend Mother said with a sigh.

Sister Agatha recounted the conversation she'd had with Sister Bernarda about the electrical work.

Reverend Mother nodded. "That's a good idea. Go ahead and speak to Mr. Fiorino and let me know as soon as possible if he agrees." Reverend Mother paused, then continued. "That NexCen contract is turning out to be a blessing for us. I never realized how crucial that income would become. That, God willing, will pay for the monastery's repairs."

Sister Agatha started to tell her about the latest problems in the scriptorium, then changed her mind. It was being handled, and she knew that there was something else on Reverend Mother's mind. That was why she'd originally been called to this meeting.

"The winery next door has been put up for sale by its owner, John Gutierrez," Reverend Mother said at last. "The Archbishop called this morning to tell me himself. He'd heard that the buyer interested in the property wants to put up apartments or townhomes there. He contacted Mr. Gutierrez on our behalf, hoping to convince the man to give us some kind of buffer zone so we can maintain our privacy . . . and silence."

"The name sounds familiar. John Gutierrez . . . hasn't he donated funds to us in the past?" Sister Agatha asked.

Reverend Mother nodded. "Yes, and he's consented to meet with one of our externs to discuss the issue. I'd like you to go. I'll have the time and place for you later today."

Sister Agatha left Reverend Mother's office with a heavy heart. Between the wiring, their finances, the hacker, and now this, it felt as if their monastery was under siege . . . and maybe it was.

Fortunately, the rest of the day proved to be less stressful and, except for a few more power fluctuations, the work in the scriptorium proceeded in a timely manner.

After Compline, the last liturgical hour of the day, the Great Silence began. Sister Agatha had remained with Sister Bernarda in the small chapel, kneeling near the altar in private prayer. Sister Bernarda had been troubled about something all week. Knowing her prayerful support was needed, Sister

Agatha stayed with her sister in Christ. Attending to the needs of another was at the heart of the second most important commandment—to love thy neighbor as thyself.

Although she'd come with the best of intentions, as time passed, Sister Agatha had to force herself to stay awake. Duty was paramount, yet the stillness in the monastery after Compline was absolute, and it made remaining alert a monumental challenge.

Sister Agatha took a deep breath. Although she had no idea what was bothering Sister Bernarda, God did, and He'd know how to fix things. Better to pray this way—without knowing. But she would make one plea—*Blessed Lord, don't let me fail her and you by falling asleep during my watch.*

Suddenly a thunderous crash shook the entire building. For a moment, the possibility that she'd received an instant answer to her prayer left Sister Agatha dumbstruck. Then she heard the ragged rhythm of a car motor somewhere close by and saw a light shining through one of the back windows of the chapel.

There'd been an accident. Sister Agatha jumped to her feet and hurried toward the door, Sister Bernarda a few steps behind her. Almost immediately Sister Agatha detected the smell of motor oil. In the glare of a bright light, she saw a cloud of dust around the twisted metal and adobe bricks that had comprised the monastery's wall and gates. In the haze, jammed into the ruined barrier, was a big sports utility vehicle, one of its headlights still working.

"We need to help whoever's inside," Sister Bernarda said, hoisting her long skirt and sprinting toward the vehicle.

Sister Agatha saw the SUV's driver's side door burst open. A tall, shadowed figure in a hooded sweatshirt jumped out of the vehicle. Shielding his eyes with his forearm, he ran away from them, quickly disappearing into the dark beyond the scene of the crash.

"Did you get a look at his face?" Sister Agatha asked, catching up to Sister Bernarda.

"No, but don't worry about that now. We need to see if there's a passenger," Sister Bernarda said, racing around to the open door and checking inside.

A moment later she eased back out of the SUV, shaking her head. "There's no passenger, but there are a bunch of empty beer cans scattered on the floor," she said disgustedly. "The emergency airbag was set off, but I didn't see any blood anywhere, so the driver probably wasn't badly injured."

"I'll call the police," Sister Agatha said. "Maybe you should switch off the ignition and light in case there's a fuel leak."

Sister Agatha hurried back inside the monastery's parlor. Although she was sure that the cloistered sisters had been awakened by the crash and would be worried, the Great Silence made its own demands. She couldn't exactly run around making an announcement now.

Wondering how to handle the situation, she walked quickly through the chapel. Then, at the entrance to the corridor, she found Pax, the monastery's large white German shepherd dog, pacing nervously back and forth. Although alerted by the noise, Pax had learned not to go into the chapel or make any sounds after Compline.

Pax stayed with her as she hurried to the parlor and dialed the county sheriff's office. Since there weren't any victims at the scene, the desk sergeant warned her that it would be at least twenty minutes before a unit would respond. She wasn't surprised. The sheriff's department had been forced to implement new budget cuts and was chronically understaffed these days.

Sister Agatha grabbed a flashlight from the desk drawer. She was about to go back outside when she heard a light rap on the grille that separated the cloister from the monastery's front parlor.

Reverend Mother was standing there, silently waiting for an explanation. After living with her for more than a decade, Sister Agatha could almost hear the thoughts that reverberated behind Reverend Mother's silences as easily as she could her spoken words.

"A big passenger vehicle crashed through the front gates, Mother," Sister Agatha whispered. The Great Silence could be broken in case of emergencies, and informing Reverend Mother of the crisis at hand was not only justified, it was imperative. "We think the driver was drinking, but he's run off. Fortunately, there were no passengers. I called the sheriff's department and now I'm going to join Sister Bernarda outside to wait for an officer to arrive."

Reverend Mother nodded. "*Benedicemus Domino*," she said, praising God before breaking Silence. "Will you be able to close the gates once the car is removed?" she asked softly.

"No, Mother, the gates are in pieces. But I'll make sure Pax has free run of the grounds tonight, and I'll sleep in the parlor until everything's fixed. He'll bark if he sees a stranger, and I'll be able to hear him clearly from here. We'll be safe."

With a nod, Reverend Mother slipped away into the cloister as silently as she'd come. Their *alpargates*, rope-soled sandals, made almost no sound on the brick floors.

Sister Agatha flipped on the floodlights that illuminated

the gate area and parking lot, then hurried back outside to join Sister Bernarda, Pax at her side.

"Twenty minutes," she told Sister Bernarda, who understood without further explanation. "Reverend Mother's been told."

"The driver won't get away. They'll track him down easily enough from the registration."

"Unless the SUV was stolen," Sister Agatha replied. Using the flashlight, she moved farther down the road, beyond the gravel, examining the footprints the driver had left in the dirt.

"I think we had a visit from Bigfoot," Sister Agatha said, pointing.

Sister Bernarda glanced down and nodded. "*Drunken* Bigfoot."

"But he didn't run like someone who was *that* drunk. . . . He never staggered or stumbled as he raced out of here," Sister Agatha said, recalling what she'd seen.

Sister Bernarda shook her head. "Don't complicate things. Take one sniff inside that SUV and the smell of beer will tell you the whole story. If the driver hadn't been drunk he wouldn't have lost control of the car." She paused then added, "What we have to do now is figure out a way to restore the gates. The next drunk that comes along might end up in our parlor. Have you thought of that?" she added brusquely.

The harshness of Sister Bernarda's tone surprised Sister Agatha. She looked over at her fellow extern nun, trying to figure out if it was just a reaction to the shock—or something more. To her, Sister Bernarda, their ex-marine, had always been the toughest of the tough—unbreakable. But the truth was that, lately, she hadn't been herself.

Pushing those thoughts aside and concentrating on the problem at hand for now, Sister Agatha added, "Do you think that the hacker who has been harassing us is somehow responsible for this? Maybe he decided to go for a more hands-on approach."

"But how would he even know that the monastery's handling NexCen's orders?" Sister Bernarda countered.

"There was a notice in the business section of the local newspaper right after we got the contract," Sister Agatha answered, then shook her head. "No, you're right. I'm just complicating things. This was undoubtedly just the work of a drunk."

Sister Bernarda remained silent for a moment, then gestured to flashing lights in the distance. "Looks like we got lucky. There's the police."

Sister Agatha glanced back at the monastery, worried. "They're all awake in there now, praying their hearts out."

"That's a good thing. Heaven knows prayers are needed now, not only for the person who did this, but for our monastery, too," Sister Bernarda said, walking to the crumbled wall and staring at what was left of several dozen big adobe bricks. Both sections of the steel gate were on the ground—bent or snapped in two. Welds had parted and bare metal was showing in several places. The locking mechanism in the center had been mangled and was now useless.

"How are we ever going to get the money to fix this, on top of everything else?" Sister Bernarda added, not really expecting an answer. "We got a new roof last year, but now the rest of the place is falling apart. That electrical fire we had in the kitchen wall was just a wake-up call. Dealing with this mess on top of getting new wiring is going to take far more than we have available in our sinking fund."

"Aluminum wiring . . . all the time we've been here it's worked for us—until now. Who knew it was a potential fire hazard?" Sister Agatha replied with a sigh.

"We might have gotten away with it for another twenty years if we hadn't overloaded the system by adding computers, printers, work lights, and the air conditioner in the infirmary."

"The air conditioner was a necessity now that Sister Gertrude's heart condition has worsened. As far as the scriptorium equipment—well, what choice did we have? We have to support ourselves by the work of our hands. That's part of our Rule," Sister Agatha answered. "But there's no sense in worrying about this. We've done all we possibly can. Now the rest is up to God."

"You're right. He'll provide whatever we need."

"He always has and He always will," Sister Agatha said.

Sister Bernarda scrutinized the immediate area. "Right now you and I have to find a way to secure our perimeter," she added, sounding very much like a marine again.

"I've got that covered," Sister Agatha answered. "I'm going to sleep in the parlor tonight, and Pax'll stay outside. If anyone wanders into our grounds the dog will let us know."

"Good plan," Sister Bernarda said. "But I should be the one to sleep in the parlor," she added, glancing down at Sister Agatha's hands, which were swollen from rheumatoid arthritis. "You did something for me by joining your prayers to mine in chapel earlier. Let me do this for you."

"I'm okay. This looks a lot worse than it feels," she said, glancing down at her hands. "But I sure wish you'd tell me what's been troubling you. Maybe I can help."

"We'll talk later. Here comes the deputy now," Sister Bernarda said as a patrol car came up the road.

Seconds later, a woman in her late twenties, with brown

hair tied back into a ponytail, climbed out of the squad car. She left the engine running and the headlights on to illuminate the crash scene. Clipboard in hand, she approached them. "Sisters, I'm Deputy Susan James. Did either of you see what happened here?"

Sister Bernarda briefed her in clipped sentences. "You'll notice the smell of beer and the empties in the SUV. The driver's gone—ran off as soon as we came outside. He left the key in the ignition, and I switched off the power and lights," she said, and gave her a description of the man.

"I'm going to call it in, then take a look around," Deputy James said, picking up her handheld radio and making her report.

"It won't be hard to figure out who this SUV belongs to once you pull out his registration. After that, we'd like the man arrested," Sister Bernarda said in her usual no-nonsense style. "We need our gate fixed on the double, and the person who did this has to make things right."

"You may have trouble collecting if he has no insurance. One out of three New Mexico drivers still aren't covered." As her radio came to life, Deputy James held up a hand, then answered the call.

To Sister Agatha and Sister Bernarda the transmission sounded garbled and virtually incoherent, but the deputy appeared to have no trouble deciphering it.

"Did ya'll get that?" she asked, looking at Sister Agatha and Sister Bernarda.

Sister Agatha shook her head and looked over at Sister Bernarda, who shrugged. "Sorry," Sister Bernarda said. "It's been a while since I've tuned in on radio chatter. You better translate for us."

"This particular SUV was reported stolen earlier tonight."

"Terrific," Sister Bernarda muttered sourly. "Guess I shouldn't have touched the key."

"At the time it was the right thing to do," Sister Agatha said. "Besides, the beer cans in there can also be checked for fingerprints. And that air bag, too. He had to push it away to get out. We found his footprints, too, Deputy James," Sister Agatha added, pointing to the ground. "They're distinctive because of their size."

"A man's shoe, size twelve or bigger. I'll take some photos." Deputy James brought out a camera with flash attachment, put her pen alongside for scale, then took several photos. She then took shots of the interior and exterior of the SUV. Finally she gathered all the cans, handling them by the edges, and placed them into evidence sacks, labeling each.

Deputy James cut away the deployed air bag from the center of the steering wheel with a big folding knife, rolled the bag up, and placed it into a large grocery bag, labeling it with the time, date, and her initials. She then slipped behind the SUV's wheel and took a quick inventory of the interior at a glance. "No key ring. The thief must have found a spare hidden on the vehicle."

"When are you going to tow the vehicle away? It's blocking our entrance," Sister Bernarda said.

"The department will send a wrecker over, but probably not before morning."

"We'll need our driveway cleared as soon as possible," Sister Bernarda said. "What if, God forbid, we have an emergency and can't get out in our own vehicles? We have a few elderly sisters here, and all the commotion might have upset one or two of them. We should at least try to push the SUV to one side so our station wagon can get out."

Deputy James nodded. "I understand, Sister. Let me see if I

can get this hunk of junk running," she said, then moved the seat forward. The seat had been set so far back that her feet barely reached the pedals.

The engine started on the first try and, although it sputtered all the way, they succeeded in getting it to the side of the road.

"Expect the wrecker in the morning," Deputy James said, taking the key and bagging it as evidence. Moments later she drove off.

Sister Bernarda glanced at Sister Agatha. "We might as well go back inside. We have a long day ahead of us tomorrow."

2

THE RHYTHMIC, DEEP PEALS OF THE GABRIEL BELL
woke up Sister Agatha the following morning. Her body
ached but, mercifully, not much more than usual. A few
minutes later, before she'd had a chance to roll up the air mattress she'd placed in the parlor, Sister Bernarda came in.

At first, Sister Agatha assumed that she'd washed up early
so she could relieve her as soon as the bell rang. But once she
saw the darkened circles under Sister Bernarda's reddened eyes,
Sister Agatha realized that her fellow extern had probably had
another sleepless night.

Sister Bernarda crouched by the mattress and gestured by
cocking her head that she'd put things away while Sister
Agatha went to wash up. The Great Silence was still being observed so, with only a nod, Sister Agatha hurried down the
corridor.

They met again shortly thereafter in chapel. Matins was

chanted before daybreak as a counter to the evils that gathered strength during the night. That ritual was followed by Lauds at sunrise, when light returned to the earth. It was the hour of praise—a commemoration of the Light that had come to the world through Jesus Christ. Their voices rose in the stillness, adding texture to what was in their hearts—an immeasurable love for the One God and His Son. After Mass came breakfast and Morning Prayers, which signaled the end of the Great Silence.

When Sister Bernarda came to find her sometime later, Sister Agatha was back at her post as portress, dusting the room with meticulous precision. If it was done for His glory all honest work was a continual prayer.

"One of us has to take Sister Gertrude to the doctor's this morning," Sister Bernarda said. "Last night, Sister Eugenia noticed that Sister Gertrude was holding her arm against her side. When she asked Sister Gertrude about it she found out that Sister has been having sharp pains in her arm and back. Both are symptoms of a heart problem, so Sister Eugenia called the doctor immediately. Sister Gertrude's better this morning after a new round of medication, but the doctor still wants to see her."

Sister Agatha knew that Sister Gertrude's heart was slowly wearing out and there was little that could be done. Sister Gertrude was in her midseventies. Although not nearly as elderly as Sister Clothilde, who they all suspected was in her nineties, Sister Gertrude's health was failing. For a while, Reverend Mother had tried to forbid her to do any work whatsoever, but that had made things worse. Stripped of all the tasks that defined her, Sister Gertrude had sunk into a deep depression. Habits of a lifetime were hard to break. These days Sister

Gertrude attended each liturgical hour and helped Sister Maria Victoria with the job of cellarer, the monastery's bookkeeper.

"Her body's turning traitor," Sister Agatha said sadly. "Good thing she agreed to move into the infirmary so Sister Eugenia could keep a closer eye on her. But going back to what you were saying, would it be possible for you to take her in to the doctor? The owner of the SUV has been located and he and Sheriff Green are coming over this morning. The owner wants to tow the car away himself once the sheriff's department releases it."

"I'm glad the sheriff is handling this personally," Sister Bernarda said.

"He's taken it upon himself to watch over our monastery," Sister Agatha said. But it hadn't always been that way. Many years ago, he'd seen it as an adversary. It was no secret that she and Tom had enjoyed a close relationship before she'd become a nun. But that was all ancient history.

"Sheriff Green values your feedback and your observations, so you're right to stay," Sister Bernarda said. "If you need help in the parlor, Sister de Lourdes is outside, clearing the area next to the north wall. She's concerned that all the dried leaves that have collected are a fire hazard, particularly after she spotted several discarded cigarette butts there yesterday. Obviously someone working at the vineyard next door flicked them over."

"That's strange. I don't remember ever seeing a worker in that section. There are no grapevines even close to the property line."

"Someone's been hanging out around there, so we should speak to Eric about it. As caretaker he's responsible for whatever happens there."

"I'll see what I can do," Sister Agatha said. "I have a feeling it might be one of the homeless people passing through."

Hearing the sound of a car driving up, Sister Agatha glanced out the parlor window. "It's the sheriff."

"Go take care of that and I'll drive Sister Gertrude to the doctor's," Sister Bernarda said.

Sister Agatha switched on the answering machine and walked outside. She had to force herself not to cringe as she saw the damage to the gate and wall in broad daylight. The monastery was kept in perfect order for a reason. Living in the presence of God meant that everything—from sweeping the floors to painting a wall—was done in service to Him.

As nuns, they lived simple lives centered on prayer. But now a vital barrier that allowed them to remain separate—to maintain that single-minded purpose that helped them draw closer to the Divine—had been breached.

Nuns were only human, and their prayers for an unrepentant world would now be tainted with negative emotions like anger. The inescapable fact that many on the outside didn't understand or value the importance of what they did had just been brought home to them in a very personal way.

As Tom came over to greet her, she made up her mind. Today, with God's help, she'd find someone willing either to take responsibility for fixing their wall, or donate funds for the repairs. That would help everyone at Our Lady of Hope Monastery put the accident behind them.

Tom Green was a tall man with brown hair that had turned almost white around his temples. His tanned face was weathered, his green eyes filled with the perpetual wariness of one who'd seen too much of the world.

The sheriff nodded a greeting. "Jack Miller's on his way over to pick up his stolen vehicle. I checked his whereabouts last night just to make sure it wasn't him driving. Jack's got an ironclad alibi. He was at Cottonwood Mall with friends who vouched for him."

"Then who did this? Were any fingerprints left behind?" she asked.

"Nothing on the vehicle or the air bag, but we lifted a clear print from one of those beer cans and got a match. It belongs to Elizabeth Leland, a sixteen-year-old with a record for shoplifting. We also got a partial that matches another teen by the name of Leeann Karon."

"Those names sound vaguely familiar. . . ."

"Elizabeth and Leeann both attended St. Charles at one time, so they may have been students of yours. Didn't you do substitute teaching there last year?"

Sister Agatha nodded. "There was a shortage of staff, so Father Rick asked for our help," she said. She'd taught one or two days at a time whenever needed, but as hard as she tried, she couldn't put a face to the names.

"You'll probably recognize the girls when you see them, and you'll have the chance shortly because Liz refused to talk to us unless you were present. I advised her to get an attorney, but she said she trusts you more."

Hearing vehicles, Sister Agatha looked up the road and saw a beat-up heavy-duty truck with oversized tires pull up by the damaged SUV. Just then, another man arrived in a new-looking sedan and parked on the opposite side of the road.

"That'll be Jack Miller and his claims adjuster. From what I hear, Jack's already spoken to Paul Gonzales about the bodywork, so now it's just a matter of paperwork."

Sister Agatha walked over with Tom to greet the new arrivals. A thin man in his late twenties stood by the wrecked SUV, shaking his head and grumbling to himself, while the second, older man in a western suit with a bolo tie walked around the scene, taking photos. Sister Agatha studied the younger man—Miller, apparently—for a moment. He was around five-foot-six and certainly much shorter than whoever had driven the SUV last night. Miller was wearing jeans with a loop for a hammer or tool and a dusty, sleeveless T-shirt, making her suspect he'd come directly from a construction site.

"I just bought this beauty, Mr. Wade, and now look at it," Jack Miller moaned. "Will my insurance cover the damage?"

"It was used when you bought it, Jack, and the deductible is pretty steep. You might be better off selling it for parts and buying a new one," Wade answered, continuing to take photos.

"Can't afford it. If the engine hasn't been damaged the rest can be repaired little by little. But the insurance has to cover enough to put me back on the road."

"You'll have to deal with an approved mechanic if you intend on keeping it insured."

"Paul Gonzales here in town is on your list," Miller said.

"I'll go talk to him, get his estimate, then tell you how much of it I can cover," Wade said, shaking hands with Miller. Nodding to Sister Agatha and Sheriff Green, he walked back to his car and drove off.

Miller shook his head once more, then turned to Sheriff Green. "What a day. And it's just beginning."

"You've got that right." Tom said, then introduced them.

"Sorry about your wall and the gate, Sister, but we both took a hit last night, didn't we?" Jack muttered.

She nodded. "Your vehicle will be in good hands with Mr. Gonzales. But I'm concerned about the damage to our property. I assume your liability insurance will cover the damage to our wall?"

He gave her a startled look. "No way I'm taking responsibility for this, Sister. I'm a victim here, too. Somewhere out there is a car thief. *He* did this. Don't blame me, and don't blame my insurance company. Mr. Wade says that in New Mexico, *your* insurance company has to pay for the wall damage because I wasn't at fault."

"We're not a wealthy monastery, Mr. Miller, and our insurance deductible is very high. Would you be willing to make a donation to our repair fund? We would be happy to keep you in our prayers in exchange. And do remember that our Lord always looks kindly on those who help us continue to serve Him."

"I can't afford it, Sister. I'm sorry." He began hitching the wreck to the pickup with a towing rig. "A lot of the repairs that'll need to be done to provide me with transportation again will be coming out of my own pocket. I'm strapped right now." He glanced over at Tom. "But once you find the person who stole my SUV, you can nail his hide to the wall."

A few minutes later Sister Agatha watched him drive off. "Whatever happened to charity?"

"People aren't in a charitable mood when the system's about to screw them over. He pays his car insurance, but there'll be a gap the size of the Grand Canyon between the value the SUV had to him and what the insurance will cough up—unless he sics a lawyer on them. And that could end up costing him more money than it's worth."

"Do you think the girls had anything to do with the car theft? All I know for sure is that the driver was a tall man," Sister Agatha said.

"The prints put both girls in that SUV at some point," Tom said, "and Miller denies knowing either of them."

"They're both underage, and if he gave them beer. . . ."

"I thought of that and questioned the friends who were

23

with him at the mall, a husband and wife. They backed him up, and assured me that Miller seldom drinks."

"Then the girls must have been inside later on, along with the beer," Sister Agatha nodded.

"I agree. They have to know something. You want to meet me at the station?"

"Sure. I'll go find Pax and follow you in," she said.

After saying good-bye to Tom, Sister Agatha went in search of Pax. As she turned the corner of the building she found him playing tug-of-war with Sister Clothilde on the grass. The old knotted piece of rope was his favorite toy, and he usually managed to find a playmate. Sister Clothilde smiled sheepishly at Sister Agatha, then returned to hanging the laundry.

Sister Clothilde, despite her age, seemed to work harder than anyone else and was still as strong as any twenty-year-old. Playing rough with Pax could knock the wind out of anyone, but she seemed undaunted. Hard physical labor and Sister Clothilde were longtime partners, and her stamina never failed to amaze the community. Maybe it was God's special gift to her because she'd pleased him with her vow of silence. Sister Clothilde hadn't spoken a word for more than fifteen years, though she communicated with hand signals and cryptic notes when necessary.

Sister Agatha looked down at Pax, who sat directly in front of her now, waiting.

"We're going into town, Pax," she said, then added his two favorite words, "Road trip!"

The dog bounded ahead to where the vehicles were parked, but before they reached the Harley, he slowed down, hackles rising. He took a few more cautious steps forward, then, facing the wall, began to growl low and menacingly. It was the deep-throated sound that belonged to the police dog he'd once been instead of a gentle monastery pet.

Sister Agatha followed his gaze, trying to figure out what he'd spotted and where the danger lay.

As she approached the adobe wall, she saw someone moving behind the junipers that lined the edge of one of the vineyard's most productive fields. He appeared to be holding something in front of his face, but before she could angle for a better look, he vanished, moving in the opposite direction.

"Hello?" she called out. The one thing she was absolutely certain about was that it hadn't been Eric. The person she'd seen had been too tall. She waited for another minute, hoping the person, maybe an employee, would return. But no one came.

She knew he hadn't been one of the homeless people who occasionally passed through. He'd been too well dressed in a white shirt and dark slacks instead of jeans and a heavy shirt or jacket. But the man hadn't answered when she'd called and that bothered her. He'd heard her, she was sure of it.

As she glanced down at Pax, she noticed that his hackles weren't raised anymore, though he was still watching. "We'll check into this later, Pax," she said firmly. "For now, we're expected at the police station."

The dog's tail began to wag furiously.

"Yeah, I know. Your old stomping ground. Let's go." She pointed to the candy-apple-red 1986 Classic Heritage Harley. It was a collector's piece and worth a small fortune, but Paul Gonzales had insisted that they take it as a donation. Now that Paul had a teenaged son, he hadn't wanted the cycle around to tempt his kid. It had taken some fancy footwork—high-style tap dancing, actually—to convince Reverend Mother to let her accept it. But the cycle, complete with sidecar, was reliable, cheap transportation, and had proven to be a blessing to the monastery.

Everyone in the area knew her and Pax by now, and most waved as she passed by. The town of Bernalillo was small, and after a drive down Camino Real, which ran through the old downtown and had once been the main highway, she reached the station.

Tom Green was waiting for them in the lobby, having undoubtedly heard the bike's distinctive V-twin engine when it entered the parking lot. "I was beginning to worry. What took you so long?"

She told him what had happened. "I think the person had binoculars. . . . I'm not at all sure of that, mind you, but I've been thinking about the position of his hands and it makes sense in that context. I'll talk to Eric later, find out what's going on, and remind him that Pax is very possessive of our grounds."

"Maybe it was an investor looking to buy the place, or one of the Realtors. They sometimes use binoculars because it saves them walking," Tom said.

"The thought of heavy equipment, dust, and months of construction sets my teeth on edge. And what if they put up apartments? I just hope we can convince the owner to give us some kind of sound barrier or buffer zone. I'm supposed to meet with him to discuss it," Sister Agatha said.

"I'm sure you and Reverend Mother will be able to work something out with him," Tom said. "But right now you and I need to get started."

He led her down the hall to one of the interview rooms. "I left Elizabeth in there alone to give her something to worry about," he said, looking through the one-way glass at the teen, who was shifting in her seat and looking away from the mirror. "Hopefully, she'll be more amenable to playing it straight now."

Suddenly aware Pax was not by her side, Sister Agatha glanced down the hall. The dog had found his way into the bullpen, where he was being fed a doughnut by one of the deputies. She sighed. "He's such a mooch."

"Don't worry about him. He'll be fine. You ready to go talk to Elizabeth?"

"After you," she said, gesturing to the door.

3

AS THEY STEPPED INSIDE THE ROOM AND ELIZABETH Leland turned to face them, Sister Agatha recognized her instantly. Liz, as she liked to be called, was a petite brunette with thick, straight hair down to her waist. She was wearing jeans and a yellow T-shirt with dark blue letters that read, I SURVIVED CATHOLIC SCHOOL.

Liz's face brightened instantly when she saw Sister Agatha. "Do you remember me, Sister?"

"Sure I do. You're a student at St. Charles."

"Not anymore. Since my dad split I had to switch to public school," she said, her shoulders slumping and her voice heavy.

Sister Agatha sat across the table from her. "Liz, what's going on? Why did you want me to be here?"

"You were never too busy to talk and I've never forgotten how you helped me pass my English final. You cared about all of us, Sister."

"I still do. That's why I came. If you need to work something out with us. . . ."

Tom cleared his throat. "Liz, whatever you say is on the record, and may be used against you in court."

Liz shot Tom a look as cold as a January dawn. "I'm not guilty of anything! Stop trying to pin everything on *me*," she said, her voice rising with every word.

"Calm down, Liz," Sister Agatha said in her best teacher's voice. "Sheriff Green is required to say that in order to protect your rights. Your prints were found on one of the beer cans inside the sport utility vehicle that crashed through our gate last night."

"That's what he keeps saying, but it's all so crazy! Sister I was never inside that SUV, much less drinking. I swear. I *hate* beer. It tastes gross."

"Liz, I've heard that you're affiliated with one of the local gangs—the Diablos Locos," Tom said, capturing her gaze and holding it. "Tell me about that."

"I *don't* belong to any gang!" She looked at Sister Agatha. "See? They want me to admit to something—anything—just because I don't have a lawyer. But Mom can't afford one, and the free public defenders . . . I heard about them. They want you to cut a deal 'cause they're overloaded with clients."

Tom continued to press. "Come on, Liz, you've been seen hanging out with the Diablos. Kids don't do that unless they're wannabes or already ranked in."

Liz hesitated and glanced at Sister Agatha nervously. "Everything at public school is so different, but I'm *not* in a gang. Sure they've pressured me to hang out with them, and I even considered joining for a while. But then . . ." She stared intensely at her hands, trying to ignore everything else in the room, especially the sheriff.

"Go on, Liz," Sister Agatha said gently.

"Dad's always making excuses for not sending child support checks, so we barely have enough to get by. Mom has to work two jobs just to make the rent. She's always tired and in a lousy mood."

Sister Agatha nodded slowly. The story was all too familiar.

"Not that we ever talked much anyway," Liz continued. "We haven't gotten along for years, but things got worse after Dad took off. I wanted to get back at her, so I did a lot of crazy things—like hanging with the Diablos. But one day I heard her talking to my aunt and crying. Mom's just scared . . . like me," she said with a soft sigh. "I stopped hanging out with the Diablos after that."

"That must not have been easy," Sister Agatha said. "Changing your life around."

"No, it wasn't, but I'm working hard to get into college next year. I know I'll need a scholarship and that'll take good grades, so I have to bring my GPA back up to where it was." She looked at Sister Agatha squarely. "That's why I'd *never* do something totally dumb like stealing a car, Sister. It would be like throwing away all the work I've done this semester. You've always been able to tell when somebody's lying. Can't you see I'm telling the truth?"

Before she could respond, Tom leaned forward. "Terrific story, Liz, but the fact is that your prints *were* on a beer can we found on the floor of the SUV. If you didn't crash into the monastery's gates, who did? You must know who the driver was. You were *in* that vehicle earlier in the evening."

"No, I wasn't! *That's* what I'm trying to tell you, Sheriff," she said, her voice rising in pitch. "I spent last night at Leeann's house." She looked back at Sister Agatha. "You remember Leeann? She and I have been friends forever."

Sister Agatha nodded, her thoughts racing. She knew that Liz wasn't tall enough to have driven the SUV with the seat pushed back as far as it had been, and neither was Leeann. She remembered the girl now.

"Leeann is being interviewed elsewhere right now. We found a print that belongs to her, too," Tom said, glancing at Sister Agatha, then back at Liz, his eyes as flat as his voice. "Leeann's mother fell asleep early, so you two could have left the house later. . . ."

"But we didn't! And you can't prove we were in that car, because we weren't. Not anywhere near it, either."

"Then how do you explain your prints on those beer cans the sheriff found, Liz?" Sister Agatha said. "Or Leeann's, who you just happened to be with last night." Sister Agatha gave her a steady look, then in a softer voice added, "Liz, you're in a world of trouble and it sure looks like you're trying to cover for someone."

"I'm not! I don't know who the driver was because Leeann and I were nowhere near that SUV!" Tears ran down her cheeks freely now. "Why won't you believe me?"

"How about taking a polygraph?" Tom asked. "Lie detector."

Liz hesitated, her eyes widening, then, wiping away her tears with one hand, nodded. "Okay, but only if you promise to keep it to two questions. You can ask me if I was ever in that SUV and if I know who stole it."

"All right." Tom gestured for Sister Agatha to follow him outside and closed the door behind him.

He then led Sister Agatha farther down the hall, and stopped in front of another interview room. "I've got Leeann in here with Sergeant Banks. Both mothers are waiting in the lunchroom. We've kept it informal and, so far, the girls' stories match up. They had a sleepover, listened to music, played some games on a computer, then went to sleep. But they're both holding something back."

"Agreed. The fact that Liz was willing to take a polygraph shows she's not lying, but the way she put a limit on what you could ask cinches it. She knows more than she admits. Have you spoken to Liz's mom yet?"

He nodded slowly. "I told her that the county would provide a lawyer for her daughter if she couldn't afford one, and she told me that she didn't care what we did with Liz. She said that if Liz had broken the law she'd have to own up to it. And if Liz ended up in jail, she could plan on living with her father after she got out."

"I've seen so many situations like this before—the kid's a ping-pong ball between the parents," Sister Agatha said.

"Now here's the bad news. I've done all I can. The car's been recovered, and no one was injured, so this is as far as we can take it. I don't have the manpower to pursue this any longer. I was only bluffing when I mentioned the polygraph. We can't fund that on a case like this."

"Then who's going to replace our gates? We have to find out who's responsible before we can pressure them to make restitution. Both Sister Bernarda and I saw a big person, probably a man, running away from that SUV after it crashed. The girls must know who it was. Will you let me talk to Leeann?"

"Sure. Go for it. But I'll have to be there with you."

As they entered the second interview room, Sister Agatha saw a teen with bright red hair and a ring in her bottom lip sitting behind the table, biting her fire-engine-red fingernails. Sister Agatha noted her blue T-shirt with the image of Jesus. Below it were the words JESUS IS MY HOMEBOY.

Sister Agatha tried not to cringe. They meant well—both the manufacturers and the teens who chose to wear them—but it still seemed sacrilegious to reduce the Lord to an image on a T-shirt.

The teen gave Sister Agatha a shaky smile. "Are you here to help us, Sister Agatha? We didn't do anything wrong."

She remembered more about Leeann now—a troubled teen who'd attended St. Charles and finally been expelled after she'd brought a sharpened rat-tail comb to school and pointed it like a weapon at one of the teachers. The kid was trouble waiting to happen.

"I want to help you, Leeann, but you're going to have to tell me the truth. Someone stole an SUV and rammed it through our gates. Fingerprints found on items inside the vehicle indicate that both of you girls were inside it at some point. Tell me who was driving."

"Sister, my hand to God, we had nothing to do with any of that. Not Liz, and not me," Leeann replied.

"Then explain how the beer cans got in there," Sister Agatha said.

"I can't. Sister, we're not above trying to pick the lock on my parents' liquor cabinet, or sneaking a beer from the refrigerator, but that's about it. I don't even have my license. Liz does, but she wouldn't steal anyone's car. That's a big crime, and she's not a thief. You *know* her."

"I know she has a record of shoplifting," Tom said firmly.

"Yeah, a ten-dollar tube of lipstick. Liz needed it for a school dance and her mom wouldn't give her the money. But steal a thirty-thousand-dollar SUV and go joyriding? Give me a break!"

"Tell us how those beer cans got there then," Sister Agatha pressed.

"I can't. But really, Sister, do you think that either of us would be dumb enough to leave our prints inside a car we just stole? We watch TV. Fingerprints always lead to the bad guys. Just because we're kids don't think we're *totally* brain-dead."

"Maybe you were riding around with your friends and things got out of hand," Tom insisted. "People don't think about fingerprints when they've been drinking."

"It wasn't us. No way we left the house last night. If we'd snuck out for even a quick smoke my mom would have known. She has radar. Trust me," she said, but avoided looking at either of them.

Leeann was holding back information and one look at Tom told Sister Agatha that he knew it, too.

"Who are you covering for, Leeann?" Sister Agatha pressed. "The car thief? It'll make your life a lot simpler if you come clean."

Leeann slumped down in her chair and shook her head, avoiding eye contact with either of them. "We're *not* guilty. Why won't you believe us?"

Sister Agatha followed Tom out of the room. "They didn't steal the SUV, Tom. I'm sure of that, though they probably know who did. Those beer cans didn't move by themselves into that vehicle."

Tom nodded. "I buy their argument about being too bright to have left those cans behind, too. Especially in a stolen vehicle."

"So what can the monastery do about the damage to the gate and our adobe wall?" Sister Agatha asked in a weary voice.

"You could sue Liz's or Leeann's parents, but on the basis of what we have so far, you'd probably lose. Truth is, even if you won, they'd probably be unable to come up with the money."

"It does sound like Liz's mother barely gets by," Sister Agatha said regretfully. "And I know Leeann's family is no better off. Miller, the owner of the SUV, won't help out, either. But *someone's* got to make things right. We need to lock our grounds, Tom. We're out in the country with few close neighbors and it's a matter of security. Without those gates we're very vulnerable. Anyone could walk in and break into our outbuildings like St. Francis's Pantry, or come peep in our windows. The monastery's a source of curiosity to many, you know."

"Maybe you can persuade one of the local construction companies to donate the materials and labor, or at least the labor."

She shook her head slowly. "These are tough times, Tom. Getting corporate donations quickly, without months of requests and paperwork, is nearly impossible. Most companies in our area don't have it to give, and the ones who do want to hold on to their money."

When a deputy approached Tom stepped aside to speak to him, then returned a second later. "We've got another problem brewing, Sister. I've got to go, but I'll be in touch if anything new crops up on this."

"Thanks." Sister Agatha went to get Pax, who'd been playing with some of the office staff, then left the station.

Once outside, the big dog jumped into the sidecar, then nuzzled her hand, waiting for a pat of approval, which she gave. "Good boy. Ready to go?"

She glanced at her watch. It was only ten thirty, so there was plenty of time for her to go by the bakery. They'd licensed their locally famous Cloister Cluster Cookie recipe, and it was time for their royalties. Our Lady of Hope Monastery's material needs were humble, but the very act of living made them subject to bills every family experienced. Yet despite a fully functioning scriptorium and the money from licensing their recipe, funds were always tight.

The ride to the bakery was much shorter than Sister Agatha would have liked. It was a typically beautiful fall New Mexico day. The savory, smoky scent of roasting chiles filled the air, and the leaves on the cottonwoods were starting to turn gold around the edges. Less than ten minutes later, Sister Agatha pulled into the parking area beside Bountiful Bakery. Leaving the motorcycle and Pax in the shade of the big green and white awning in front of the business, she went inside.

Jerry Dexter and his wife Sally greeted her warmly—a miracle on its own. Not so long ago the monastery had done battle with them after the Dexters had begun to market a cheaper version of the monastery's popular Cloister Clusters. The Dexters had called their cookies Coconut Clones, which hadn't fooled anyone. Most of their regular customers had sided with the nuns and boycotted the bakery. Eventually, Jerry had agreed to license the nuns' recipe.

It had been a blessing for all concerned. The nuns still earned some extra income, but the round-the-clock baking that increasing orders had required—and which had so interfered with their prayer schedule—was now a thing of the past.

Jerry escorted her to his office. "Your quarterly royalty check is ready, but I'm afraid you might be disappointed. The sales are steady, but won't start climbing until the winter holiday season." He reached into the top desk drawer. "I was going to mail the check to Ms. Fuentes, your attorney, but I'll be happy to turn it over to you. Just make sure you let her know you've been paid for this quarter."

"Of course I will." Sister Agatha took the envelope and opened it. The check was for only a few hundred dollars. "It'll help," she said, refusing to worry. God *would* provide for them.

"Listen, I heard the monastery had a problem with that SUV crashing into your wall and all. The news is all over town. So if you need to host a few special bake sales, go for it."

"But we signed the contract. . . ."

He held up one hand. "Contracts are binding, but God-fearing people follow higher laws. Tell Ms. Fuentes to find a way to make it legal. I'll sign off on it, and even bake some extra cakes and brownies and donate them to the cause."

"I really appreciate the gesture, Mr. Dexter. I'll let Reverend Mother know."

Pax, who'd waited by the motorcycle the entire time without moving, barked as she approached and sniffed the air. The scent of freshly baked bread was very inviting.

"Sorry, Pax. I didn't bring you anything this—"

Before she could complete the sentence, Jerry Dexter came rushing out. "Sister, I almost forgot. Here's a sampling of our new doggy cookies. All-natural ingredients. You wouldn't believe the demand for them!"

He tossed Pax two of the bone-shaped cookies and Pax gulped them down with quick chomps.

"Judging from his reaction, I think you've got a hit on your hands, Jerry," she said.

"I'll have a bag for him next time you come around."

As they climbed aboard the Harley, Sister Agatha looked at Pax's satisfied canine grin and laughed. "You're a pig, Pax, but I love you anyway."

Despite her struggle to keep her thoughts hopeful and centered on God, the monastery's situation weighed heavily on her as she drove back home. Neither the cool air sweeping past her nor Pax's insatiable doggy grin as he held his muzzle into the wind soothed her.

A short while later, Sister Agatha drove through the opening in the wall where the gate had been. She slowed, noting the piles of broken adobes on both sides of the drive. Everything had been swept up, and the pieces of the damaged gate had been dragged out of the road and were now resting against the wall. Yet despite the order they'd tried to impose, the destruction lay there for all to see—open wounds in God's house that silently demanded their attention.

Sister Agatha parked the Harley beside the Antichrysler, then released Pax, who immediately raced around the building toward the kitchen. Sister Agatha's footsteps were heavy as she made her way to the parlor door. The knowledge that all she brought with her was another disappointment stung.

Sister Bernarda stood as she came in. "I can tell from your expression that the news isn't good. Tell me what happened."

As always, the ex-marine's tone of voice made it sound less like a request and more like an order, but she'd grown used to that and it didn't bother her. Sister Bernarda's heart was in the right place. "No one's admitting a thing, and the sheriff doesn't have enough evidence to make an arrest. If we want the gate fixed before winter, we're going to have to find a way to do it on our own. Our insurance deductible is just too high to file a claim."

Sister Bernarda pursed her lips. "I should have expected as much. You better go tell Reverend Mother."

Sister Agatha nodded. "How's Sister Gertrude?"

Sister Bernarda's eyes narrowed with emotion and she shook her head. "Our old friend's on a new anticoagulant be-

39

cause she's still throwing clots. Her heart has continued to deteriorate since her last checkup," she said. Then, in a voice thick with emotion, she added, "The prognosis wasn't good."

A lump formed at the back of Sister Agatha's throat, and for a moment she didn't trust herself to speak. "And Reverend Mother knows?" she whispered.

Sister Bernarda nodded.

Sister Agatha felt her chest constrict. "And here I am bringing her even more bad news. I wish I had something positive to tell her."

As Sister Agatha walked down the long, narrow corridor, she prayed silently that she'd find the right words to soften the blow.

Sister Agatha knocked lightly at Reverend Mother's open door and spoke the customary greeting. "Praised be Jesus Christ."

"Now and forever," Reverend Mother answered. "Enter, child." Reverend Mother waved her to one of the straight-backed wooden chairs before her desk.

"I've got bad news, Mother," Sister Agatha said, getting right to the point. Drawing it out would only make the news more difficult.

"I read as much from your face when you came in," Reverend Mother said and walked to the statue of the Blessed Virgin that rested on a stand in the far corner. The only other decoration in the spartan office was a simple wooden crucifix hung on the white stucco wall directly behind her desk.

Sensing that Reverend Mother was asking The Lady for the strength to bear the news, she waited silently. After a long moment, Reverend Mother turned around. "Now tell me what you've learned."

Sister Agatha recounted the morning's events succinctly, then placed the cookie royalty check on her desk. "This money will help, but it's not nearly enough," she said. "On the positive side, Mr. Dexter predicts that our earnings will go up next quarter."

"Money's always a struggle," she said in a weary voice, then straightened her shoulders and looked at Sister Agatha directly. "We'll meet this new challenge with His help. Call everyone to the community room. We're facing a serious situation and prayers are needed. I'd like the externs to join us as well. Lock up the parlor for now."

"Right away, Mother," she said and left.

Sister Agatha found Sister de Lourdes in the hall. Respecting the need for quiet, Sister Agatha kept her voice low. "Ring the Maria bell, Sister. Everyone must attend a special meeting in the communal room."

"Right away, Your Charity," she said and hurried off.

The bells were at the heart of everything that defined their monastery. They called the sisters to Mass, to special prayers, and, on certain sad occasions, rang a death knell that announced a passing. The times the bells rang were, by and large, fixed in stone. When a bell rang at an unscheduled hour, it instantly commanded the sisters' attention, warning all that trouble was near.

4

L ESS THAN FIVE MINUTES AFTER THE MARIA BELL'S summons—three consecutive peals meant a special meeting—the nine nuns filed into the communal room. Elderly Sister Clothilde was one of the first, her hands still dusted with bits of flour. Aware of the many blessings her Cloister Clusters had brought to the monastery, Sister Clothilde had begun experimenting with a new cookie recipe.

Sister Eugenia, their infirmarian, came in next, pushing Sister Gertrude in her wheelchair. Sister Eugenia had been a nurse before joining the order and continued to serve the monastery in that capacity. It took patience and a great deal of love to serve as infirmarian. Sister Agatha believed that it was the hardest job of all. If she had to vote on which one of them exemplified the virtues of Our Lord best, she would have chosen Sister Eugenia in a heartbeat.

Sister Bernarda and Sister de Lourdes sat in two of the wooden chairs that surrounded their well-worn burgundy and blue sofa. The much-used donation had been repaired so many times by Sister Maria Victoria, their resident seamstress, that the upholstery fabric now resembled a patchwork quilt.

Seeing Sister Agatha staring pensively at the sofa, Sister Ignatius smiled. "Remember how badly we'd all wanted a comfortable couch down here and how one was donated to us when we least expected it? Have faith. Whatever brings us here today is just another opportunity to prove that God's love is an ever present help."

Sister Agatha smiled at her. Sister Ignatius was the most devout among them, often finding sought-after signs in the most ordinary things, like a dandelion growing in the rock garden or a colorful butterfly. Sister Ignatius's faith was unshakable, and there was a joyousness and peace about her that nothing seemed to disturb. Sister Agatha had no doubt that Sister Ignatius held a very special place in the Lord's heart.

Everyone stood as Reverend Mother came into the room. "Praised be Jesus Christ," Mother said, nodding at the sisters.

"Now and forever," they replied in unison.

Reverend Mother Margaret Mary carried the weight of their world on her shoulders. The office of Prioress was an elected position, but every three years for the past fifteen she'd been reelected without opposition. None of them felt as qualified as she was, so the decision was always unanimous.

The meeting opened with a prayer to St. Joseph, the Prior of their monastery. They asked that he, who had taken care of the Holy Family, intercede for them with God and help them find a way to help themselves.

Then Mother read from Isaiah, "He gives power to the

weary and to those who have no might he increases strength . . . they that wait upon the Lord shall renew their strength."

They finished with a Hail Mary, and a brief silence followed as they waited for Reverend Mother to speak.

"We have a serious financial crisis facing us," Reverend Mother said at long last. After telling the sisters that the winery next door was for sale, she continued. "We are asking that we be given a buffer zone and will continue to work for that. In the meantime, we also have other pressing business. In addition to the rewiring work that needs to be done, we now have to find a way to pay for the repairs to our wall and gate. I'd like our cellarer," she said, using the name given to the monastery's bookkeeper, "to tell us all exactly where we stand financially."

Sister Gertrude glanced around the room. Her voice was soft but never faltered. "Our situation is *not* good. Our health insurance premiums were due this month and that depleted our available funds. We don't have enough left over to cover the electrical work needed, let alone the repairs to the wall and gate. Since our scriptorium business is still fairly new, we can't borrow against future earnings without collateral. Sister de Lourdes offered to turn over the title to our station wagon, but our banker, Mr. Jenkins, just laughed. The motorcycle is worth quite a bit more to collectors, but only if we sold it outright, and that still wouldn't bring in the amount we need. The only thing the bank will accept is a mortgage on this property."

"Putting our home on the line has to be our last option," Reverend Mother said. "Remember St. Paul's words, 'Owe no man anything, but to love one another.'" She took a deep pensive breath and looked around the room. "Any suggestions? Anyone?"

"Our Lord will provide for us as he's always done. We just have to be patient, Mother," Sister Ignatius said softly. "Remember the words from Philippians that were part of our morning prayers today," she said, and brought out her breviary. "'Never worry about anything, but tell God all your desires of every kind in prayer and petition shot through with gratitude'. . . . That's all we have to do. He *will* take care of the rest. Remember the coin in the fish's mouth. All we have to do is stay alert for the opportunity that's sure to come our way."

Reverend Mother smiled. "You're right, child. Let's all pray with gratitude for the gifts we receive daily. This trial will be our opportunity to draw even closer to Our Lord."

She stood, then concluded the meeting with a Bible verse. "We do not fix our gaze on what is seen but on what is unseen. What is seen is transitory; what is unseen lasts forever." She paused, then looked at the sisters. "Let us now continue our work with the blessing of God."

As their business came to a close, Sister Agatha met with Sister Bernarda and Sister de Lourdes. "Maybe it's time for us to go out into the community and see if we can solicit a few cash donations, materials, or volunteers to help us with the repairs to the gate and wall. We'll take the novena cards that assure people we'll be praying for them and their intentions as a thank-you for their donations."

"The merchants don't listen to me like they do you and Sister Agatha," Sister de Lourdes said. "Last time I tried to get a donation of white paint for our walls, but the best I could get were two gallons of mauve and light green."

"We made do," Sister Bernarda said flatly. "It was enough."

Sister Agatha smiled. Her own room—a cell, as they were called here—was now a blend of both colors. Leftovers of each had been combined, yielding a pleasant, light coffee tone. "There's no rule that requires us to have white walls. And the walls really needed a coat of paint."

"But *you* were able to get Mr. Joyner to give us white when we needed to do the halls," Sister de Lourdes said, looking at Sister Agatha.

"That's only because he had plenty sitting around when I came by, that's all. Timing is important."

"I think *my* time will be better spent in the scriptorium. We're backlogged there at the moment, but I think I can catch up today if I get down to it. Our system is now more hacker resistant, according to Merilee."

"Get to work then," Sister Agatha said.

"I'll take the first shift in town if you'll stay in the parlor, Sister Agatha," Sister Bernarda said.

"That's fine," she answered.

"I'll find out if Sister Eugenia needs me to pick up anything from the pharmacy, then I'll be going."

"May The Lady and her Son bless your efforts," Sister Agatha said, then hurried to the parlor.

The first thing Sister Agatha did when she arrived was unlock the front doors. By then, it was noon and the bells were ringing the Angelus, a devotion to honor the angel Gabriel's joyous message to the Virgin Mary. Then came Sext, one of the three little liturgical hours, so-called because they were of shorter duration.

Sister Agatha sat at the desk and began to honor the liturgical hours with a series of Pater Nosters. She'd only just begun when there was a knock at the parlor door.

"*Deo Gratias*," she said, honoring God first, then opened the door and invited the well-dressed stranger inside.

"Welcome to Our Lady of Hope Monastery. I'm Sister Agatha. How may I help you?" she asked, inviting their guest to take a seat.

He was pleasant looking, some might have even said handsome, and was wearing a brown, western-styled suit and cream-colored tie. His eyes were dark brown and his hair a shade too dark to be genuine for a man in his midforties. Her first impression was that the visitor was a salesman but, if so, he had no sample case and no business card in his hand—yet.

"My name's Ralph Simpson, Sister. I'd like to speak to Reverend Mother," he said, flashing her an engaging smile.

People who came to the monastery on business for the first time weren't always aware of the rules. "I'm afraid an audience with Reverend Mother is not as simple as all that," she said patiently. "Extern nuns like myself—those of us who don't take a vow of enclosure—are here to handle all the monastery's day-to-day business. Only on rare occasions does Reverend Mother actually come to the grille," she said, pointing to the latticed ironwork that separated the enclosure from the outer room.

"I understand," he said, nodding. "I represent one of your contributors, John Gutierrez. He owns the winery adjacent to this monastery. No date was set, but I believe Reverend Mother was interested in discussing the possibility of a buffer zone along the property line to protect the monastery from any pending development."

Sister Agatha gave a silent thanks to God. "Yes, that's true. As a matter of fact she's authorized me to meet with Mr. Gutierrez."

"Good. John actually sent me here to make you an offer on his behalf. What he's proposing is an exchange, really. John's heard of your skills as an investigator, Sister Agatha, and he'd like you to help him with a problem. In return, he's prepared to make a very generous donation to this monastery—the title to a fifty-foot-wide stretch of land along our common property line."

Sister Agatha smiled, excitement pulsing through her. "I

would like to speak to Mr. Gutierrez directly. Will this be possible?"

"He would have come here himself, but John's sick and he's having difficulty getting around. The trip from Colorado proved more difficult for him than he'd anticipated. Can you meet him at the Siesta Inn?"

"Yes, but first I'll have to make arrangements for someone to take over as portress, and I'll need Reverend Mother's permission before I leave the monastery. I'll be happy to give you a call later today and let you know when I can come."

"All right then. We'll look forward to hearing from you."

After saying good-bye, Sister Agatha watched Ralph Simpson climb into a large blue van and drive away. Unlike their Antichrysler, his car scarcely made any sound at all. Feeling envious and knowing it was a sin, she pushed back the emotion and sighed as the vehicle disappeared from sight.

It was shortly after noon when Sister Agatha locked the parlor doors, switched on the answering machine, and hurried down the hall to Reverend Mother's office. Her superior had just returned from Sext and was there with Sister Gertrude.

Hating to interrupt, but knowing Mother would want to know the latest news right away, Sister Agatha knocked lightly on the open door. After the usual greeting, Sister Agatha quickly explained what had transpired.

"I don't quite know what to make of this," Reverend Mother said slowly. "Mr. Simpson didn't give you much information. What could Mr. Gutierrez want you to do, identify some crooked employee of his?"

"I recognize Mr. Gutierrez's name, Mother," Sister Gertrude said. "He's sent us a few generous checks since he took over ownership of the vineyard, so it can't be because he can't afford to hire a private investigator."

Reverend Mother lapsed into a thoughtful silence. At long last she looked at Sister Agatha. "The future of that land affects us directly. The problem is we don't know much about this man. We need to check him out with Sheriff Green first. If the sheriff feels it would be safe for you to go, then do so, and take Pax with you."

"All right, Mother. I'll report back to you as soon as I know more," Sister Agatha said.

When Sister Eugenia showed up to wheel Sister Gertrude back to the infirmary, Mother signaled Sister Agatha to remain.

"Sister Gertrude looks so much better since she moved into the air-conditioned infirmary, Mother," Sister Agatha observed as soon as they were alone. "I don't think she would have made it through this past summer if she hadn't."

"What almost killed her wasn't the heat, it was not feeling useful. Forcing Gertie to rest and keeping her from the tasks she'd performed all her life did her more harm than good."

"You had the best of intentions, Mother," Sister Agatha responded. "After all, you were following her doctor's orders."

"Yes, but I should have remembered that work is a vital part of everything we are. Purpose and happiness are inexorably linked," Reverend Mother said as she walked with Sister Agatha to the door.

Sister Agatha returned to the parlor worried, and aware of how much depended on her now. Looking up Sheriff Tom Green's number, she dialed his direct line. It took a few minutes for him to answer and, when he did, he sounded tense and rushed.

"Did I call you at a bad time?" Sister Agatha asked.

"No, it's fine," he answered, an edge in his voice. "I just had a run-in with a defense attorney and they're seldom the bright spot in my day. What's up?"

She told him about their visitor and his offer. "I was hoping you could check out Ralph Simpson and John Gutierrez for me before I go over there."

"That's a good idea—safe and smart. Give me about a half hour, then I'll call you back. Sound good?"

"Wonderful. Thanks, Tom!"

Lunch, the main meal of the day, had already been served in the refectory, but portresses usually stayed at their desks. Today it was Sister Ignatius who brought a plate of spaghetti to the inner door leading into the parlor. As usual, Sister Agatha nearly missed her whisper-soft knock.

"Thank you," Sister Agatha said, taking the warm plate from her hands, and closing the door separating the parlor from the cloister again.

At her desk, she stared at the spaghetti unenthusiastically. Since there had been another bumper crop of tomatoes this year and Smitty's Grocery had also made a large donation of pasta to the monastery, meals would be predictably Italian for the foreseeable future.

A half hour came and went, but the phone remained silent. Around one thirty Sister Bernarda came into the parlor. "Your Charity, I'd be happy to take over your duties here if you could help Sister de Lourdes in the scriptorium. She's been getting a lot of customer complaints today. According to our records, we're shipping and billing properly. Yet some of NexCen's clients are telling us that we're sending them more than they ordered. Sister de Lourdes thinks it may be a bug or an incorrectly entered value in the program. But NexCen is extremely upset and sent us a very harsh letter. Their sales manager thinks we're trying to cover up for our own incompetence. Apparently their Web site records match that of the customers', so they're convinced the error is ours."

"Maybe the hacker is responsible. I'll go try and help her." Sister Agatha headed to the enclosure door, stopped, and glanced back at Sister Bernarda. "How did it go in town? Were you able to get any donors?"

She shook her head. "I had a few who said they'd get back to us, but it didn't look promising."

"You did your best. That's all any of us can do." She glanced at the phone for a moment, then looked back at her fellow extern. "I'm waiting for a call from the sheriff regarding our benefactor, Mr. Gutierrez. Let me know what he says as soon as you hear. It's important."

Sister Bernarda nodded. Elaborate explanations were seldom necessary here.

5

SISTER AGATHA STOOD BESIDE SISTER DE LOURDES, who was seated at the computer keyboard, and read aloud the directions in the software manual. All five computers were networked, so programs on the server—the main computer—could be accessed from any of the terminals.

"If this doesn't work, we'll have to call in the tech from NexCen again. But I'd rather avoid that, considering all the time she spent here before," Sister de Lourdes said.

"Maybe what you've already done has fixed the problem. If we don't get any more complaints, let's call it a win," Sister Agatha said. The last thing they needed now was to lose the NexCen contract.

Sister de Lourdes nodded. "I'll monitor everything from the server, and call the clients and verify their orders before we get anything ready to ship. If the problem's still there, I'll ask

NexCen to reissue us the software just in case something's been damaged or there were bugs in the versions we've installed."

"Could this be the result of the hacker's work again?"

"If it is, he hasn't bragged about it like before so there's no way I'd be able to say for sure. We're *supposed* to be protected with that new firewall. For now, I'll go ahead with our plan and hope it was just a software glitch."

"Sounds good." She was about to say more when Sister Bernarda came in, nodded once, then left.

"I'm needed back in the parlor. I'll be back as soon as I can." Sister Agatha found Sister Bernarda on the phone as she went into the room.

"Here she is now, Sheriff. Would you like to talk to her yourself?" After a second's pause, Sister Bernarda handed Sister Agatha the phone.

"'Afternoon again, Tom," she said.

"I had my deputy stop by the Siesta Inn, and he confirmed that John Gutierrez is there and bedridden. At first the motel's manager refused to have oxygen tanks in the room because they're highly combustible, but they worked it out after Gutierrez gave her an unbelievably hefty deposit."

"If he made the trip all the way from Colorado to get our help under those circumstances, I'm going to accommodate him and go by his room."

"It sounds legit, but if you have a problem, call me."

As she hung up, she glanced at Sister Bernarda. "I'm heading into town to talk to Mr. Gutierrez. He wants to negotiate a deal that might result in our monastery getting that strip of land Reverend Mother spoke about during Chapter."

"I figured as much from your side of the conversation," she said, then added. "Can you run an errand for me on the way?" Seeing Sister Agatha nod, she continued. "Stop by Catholic

Charities and ask them to arrange for some help for Mrs. Griego. The poor lady broke her leg last week and desperately needs someone to bring her a hot meal and do some cleanup. Her neighbor called earlier on her behalf." She handed Sister Agatha a slip of paper with Mrs. Griego's address and home number.

"I'll take care of it," Sister Agatha said, recognizing the name of one of their few regulars at Mass. "That explains why we didn't see her Sunday."

Sister Agatha grabbed the donated cell phone they always took with them when away from the monastery, stepped outside, and whistled. A heartbeat later, Pax came running around the corner of the building.

She smiled as he continued toward her at full speed. He looked as graceful as a cougar when he ran. Then, just when it looked like he'd be crashing right into her, he suddenly stopped and dropped his hindquarters in a perfect "sit" position.

"Come on. Get into the Harley. Road trip!"

They were on their way to town a minute later, Pax seated in the sidecar to her right, enjoying the blast of air.

It was almost four, and the air was starting to cool. In September, evenings tended to be brisk, though the days were warm unless it was raining and gusty.

Minutes later, as she passed the familiar, colorful storefronts, many dating back decades, people on the sidewalk saw them and waved. The Spanish-style cantinas, gas stations, and even the feed store were all part of the old downtown Bernalillo she'd come to love and include in her daily prayers.

Sister Agatha drove directly to the Catholic Charities office near the old church. She parked in the staff slot next to a silver Toyota with a rosary hanging from the rearview mirror and walked inside the former employment agency building.

The first thing that struck her was that the staff of four was down by two. Cutbacks had affected everything here recently. Harder times meant fewer donations and volunteers, and that, in turn, meant services had been curtailed.

The desk closest to the door was manned by a woman in a ruffled blouse typing at breakneck speed. As Sister Agatha approached, the brown-haired lady glanced up and then smiled when Sister Agatha introduced herself.

Going around the desk to pet Pax, she looked up at Sister Agatha. "I've heard so much about you, Sister! The dog, too! I've been dying to meet you. I'm Terri Montoya."

Sister Agatha had Pax shake hands and from Terri's enthusiastic response, Sister Agatha had no doubt she was a dog person.

"So how can I help you, Sister?" Terri asked as she scratched Pax behind the ears.

Even though she was a good one hundred pounds overweight, Terri moved fluidly and with grace. She had a lovely face, too, with beautiful, almond-shaped eyes and an easy smile.

Sister Agatha told her all she knew about Mrs. Griego. Throughout, Terri chewed her gum loudly and with an open mouth, a habit Sister Agatha detested, though she tried not to show it.

Terri wrote down the information, then glanced up at her. "I'll send a caseworker over to assess the need as soon as we can. But it may take a few days. As you can tell, we're understaffed."

"With all the cutbacks, I'm surprised you'll be able to get to her so quickly," Sister Agatha said, glancing at the two empty desks.

"The senior people just quit," she said pointing to the

empty desks. "I was hired after they left and pretty much had to figure out the job on my own. I've only been here three weeks, and I can see now why someone might want to just give up. The workload is staggering. But I'll stick it out. I need the job."

"Things will get better. They always do. Just remember to keep praying," Sister Agatha said.

"I will, Sister. You pray for me too, okay?"

As Sister Agatha walked back outside, she checked her watch. It was almost four thirty now. She'd head over to see Mr. Gutierrez next.

The Siesta Inn was less than five minutes away, west of Camino Real and adjacent to one of the ancient irrigation ditches dug by farmers perhaps four hundred years earlier. Sister Agatha parked near the office of the long, one-story, pueblo-style building that circled a small interior courtyard. Freshly stuccoed and well maintained, the inn stood as a silent testimony of days gone by, when it had been the hacienda of one of the wealthiest Hispanic families in the area.

Leaving the Harley in front of one of the large, peeled-log parking lot barriers, she climbed off the cycle and started toward the front door of the office. She'd just reached the steps when she spotted Ralph Simpson beyond the entrance to the interior courtyard, leaning against an old cottonwood, having a smoke. Seeing her, he crushed his cigarette with his heel and came outside the enclosure to greet her.

Sister Agatha stopped and waited for him to reach the brick-lined walk and join her. "Good afternoon, Mr. Simpson."

"Just Ralph, Sister," he answered. "I was on break, so I decided to have a smoke outside and wait for you. I spoke to Sister Bernarda earlier, and she said you'd be by within the hour."

He paused, frowning, then continued. "I'm sure glad she has the cold and not you. It wouldn't be a good idea for anyone with a respiratory virus to get near Mr. Gutierrez right now."

"What makes you think Sister Bernarda has a cold?" she asked, genuinely puzzled.

"I just assumed . . . well, her voice sounded choked up, you know? Maybe it was just allergies."

Sister Bernarda had no allergies as far as she could recall. Sister Agatha thought it over, and realized that Sister Bernarda had probably been crying in the privacy of the parlor. After the accident the other night, they'd never discussed what was bothering her. Sister Agatha made up her mind right then to find out as soon as possible what was getting her so upset.

"I'm glad you've accepted my boss's invitation," Ralph said, bringing her focus back to the business at hand. "But I'm not sure your dog should go into the room with us," he added, glancing down at Pax. "John's respiratory problems . . ."

"Say no more. Pax will understand. I'll leave him at 'stay' outside in the hall. He'll wait for me."

Once inside the inn they walked down the hall, passing tall, hand-carved pine doors with names like "Sage" and "Chaparral" instead of numbers. Noticing that Ralph was holding his shoulders rigid, and every once in a while cast a nervous sideways glance at the dog, she added, "Relax, Ralph. Pax is harmless." Making sure she remained between the dog and him, she continued. "But he's picking up on your anxiety and that's making him a little tense."

He gave her a taut smile. "Sorry, I'm just not that crazy about dogs," he muttered.

As they reached the final door, which had a sign proclaiming they'd reached the "Chamisa" room, Ralph reached for a card with a magnetic strip and opened the door.

Sister Agatha gave Pax the hand signal to "down and stay," then went inside. The suite was large, and at quick glance appeared to be divided into the sleeping area, a sitting room, bathroom, and a small kitchenette in an alcove. A man propped up by pillows sat up on a high four-poster bed, his breathing loud and labored. He was hooked up to a pulse oximeter, an oxygen and heart monitor that was attached to his finger. Its steady, rhythmic beeping echoed in the background.

"Wonderful, Sister, you're here," Mr. Gutierrez said in a stronger voice than she would have expected under the circumstances. "Please make yourself comfortable."

She stood near the door, not wanting to be too far away from Pax in case someone came down the hall and reacted to him.

"Don't keep John talking too long, Sister. He tires easily, though he'd cut out his tongue before he'd admit it," Ralph whispered, leaning into her.

"Will you take a seat here by the bed, Sister?" John said.

"Thanks, but our monastery's dog is right outside at 'stay' and I'd like to remain close by."

"Why don't you bring him inside the room? It's okay," John added. "I have difficulty breathing, but it's from physical deterioration, not allergies. As long as he doesn't try to get up on the bed, he'll be fine."

"Thank you, Mr. Gutierrez." Sister Agatha opened the door, gave Pax the command to "come," then placed him at "down" and "stay" just inside. "He'll be fine right there."

Ralph pulled a chair closer to the bed for Sister Agatha then retreated silently.

"Make yourself comfortable, Sister," John said, then coughed, the sound deep and ominous.

As Sister Agatha took a seat, she studied the man before

her. In contrast to his manicured nails and expensive gold ring, John's face attested to a rough life lived with a ready fist. His nose had been broken more than once, and there were little scars on his left cheek as well as one long one by his chin. His eyes were heavy-lidded, dark circles rimming each. Though he couldn't have been more than fifty-five, he was pale and didn't inhale as much as gulp in a breath and then let it out in an uneven gasp. Yet he seemed to be struggling less than a cardiac patient like Sister Gertrude did at times, or the asthmatic roommate she'd had in college.

"I've read a great deal about you in the local paper," John said, then added, "I lived in this area some years ago, and when I moved away to Colorado I missed it, so I decided to subscribe and keep up with the news."

She nodded politely, hoping he'd get to the point of the visit soon—the job she was supposed to do. Curiosity was nipping at her heels.

As if reading her mind, he continued. "I'm a dying man, Sister Agatha—big C. My niece is my only living relative, and I've got reason to believe that she's living in this area now. I've hired private investigators, of course, but they've only come up with strangers who have the same name. It's possible she's gotten married, but if she has, there's no record of it in this state or any of the adjacent ones. I have no leads, but you seem to be very resourceful. After reading about your exploits working with the police, I knew you were just the person to help me."

"I'll need to know a lot more, Mr. Gutierrez," she said cautiously.

He nodded and continued. "My niece and I lost track of each other several years ago, not on the best of terms, and it's important that I find her quickly. I have no children of my own, so she'll be inheriting everything I've worked for—my corporation and its assets. But my reasons for needing to find her go beyond that . . . it's about continuity and family. I can't die in peace until I've had a chance to talk to her again." He paused, as if gathering his strength, then glanced at her and continued. "I'm prepared to offer you—well, the monastery— that strip of land the Archbishop and I discussed briefly over the telephone. I'll also pay for any expenses you may incur if you accept the job."

Ralph Simpson stepped over and held out a check from a Denver bank that had already been made out for five hundred dollars.

"That's just to cover your initial expenses," John said. "I've also had the necessary papers drawn up to transfer ownership of a substantial portion of land to the monastery—should you find my niece—along with a generous check for your services."

He waved toward the night table, where a thick manila folder was resting. "That deed would expand your borders and give you a very effective buffer zone against any possible future development. Go ahead and look for yourself, then take it with you and have an attorney vet it out."

Sister Agatha reached over and skimmed through the papers, which appeared authentic and accurate from her limited knowledge of legal documents. Although she knew enough about business not to allow her enthusiasm to get the better of her, this was clearly a Godsend. Knowing honesty was called for now, she fought the temptation to keep her mouth shut about any misgivings and take the deal immediately.

"I don't know what you've read about me," Sister Agatha said, "but have you considered the possibility that I may not be able to find your niece?"

"I have full confidence in your abilities, Sister Agatha," John said simply. "But even if you fail, you'll still get to keep whatever remains of that check. I'm sure your order can always find a use for the money. And by at least trying to find her, you'll be helping a dying man."

Christian charity almost compelled her to accept on the spot. But she knew better. The vow of obedience bound her. "I'll talk to Reverend Mother this evening. The decision is totally up to her. But, tell me, what makes you think that your niece is in this area, and what's her name?"

"Her maiden name was Angela—Angie Sanchez. She's my late sister's daughter. She was fresh out of high school when her mother and father died in an auto accident on Highway 528. Angie's the only family I have now. Several months ago, after giving up on private investigators, I put out feelers through my business associates and one of them—a local Realtor—told me she'd seen Angie at the Cottonwood Mall, the shopping center on Albuquerque's northwest side. You've probably heard of it."

Sister Agatha nodded. "Go on."

"She saw Angie through the store window as she passed by and they made eye contact. My associate paid for her purchases and hurried out of the store, intending on catching up to her but, by then, my niece was nowhere in sight. It happened so fast she was sure she'd spooked Angie somehow."

"What kind of work does Angie do?"

"She has a degree in business and has worked in real estate. What she's doing now . . . ," he shrugged.

"I could use a photo if you have one," Sister Agatha said.

He motioned toward an envelope on the nightstand next to him and she reached for it. Inside the inn's stationery was a small snapshot. "That's a copy I made from the original. It's five years old."

Sister Agatha looked at the grainy image, cropped and enlarged from an apparent group photo. The face looked vaguely familiar. Maybe she had seen Angie in the Bernalillo area. The knowledge made Mr. Gutierrez's offer even more tempting.

"What have you done to try and find her?"

"According to my investigators, every phone book and journal in four states has been checked, including all the databases online that we can access. If Angie's married and has a new name now . . . well, it's not possible to check out every Angela in the country, is it? But this new lead is the best I have. It makes sense that she'd return to Bernalillo. Angie lived in the area for many years and she has some very happy childhood memories of this place."

"What were her interests and hobbies?"

"She loved country-western dancing and used to frequent some of the local nightclubs. And, as far as hobbies, she always liked hiking in the bosque." A faraway look came over him as he continued. "I still remember the first hike Angie went on with her father and me. We'd decided to spend the night in the Manzanos, south of Capilla Peak. I used to love that area, and at that time I was still working as a hunting guide. Halfway down the trail to our planned campsite, Angie realized that her favorite stuffed animal was missing from her backpack—a raggedy, pitiful-looking white rabbit. We offered to buy her a new one when we returned to town—then a dozen new ones—but she wasn't having any of it. Her dad and I ended up walking almost the entire distance down the mountain trail to where we'd parked the car, searching for that thing," he said then began to cough. After taking a sip of water, he continued. "By the time we found it, it looked chewed up, like a wild animal had played with it, but it didn't make any difference to her."

He paused until his breathing evened again. "Memories

like those are what I hold most dear right now—and if there is an afterlife, that's what I'm taking with me. Family matters to me, Sister, though it took me a long time to realize that."

Sister Agatha returned the photo to the envelope and placed it back on the nightstand. "If Reverend Mother says I can take the job, I'll be back for the photo and that check. But I don't feel right taking either until she gives me permission."

"That's fine," he said, then went into a long coughing spasm that left him shaky and breathless.

She walked to the pitcher and refilled his water glass without being asked. "Are you all right?" she asked, as he took it from her hand.

He nodded. "It's uncomfortable, that's all," he managed.

"I do have one more question," Sister Agatha said. "How close are you to selling the vineyard?"

"Eric Barclay's interested in buying it back from me. I took it off his hands a few years ago when he was having financial troubles. He's already offered me what I paid for it plus five percent, but the truth is that my own financial advisers insist I can do better. There's another party putting together an offer I believe will be much more lucrative."

"And what do the other prospective buyers plan to do with the vineyards?"

"I have no idea, but I do know the individuals have two significant rental apartment structures within the Albuquerque area."

Sister Agatha managed not to groan. "I'll be in touch again as soon as Reverend Mother makes her decision, which I expect will be shortly," she said, standing.

"I'll look forward to hearing from you, Sister."

Soon she and Pax were on their way back to the monastery. As she sped down a long curve in the road, Sister Agatha spotted a sedan quickly closing in on her. It was no one she recognized, but as the distance between them narrowed, a sixth sense warned her of danger. Sister Agatha glanced at Pax, who seemed to sense her abrupt change of mood, and now sat fully alert.

"Hang on," she said. Accelerating, she zipped into a side street that wound its way back around to the main highway. When the sedan didn't follow, she breathed a sigh of relief. Maybe she was getting paranoid.

Then she spotted the sedan again. It was coming up the side street and once again closing in on her. She thought about the hacker who'd been causing so many problems for them, remembering that he or she was a local. Maybe he *had* read that old article in the paper and knew that the nuns were now managing the NexCen Web site. If he'd also grown tired of those impersonal computer attacks . . .

"I don't like this, Pax. Hang on, boy," she yelled over the rumble of the motorcycle as she accelerated.

Sister Agatha moved out, heading down one of the back roads that ran toward the river. By the time she doubled back, circled around, and reached the main road, now south of Bernalillo, no one was behind her.

She smiled, satisfied, but then, a second later, she heard a siren and, as she slowed down and pulled over, she saw the sedan she'd tried so hard to avoid coming up behind her.

"Hey, what are you doing?" Sheriff Tom Green called out as he parked and got out of the unmarked sedan. "Practicing how to lose a tail?" he added with a grin.

She removed her helmet and glared at him. "You knothead! Why didn't you use the emergency lights or siren before now? You almost gave me a heart attack!"

"I just wanted to show you my new car so you'd recognize

it. What's making you so jumpy?" he asked, his eyes narrowing. "What are you up to?"

"Nothing. Really," she added, seeing the open look of skepticism on his face. She didn't expect him to talk about police business that didn't concern her, so there was no reason why she should discuss monastery business with him—or the problem with their computers. "Have you found out anything that might help us get compensated for our broken gate?" she asked, changing the subject quickly.

He shook his head. "I know how important that is to all of you, so I'm not ignoring it. But the only thing I've got is some scuttlebutt. Jack Miller's planning to sue Liz and Leeann's families."

"That's a waste of time. They have no money to give him. I'd pressure them myself if I thought it would get me the name of whoever was behind the wheel of that SUV." She paused and then holding his gaze, added, "We've got to find a way to get those kids to tell us what they know."

"The problem is that neither girl is in custody now so—" Before he could say anything else, he received a call on his cell phone. Tom stepped away from the Harley, spoke hurriedly for a moment, then closed up the phone. "Gotta go. There's a problem back at the station."

After he drove off, Sister Agatha fastened her helmet and continued north through town, intending to return to the monastery. As she passed the Burger Biggins, the new local hot spot for the town's teens, she caught a glimpse of Liz standing beside a customized car talking to some tough-looking kids.

Away from authority figures like the police and her mother, Sister Agatha suspected that she would have a better shot at getting answers from Liz—that is, of course, providing she could find a way to separate her from her friends for a few moments. To that end, she came up with an idea that was practically foolproof. With a smile, Sister Agatha made a left turn. She had work to do at the Burger Biggins.

6

L IZ STOOD WITH THREE BOYS WHO WERE WEARING EX-
tremely baggy pants, dark, sleeveless T-shirts, and ama-
teur tattoos with a stylized font that reminded her of old
English.

As Sister Agatha pulled into the parking slot next to them
and stopped, one of the boys whistled. "Hey, Sister, primo set
of wheels there!"

Sister Agatha removed her helmet and placed a hand on
Pax, making sure he stayed inside the sidecar at sit. "Ernesto, I
haven't seen you in years," she said, recognizing him from his
grade-school days at St. Charles despite the peach fuzz haircut.

"Nobody but Tia Rosita calls me Ernesto anymore, Sister.
My name's Macho."

"Really? Well, I have to agree with Tia Rosita. To, me,
you'll always be Ernesto." She looked at each face, making eye

contact with every member of the group. "I was just talking to Sheriff Green, and I believe he's looking for some volunteers to help scrub off some of the graffiti on the sides of buildings downtown. Would you guys like to lend a hand?" she asked. Tom had said no such thing—not this time—but there was a project going on, sponsored by the Police Athletic League, so it wasn't a total lie.

Ernesto and his two male companions reacted exactly the way she'd hoped.

"Uh . . . okay, Sister. Maybe later. But I gotta go now," Ernesto said, reaching for the door handle on the low-slung car just behind him.

The other two boys with him avoided eye contact with her as well and, muttering excuses, shuffled toward an adjacent vehicle as quickly as their "cool" walk would allow.

By the time Sister Agatha looked back at Liz, she saw the girl was trying to slink away. Using her best teacher/nun voice, she snapped, "One moment, Liz."

The girl stopped in her tracks, rolling her eyes as Ernesto drove away, in case he was watching, then finally turned to face her. "You want me for something else, Sister? Please tell me it isn't that gate thing again!"

"Liz, it's just you and me here now . . . well, and Pax," she said, noting that the girl had her eyes on the dog, who was still in the sidecar. "Relax."

"You're so lucky to have him, Sister," Liz said, going over to pet him. "He's really beautiful. When I leave home that's one of the first things I'll be getting," Liz said, then started to put her hands into her pockets before she realized her slacks had no pockets. Awkwardly, she crossed her arms in front of her chest.

Sister Agatha allowed the silence to stretch out between

them, sensing Liz wanted to tell her something, but was finding it difficult to put into words.

"You *know* I'm not involved in what happened at the monastery, right, Sister Agatha?" Liz said. "And I don't drink or go cruising with anyone who would do that either."

"You're still hanging around with the wrong crowd," Sister Agatha said softly. "And when that becomes a habit, you can get caught up in trouble you never intended."

"I'm not part of a gang, honest. But the people I *thought* were my friends at St. Charles just don't want to hang with me anymore. Guys like Ernesto at least don't look down their noses at me."

"Liz, you're still dancing around the big issue. You *know* something about the accident at our gates that you're not telling me."

"You're wrong, Sister. I don't know anything about who stole that SUV, and I wasn't there when someone used it to ram your gates. I swear! I can't figure out how those beer cans got there. Maybe someone put my prints on them. It's possible to do that, you know. I saw it on TV."

Sister Agatha gave her an incredulous look. "Come on, Liz. Give us both a break."

Liz sighed and stepped closer to Sister Agatha. "Okay," she whispered, "but you can't tell anyone."

Even under these circumstances Sister Agatha couldn't bring herself to purposely mislead Liz. "Will Sheriff Green need to know what you're going to tell me in order to make an arrest?"

"No," Liz answered flatly.

"Okay—go for it then. I'm listening."

"Leeann and I got invited to Sheila Conner's house that night for a kind-of party. Sheila's parents were out of town, so we snuck out after Leeann's parents went to bed. One of the guys Sheila invited brought a six-pack and we each had *one* beer. That's it, Sister. And I didn't even finish mine. I just sipped it for a while. I hate beer, and this wasn't even cold. It almost made me gag."

"Then how does the wrecked SUV fit into this? I don't understand," Sister Agatha asked.

"Neither do we. We never left her house—well, except for one time—until we snuck back into Leeann's at around two in the morning."

"What happened that one time, Liz? What did you do?"

She tugged at her ring and stared at her hand. "That was when Sheila and I dumped the empties in her neighbor's trash can across the street," she muttered. "If Sheila's dad had seen the cans in *their* garbage, he would have grounded her until after the Second Coming."

Sister Agatha nodded thoughtfully. She knew the Conners. Sheila's dad had been arrested for domestic abuse, and his wife had spent time at the battered-woman's shelter. "Sheila took quite a chance," Sister Agatha said softly, "and so did you and Leeann."

"I know, but we all feel sorry for Sheila. Sheila's parents don't allow her to do *anything*. I don't blame her for cutting loose once in a while. But as God's my witness, Sister Agatha, none of us have the remotest idea how those cans got into that SUV. We put them in the neighbor's recycle bin. There was no lid, and it was full already, so the cans were on top. But why would anyone go pick them out? To take the last sip? Yuck."

"That still sounds like a strange story, Liz. Someone stealing basically empty beer cans?" Sister Agatha challenged her with a long, skeptical gaze.

"Sister, I'm telling you the truth. Macho—Ernesto—was

there trying to make his move on Leeann. And, yeah, we were drinking beer. But *no way* we'd steal a car."

"Gangs have been known to do that, and Ernesto's in a gang," Sister Agatha pressed.

"The Diablos Locos act tough and all that, but none of them will risk the D-home or jail. Macho's uncle is a cop, and he leans on Macho pretty hard. That's why Macho stays clean—not including the beer, of course."

Sister Agatha heard voices, one she recognized, and turned to look. Macho had returned, and appeared to be arguing with another teen—a slender kid with styled hair and clothes that didn't suggest a gang affiliation.

Liz saw what was going on, too. "Don't worry, Macho won't throw blows. Not here in public, anyway."

The boy Macho had been confronting walked away quickly, not running but close to it.

"See?" Liz lowered her voice. "Macho got arrested once and his uncle took him to the D-home. He left him there overnight just to show him what jail was like. Then he told Macho about prison and made sure he met a couple of ex-cons. Since then, Macho has been straight—well, except for a little drinking, and giving some of the kids at school a hard time."

Hearing footsteps on the asphalt, Sister Agatha turned her head and saw Macho approaching. Pax got to his feet suddenly, his gaze on the boy, but Sister Agatha reassured him quickly. "It's okay, boy."

"Noticed you stuck around, Liz. You guys talking about the beer cans again?" Seeing Sister Agatha nod, he added, "I don't know what Liz told you, Sister, but someone set us up."

"She knows what happened," Liz confirmed.

He looked at Liz then back at Sister Agatha. "Did she tell you where she and Sheila left the empties?"

"Yes, she did," Sister Agatha answered.

She knew that it was almost a direct route from where the cans had supposedly been dumped by the girls to the site where the SUV had been stolen. The beer cans *could* have been picked up en route by the SUV's driver. She wouldn't rule out the possibility that it had been a deliberate act to target the kids.

Knowing how easily violence could escalate between rival gangs, she added, "But if someone had wanted to deliberately frame you or your friends, they would have been more careful handling the cans. Most of the prints were lost—smeared. The police only got one partial and one full print."

"Yeah, maybe you're right, Sister, but it could be they weren't too smart about it. You never know," Macho said. "I'm going to keep my eyes and ears open. If I hear anything, I'll let you know."

"Thanks," Sister Agatha replied.

"You coming, Liz?" Macho pointed toward his car, which was parked several slots down.

"I'll meet you there in a sec."

As he strolled away, Liz turned to Sister Agatha and in a whisper-soft voice, added, "There's something I've been meaning to tell you. The nuns have made some enemies in town, so watch your back."

"Enemies? What on earth are you talking about?"

"That's all I've got to say, Sister." Liz started to walk away, but Sister Agatha placed a hand on her arm.

"Tell me what you've heard, Liz," she pressed.

"That's all I know, Sister. Just remember what I said," she whispered urgently, then jogged over to join Macho, who'd stopped to wait about halfway to his car.

Sister Agatha watched Liz for a moment, trying to figure

things out. Liz wouldn't have said something like that without reason. She suddenly had a strong feeling that the monastery's problems were just beginning.

By the time she returned to the monastery it was after six. Although the parlor was locked to visitors now, she knew that either Sister Bernarda or Sister de Lourdes would be there, waiting for her return.

Sister Agatha knocked lightly and Sister Bernarda came to the door immediately. "We were beginning to worry about you," Sister Bernarda said, her voice hard.

"I'm sorry. I was delayed," she answered. "Let me help you lock up and then we'll go to recreation. It's been a long, tough day and you and I could both use some time to unwind," Sister Agatha said.

Sister Bernarda shook her head. "I'm going to chapel. I need to sort some things out."

"Your Charity, won't you tell me what's bothering you?" she asked, pleading with her eyes as well as with her words. "You've been so upset lately and I'd really like to help."

Sister Bernarda stared thoughtfully at the gold band around the fourth finger of her left hand, the symbol that distinguished her as a Bride of Christ. "I need to get a better handle on this before I can talk about it. But there *is* something you can do."

"Name it."

"Pray that I can find peace again."

"I will, Sister Bernarda. And remember our Lord always takes care of his own."

After making sure the parlor was locked up, Sister Agatha went to the communal room. When she arrived, Reverend

Mother and Sister Gertrude were preparing for their daily walk. Sister Gertrude's doctor had advised her to find an "exercise buddy" for the times she left her wheelchair so that she wouldn't overexert herself. Reverend Mother had insisted on taking the job.

Before Sister Agatha could join them, Sister de Lourdes took her aside. "Your Charity, I need to speak to you. Something's been weighing heavily on Sister Bernarda. I found her almost in tears earlier today, though she tried to hide that as soon as she saw me. She instantly muttered something about hormones acting up, and said I shouldn't give it another thought."

Mood swings and emotional outbreaks were part of menopause, and Sister Bernarda was the right age for that, but it wasn't really something they'd ever talked about. Before she could answer Sister de Lourdes, Sister Clothilde came up, and, mindful of her vow of silence, signaled for Sister Agatha to follow her. They ended up in the kitchen, where Sister Clothilde placed a bowl of vegetable soup and a slice of bread in front of her.

"Sister Clothilde, this is very kind. You saved me something from collation," Sister Agatha said, using the term for dinner. "But it wasn't necessary."

"Yes, it was," another voice piped in from behind her.

Sister Agatha turned her head and saw that Sister Eugenia had followed them in. "You've been neglecting your arthritis medication, Sister Agatha, and tonight I intend to see to it that you take your pill. We're expecting rain, and you know how your hands swell when the humidity is up."

"It really hasn't been bothering me so much lately," Sister Agatha protested. "I don't want to take any medication unless there's a need."

"If you wait until the symptoms start, you're in for a rough time, and I'm here to make sure we avoid that."

Sister Agatha glanced down at her hands. Her joints were misshapen but not badly. Still, arthritis made her feel ancient and far older than her midforties. As she glanced up at Sister Eugenia, she saw her bright blue eyes shimmering with uncompromising determination—a sure sign that any argument would be futile.

As Sister Agatha began to eat, Sister Eugenia took out the medicine bottle from her pocket and placed one pill before her. "Take it after you finish eating—not during. And *don't* forget!"

Sister Agatha felt guilty sitting there eating while Sister Clothilde gave up recreation, but the older nun refused to leave her side. After she finished, Sister Agatha washed the dishes and helped sweep up and clean the kitchen. They were nearly done and anticipating the bell for Compline when Sister de Lourdes came in looking for her.

"Sister Agatha, tomorrow after morning prayers, will you come help me in the scriptorium? The orders are getting all fouled up again. We've also received some letters that I need to talk to you about. They're very—"

The bell for Compline rang, and immediately they stopped speaking. Their bridegroom called. Heads bowed, they silently made their way to chapel.

7

T HE NEXT MORNING SISTER AGATHA MET WITH REV-
erend Mother and went over the details of her meeting
with John Gutierrez.

After reading the copies of the legal agreement, Reverend
Mother looked up. "This looks like a great opportunity, but do
you think you'll be able to find Angela Sanchez? Private investigators weren't able to help Mr. Gutierrez. What makes you
think you'll be able to do what they couldn't?"

"Many people around here would be reluctant to speak to a
stranger. But most everyone knows me and, by and large, I'm
trusted."

"Go ahead and give it your best try then, child. You have
our blessings and Our Lord to guide you."

"I'll get right on it. Mr. Gutierrez's check will help our
cash-flow problem, too. It's the proverbial coin in the fish's
mouth—coming when it's most needed and out of the blue."

"That sum would have paid for the gate and then some when I was a girl. Nowadays, it doesn't go very far—not with health insurance, car insurance, and monthly utility bills," she said, then added in a stronger voice, "But we'll take things one day at a time. 'Sufficient unto the day is the evil thereof,' as Our Lord said."

By the time Sister Agatha made it to the scriptorium, Merilee Brown was there with Sister de Lourdes. The NexCen tech had shown up once again to help them out. Aware Sister Agatha had joined them and, not wanting to interrupt Merilee at the keyboard, Sister de Lourdes took Sister Agatha aside.

"She's checking out the system again, trying to find the source of the latest glitches. This might take hours," she said in a whisper-soft voice, "and I'll need to stay here with Merilee. Do you think Sister Bernarda can cover my shift in the parlor?"

"If she can't, I will," Sister Agatha said.

Sister Agatha hurried to the parlor and found Sister Bernarda sorting through some hand tools in a plastic container. Tears stained her face. Seeing Sister Agatha, she looked away quickly and wiped her face.

"I've checked with Mr. Fiorino and he's agreed to inspect the work I do with the outlets," she said, her tone preempting any questions. "I'm now checking to find out what else I'll need to start work."

Sister Agatha touched her arm lightly. "I sure wish you'd tell me what's bothering you, Sister. Talking about things may help."

Sister Bernarda's shoulders sagged as if she were carrying an unbearable weight, but, this time, she nodded. "I'm going through menopause and it's been forcing me to take a hard look at everything—mostly myself," she admitted reluctantly.

"I know this sounds crazy, but the worst of it is knowing that even if I left my vocation—which I never would—I still wouldn't be able to have children now. When we're young, no decision seems irrevocable. Then, as we get older, we have to live with the consequences of the choices we made. As a nun, I've lived with that sacrifice and never questioned it. But once my periods stopped, the awareness of what I'd given up started eating at me. Sometimes it feels like there's a huge hole inside me. I think it's the emptiness left by all the things that might have been."

Sister Agatha wanted to hug her but knew Sister Bernarda wouldn't tolerate it. "Knowing we'll never have kids is the biggest sacrifice we all make. None of us ever really gets over it," she answered gently.

"But when you face the fact that there's no turning back—*that's* when the cost hits you the hardest."

"When you became a nun you submitted everything you are to His care. Put this longing and your tears before Him now. He promised never to leave us comfortless. You need to trust Him now more than ever."

Sister Bernarda nodded silently. "I am His bride."

"He loves you and He *is* faithful."

Sister Bernarda said nothing for a long time then, taking a deep breath, focused her attention back on Sister Agatha. "Enough of this," she said, sounding like her old self at the moment. "Did you stop by to let me know you were going into town?"

Sister Agatha nodded. "I'm doing a job for Mr. Gutierrez," Sister Agatha said, and gave her the highlights.

"It sounds like a wonderful offer, particularly with that parcel of land thrown in. I hope it all works out."

"Before I go there's something else. We have a potential

problem. Our monastery may have acquired some enemies in the community," she said, telling Sister Bernarda what Liz had said. "Normally I don't pay any attention to rumors, but in view of our destroyed gate, the person lurking right outside our wall, and having to deal with a hacker . . . well, I think there might be something to this. These incidents can't all be just the result of bad luck or coincidence. Liz may be on to something."

"But who are these enemies we're supposed to have?" Sister Bernarda asked. "Last year's cookie war, if we can call it that, was resolved amicably. And there's been no other source of contention between us and the community."

"It's time I headed into town and started poking around. Maybe I can pick up some hint about what's going on."

Just then Sister Clothilde came up to the grille, rapped on the bars, and extended a note to them.

Sister Bernarda read it quickly, then looked at Sister Agatha. "There's a man with binoculars looking over the wall that separates our property from the vineyard."

"I'll take Pax and go see what that's about," Sister Agatha said.

"You're not going without me. I'll lock up the parlor," Sister Lernarda said.

Heading out through the kitchen and picking up Pax along the way, the three went outside. Sister Agatha reached the wall first, stood on the *banco*, and looked over at the vineyard, studying the area. As she did, Pax continued sniffing the air and growling.

"He's still out there," Sister Agatha said softly as Sister Bernarda joined her, "and it's not Eric, or Pax wouldn't be growling. But why doesn't he come out into the open . . . unless he's up to no good?" she added, not really expecting an answer.

"We should hop over and find out for ourselves," Sister

Bernarda said. "But if we do that without permission, *we're* the ones trespassing."

"I'll take the Harley, drive around, and find Eric," Sister Agatha said. "In the meantime, call Sheriff Green and tell him what's going on. Remember that we've found cigarette butts on *our* side of the property, so we know for a fact that someone's been hanging around real close to our wall."

Seeing Pax begin to relax, Sister Agatha breathed a sigh of relief. "Whoever it was has moved on, but I'm going to go warn Eric. He needs to stay on the lookout. Or maybe he already knows who it is. Either way, he and I need to talk."

"Will you be coming right back?" Sister Bernarda asked.

"No. As long as I'm out, I might as well go pick up Mr. Gutierrez's check. Then I think I'll pay Tom Green a visit. If we've got enemies, he needs to know about it."

"I'll let Reverend Mother know what just happened. But for what it's worth, I think your instincts are right. What happened to our gate wasn't just an accident. Even if the driver was drunk, we were singled out."

"We have enemies, Sister Bernarda, but we also have friends," she said softly. "He gives His Angels charge over us. Those armed with faith have all they need."

8

WITH PAX IN THE MOTORCYCLE'S SIDECAR, SISTER
Agatha drove down the road about a quarter of a
mile, then turned up past the Realtor's sign into
the driveway that led to Luz del Cielo Vineyard and Winery.
The main house, an old Spanish-style villa with a red clay–tiled
roof and several balconies, had once been Carla Barclay's pride
and joy. But now only Eric and their daughter remained.

Sister Agatha parked in the shade, ordered Pax to stay,
then climbed off the bike. Thinking of happier days when the
large fountain had bubbled with life, she stared at it, lost in
thought. Like the vineyard, it seemed to be waiting for something yet to be defined.

Arriving on the redbrick steps, Sister Agatha knocked on
the massive carved wooden front door. No one answered. Not
so long ago this building had always been open during business

hours. Eric Barclay's daughter would greet visitors and offer to take them on a tour or invite them to sample the house wine. But then, Eric, inundated with medical bills from his late wife's losing battle with cancer, had been forced to give up his dreams and sell the property. After that, though he'd stayed on, nothing had remained the same. It was as if Luz del Cielo's heart had been broken.

When no one responded to the doorbell, Sister Agatha tried the massive iron knocker, but still no one came.

Sister Agatha glanced around, then decided to walk down the small service road to the fields. Stopping every once in a while, she called out for Eric, but either he was out of earshot or off the property completely.

Unable to locate him, she finally opted to leave a note, asking him to call the monastery, and slipped it beneath his front door. Eric had always been dependable, so she knew he'd be in touch as soon as he read it.

Her second stop was the Siesta Inn. As she headed down the hallway leading to John Gutierrez's room, she saw Ralph Simpson putting coins in the Coke machine set into a wall recess.

Seeing her, he smiled. "Sister Agatha, what a pleasure. I hope you've come with good news for us."

She nodded. "I'm ready to accept the job, but I'd like to ask John a few more questions about his niece."

Ralph shook his head. "Unfortunately, Sister, now's really not a good time. John had a rough night and he only managed to fall asleep a short while ago. I don't want to wake him up, but if it'll help, I can go bring you the photo and the check right now so you can get started."

"That would be great. Thanks."

Sister Agatha waited in the hall with Pax. A short time

later Ralph came back out and handed her an envelope. "Here you go."

Inside, she found the photo and the check made out to the monastery. "Thank you. Please tell your employer that I'll be in touch as soon as I have something."

Sister Agatha, with Pax still at heel, retraced her steps back outside to the Harley. "We're going to have to work fast on this one, Pax. That buffer zone's critical and so's getting that second check."

Sister Agatha put the cycle in gear. There was one problem with the work she'd accepted, and it nagged at her. Finding Angie Sanchez was one thing—convincing her to come to see her estranged uncle was another issue entirely. She'd assumed that John understood that, but the possibility that she'd ultimately fail a dying man made her chest tighten.

After a brief stop by the bank, she drove toward the station. Pax, recognizing the route, barked happily and Sister Agatha smiled.

She was still a few blocks away from her destination when Sister Agatha spotted Liz walking down the sidewalk. Knowing the girl should have been in school, Sister Agatha pulled over to the curb, parked next to her, and took off her helmet.

"I'm not ditching, if that's what you think," Liz said before Sister Agatha could say anything. "I don't feel good and I'm going home."

"Want a ride? You can sit with Pax, or climb up behind me."

Liz shook her head. "Mom wouldn't like it if she saw me riding with you." She cringed as soon as the words came out. "Forget I said that. I'm already in *enough* trouble with her." Liz gave a haphazard wave, then quickly headed diagonally across the feed store's parking lot and toward an opening in the evergreen hedge. On the other side was a residential neighborhood.

Sister Agatha watched her go. Whether or not Liz approved, she intended to pay Mrs. Leland a visit real soon and try to figure out what was going on. She couldn't think of any reason why Liz's mother might have a grudge against her or the monastery, but there was no better way to find out than to ask. Putting the cycle in gear, Sister Agatha continued to the sheriff's office.

They arrived a few minutes later. The bull pen was busier than usual, so Sister Agatha kept Pax with her instead of letting him roam among the deputies. As she went back toward Tom's office, a few people nodded, but no one stopped her. Tom was working at his desk when Sister Agatha finally reached his open door and knocked.

"Do you have a moment?" she asked.

"Sure," he said, leaning back in his chair and waving her in. "To tell you the truth, I need the break. Have a seat." He walked over to the coffeepot resting on a small cart in the corner of his office and poured himself a cup. "You want one? It's strong. We had a long night around here."

"No thanks, I'll pass," she said, looking at the thick liquid that was more the consistency of molasses than coffee and trying not to cringe. "What happened?"

"A new gang's surfaced, and with it a rash of vandalism, petty theft, and car break-ins." He rubbed the back of his neck with one hand. "Now tell me what's been going on at the monastery. I understand you spotted someone hanging around again just outside the wall."

"Yeah, but there's more." She told him about her conversation with Liz, and the attacks and threats they'd received via the Internet. "I think Liz's warning may have some validity. It sure seems like someone's out to make our lives difficult."

"Don't jump to conclusions. You have no proof that anything's related," he said. "Computer criminals, for instance, rarely confront anyone directly."

"Yes, but think about all the incidents we've had. The monastery's gate could have been deliberately rammed to harass us, and the beer cans picked from the trash and placed inside the SUV just to throw the police off track."

"If that's the case, then the person out to get you muddied up the threat and that's not very likely. People out to harass want their message heard loud and clear. Your hacker friend, for instance, sent very clear warnings."

"You may be right about the hacker, but I'm going to look into what happened to our gate some more. Will you give me Jack Miller's address? I want to talk to him again."

"Can't do it—for legal and ethical reasons. You know that from your old journalism days."

"How about letting me read his statement? I'm interested in his whereabouts when the crash occurred."

"We've already checked that out and interviewed the people who were at the mall with him—Randy Robertson, the cousin of one of our senior deputies, and Randy's wife. Jack was with them the entire time."

"Okay. If you've already been over that ground thoroughly, then I'm going to head over to Mrs. Leland's and have a talk with her."

"Be careful. The woman might turn out to be a crank, or maybe she's starting to crack under pressures from her own life." He stood and came around his desk to walk her to the door. "Let me know if you learn anything more substantial about these enemies the monastery's supposed to have."

"Will do. One last thing." Fishing the envelope that Ralph had given her out of her pocket, she showed him the photo of Angie Sanchez. "I'm trying to locate the niece of one of our benefactors. She looks vaguely familiar, but I'm not sure why. Do *you* happen to know her?" she asked, giving him the niece's name.

He studied the photo, then shook his head. "I don't recognize the face, but the name's fairly common. I know at least two women named Angie Sanchez, but the photo doesn't match either of them."

Sister Agatha nodded and placed the photo back into her pocket. "She may have changed her name, so think about it when you can. I'll be asking Father Mahoney later, too. He knows almost everyone around here."

"Good luck," he said.

After checking the phone book for the address, Sister Agatha and Pax were on their way to Mrs. Leland's. Less than ten minutes later, Sister Agatha pulled up by the small adobe home. The place showed stages of neglect everywhere. The ground was filled with goat heads, and a large cottonwood that had once given a wealth of shade to the property was now nothing more than dried bark. Branches, like bony arms, reached out to the sky in silent supplication.

Sister Agatha ordered Pax to remain at heel on the sidewalk as they walked up to the front entrance. Before she reached the small porch, the door opened.

"I hope you're not here to tell me Liz is in trouble again," Mrs. Leland snapped. "If you are, Sister, then you and the sheriff can just keep her this time. A mother can only do so much." She stood there, adjusting the green apron worn by employees of a local restaurant.

"Mrs. Leland, I understand that you've been through a difficult time—"

"That, Sister, is the understatement of the year," she interrupted. Margot Leland pulled back a strand of tinted brown hair that had worked loose from the bun at the nape of her neck and pinned it in place. Giving Pax a quick glance, she added, "You can both come in, if you'd like, but I've got to eat quickly before I leave for my second job," she said.

Sister Agatha followed her into the kitchen. "I saw Liz earlier, walking home. I understand she left school because she wasn't feeling well."

"Liz is fine, she just stayed up too late last night. She's asleep right now. Don't let her con you, Sister. That girl doesn't have it nearly as bad as she thinks." She pulled out a chair and sat down, gesturing for Sister Agatha to do the same. "Would you like an egg salad sandwich? I made an extra one."

"Thanks," she said, accepting, not only to be sociable but aware that she'd be missing the main meal of the day at the monastery.

"Everything is done in a rush these days," Margot said, placing a plate in front of Sister Agatha. Then, reaching into the refrigerator, she brought out two cans of soda. "When I was young my mother always had fresh cookies and a pot of coffee brewed in case a friend or neighbor dropped by. Food was an open door that led to confidences and old-fashioned girl talk. Now it's eating on the run and rushing to work. Women have lost a vital part of what made our lives richer."

"More is expected of women these days. Progress brought good things and bad."

Margot glanced around the kitchen. "Not long ago I was a great homemaker. My kitchen was the heart of our home. It was sparkling clean and there was always something cooking in the oven. But then everything changed. . . ." She shook her head, looked at the clock on the wall, and started eating her sandwich quickly. "You better tell me what brought you here today. I'm going to have to leave soon."

"Your daughter mentioned to me in passing that she believed our monastery had made some local enemies, but when I pressed her about it, she refused to elaborate. By any chance do you know what she was talking about?" Sister Agatha asked, quickly finishing her sandwich.

With a scowl, Margot took her plate and Sister Agatha's to the sink. "I have no idea why Lizzie said that to you."

"Do you recall the problem we had with our gate?" Sister Agatha saw her nod and continued. "We're still not sure what happened, but if there's a possibility that it was done deliberately. . . ."

"Move on. You'll find a way to get it fixed. Face it, the monastery has it made, Sister. The rest of us out here in the real world have to work for a living, two or three jobs sometimes, and even then it's never quite enough. All you have to do is kneel, mutter some prayers, and ask for donations. Then poof! Everything is taken care of."

The resentment laced through her words surprised Sister Agatha. "Mrs. Leland, you're wrong about us. We also work very hard. Our Rule requires that each day be divided between manual labor and prayers, just like it was for the apostles. We have to support ourselves, too."

"Maybe so, but you get charity, donations, and tax breaks the rest of us don't. Smitty, for one, is constantly making food donations, and the other merchants are always chipping in for some church project or another. The working public—the rest of us—we're on our own."

Struggling for patience, Sister Agatha took a deep breath and let it out slowly. "Mrs. Leland, our main job—what defines us—is praying and giving glory to God. We also pray for anyone who asks and, in exchange, people sometimes make donations that help us continue God's work. If you don't believe that prayers are of value, then that won't make much sense to you. But prayer is a lot like the proverbial mustard seed. It doesn't seem like much at first, but the results can be pretty impressive."

"I don't care how you phrase it, the bottom line is that you get a lot of economic breaks in return for prattling off a Hail Mary or two."

Despite her harsh words, all she could see in Margot's eyes were pain and dark emotions like anger that targeted those nearest her—her daughter, the monastery, and probably anyone else who got in her way.

Empathy and sadness enveloped Sister Agatha. Sometimes life ground a person's dreams into the dust. Refusing to reach out to God at times like those often meant they'd sink into a pit so deep and dark that crawling out of Hell would have been a snap in comparison.

"The length of a prayer isn't nearly as important to God as what's in our hearts," Sister Agatha said gently. "Prayer's about faith and, even more, about love."

"There was a time when I believed in all those things, but I prayed, went to church, gave to the poor, and still my family fell apart. Then my own child turned against me. That's when I stopped praying, and you know what? Nothing's changed. These days I work hard and try to get by, but nobody ever takes up a collection for *me*. I've never been given something for nothing."

"I'll pray for you, Margot, that's something. And I won't give up. God *will* help you, but you've got to open your heart to Him."

Margot shook her head. "Forget the sermon, Sister. You guys have learned to work the system while the rest of us have to fight for every dime. And you clearly have the advantage.

Look at the NexCen contract. You cheated but you still landed the account."

Sister Agatha stared at her in surprise. "Cheated? How? We placed our bid, just like the other companies."

"But you have no overhead, not like a *real* business does. The nuns work for free, so you can underbid everyone else. That's why you got the contract. But the company that you beat out had to lay off half their workers when they lost the NexCen contract."

Margot Leland looked around her kitchen, desperation in her tear-filled eyes. "You're taking away people's jobs and destroying their lives by going where you don't belong, don't you get it?" She stood up. "You'd better leave now."

Sister Agatha signaled to Pax, who'd been lying on the floor at her side. "I *will* keep you in our prayers, Margot. God *can* help you, but you have to invite Him back into your life."

Margot held the front door open for her. "Don't do me any favors, Sister, and don't bother coming back. You and I have nothing more to talk about."

Sister Agatha walked to the Harley with Pax. As he jumped into the sidecar, he glanced at her and whined softly.

Sister Agatha reached out to him and patted him gently on the head. "Sometimes people lose their way, Pax. All we can do is pray and leave the matter in God's gentle hands. That battle isn't ours to fight."

9

WHEN SISTER AGATHA RETURNED HOME TO THE monastery and entered the parlor, she found Sister Bernarda with the door keys in her hands, getting ready to lock up.

"Reverend Mother has called another chapter meeting," Sister Bernarda said quickly. "She's asked everyone to meet her in the community room." As she finished speaking, the bell began ringing, its deep, rich tones summoning each of them. "The door and windows are now locked, and the answering machine is on. Let's go," Sister Bernarda said, opening the door to the enclosure.

"Any idea what's going on?"

"No, not a clue, but I expect we'll find out soon enough."

By the time they reached the community room, all the other sisters and Reverend Mother were already there. Going inside as quietly as possible, they stood by the wall and joined in the opening prayer.

"God, let your love come upon us. Glory be to the Father, and the Son . . . ," Reverend Mother intoned, then, once finished, glanced around the room. "Sit down, children."

There was a flurry of activity as they obeyed, followed by an expectant silence.

"I'll begin with the good news. Mr. Gutierrez will donate the buffer zone we requested, a fifty-foot-wide strip of land, *if* Sister Agatha can help him with a pressing family matter. We all need to pray for her success."

Reverend Mother paused for several long seconds, then continued. "Now the less positive news. Our insurance company is demanding that the rewiring work be completed quickly or they'll drop coverage. Since our cash reserves are low, we'll need a loan to do this, even with Sister Bernarda doing some of the work herself. The problem we're facing is that to pay back the loan, we'll have to rely on our *future* income from NexCen and from the money Sister Agatha will be given *if* her work for Mr. Gutierrez is successful. If that money doesn't come in, we would have to default on the loan, and that'll mean a significant penalty as well as higher interest rates and payments. That's why we all have to vote on this. The choice before us is this: drop our insurance for a few months until we have the cash to pay for the repairs, or do the needed work now, and fund it with a short-term loan, counting that the money we need will come in on time."

"We have the very minimum of insurance as it is, Mother," Sister Gertrude, their cellarer said. "We can't allow it to lapse."

Sister Agatha looked at the others then back at Mother, uncertain whether to tell them what she'd learned from Margot Leland. With enemies working against them, maybe now wasn't a good time for financial risk-taking. But since her concerns were mostly based on rumor, she wasn't sure if she should bring it up or not.

"What's on your mind, child?" Reverend Mother asked, her gaze on Sister Agatha. "If you have any thoughts about this, speak freely."

Sister Agatha told them what she'd learned. "The incidents may be unrelated. But the situation still worries me. We need the protection of our walls and a solid gate, but maybe we should hold off on the rest, including the rewiring, and trust things will hold together a little longer."

"Could Mr. Gutierrez be persuaded to advance us the second check and trust you to locate his niece?" Reverend Mother asked.

Sister Agatha shook her head slowly. "I don't think so, Mother. He's a businessman. If I don't deliver, he'll use the remaining funds to hire someone else, maybe another private investigator. The blessing is that he came to us first and we did get a check that should cover a good part of the repairs to our gate."

"We need to trust God to see things through for us from beginning to end," Sister Ignatius said firmly. "He led Moses through the desert, and He'll see us through this now."

After considering all sides of the problem, they voted unanimously to take out the loan and give priority to fixing the wiring, an ever-present fire hazard. Reverend Mother called an end to their meeting and, as she walked out of the room, gestured for Sister Agatha to accompany her.

Sister Agatha silently fell into step beside her and waited for her to speak.

"Go back and talk to Sheriff Green. Make sure he understands that our monastery may need extra protection while our wall is down."

"I'll take care of that right away, Mother."

The bells were ringing for None as Sister Agatha prepared to leave the monastery again. Assured on the telephone that Tom would be in his office until late, she went down the hall to look for Sister Bernarda, who was checking out an outlet.

She explained her errand then added, "I'll need you to take over as portress."

"Will you be coming back as soon as you're finished at the station?" Sister Bernarda asked.

"Yes, but on the way there, I'll be stopping to get gas for the Harley. I don't expect this to be a quick trip, so I'll take the extra set of keys to the front door. That way you won't have to stay in the parlor to let me back in."

"All right. But a head's-up, Sister Agatha. Last time I stopped by the garage, Paul Gonzales was in a terrible mood. He said that he wasn't sure how much longer he'd be able to continue his donations of gas and car repairs to the monastery."

"Times have been tough for many of our small businessmen," Sister Agatha said, nodding. "Maybe he's having some financial problems of his own. I'll make it a point to talk to him." Mr. Gonzales's donations were more important than ever to the monastery. If those stopped, she wasn't sure how they'd manage.

It was a little past five-thirty when Sister Agatha walked out to the parking area. Seeing her, Pax bounded to the Harley and waited for her in the sidecar. Soon they were on their way to Paul's garage.

As she drove the Harley up by the gasoline pumps and parked, Paul came out from one of the garage bays, wiping his hands on a rag. A radio inside was playing a Mexican ballad, and Paul was singing along, looking as if his thoughts were a million miles away.

"Hello, Paul," she greeted.

"Hello, Sister. Do you need some help?"

"No, I just stopped by for gas and to say hi. The song you were singing sounded sad. Not your singing, the song itself," she clarified quickly. "How are things going?"

"Not good." Paul stared at the gas pumps as if they were long-lost friends, then turned to look at the building. "Fact is, I've been thinking of closing down the garage, Sister. It's a lot of work and I'm getting up in years. If I sell the business, the wife and I could retire and do some traveling together."

"You built this business from scratch, Paul," she said, surprised. "I thought you'd never give it up. Has something changed?"

"Our son has no interest in taking over the business. He says he has plans of his own, and they don't include running the garage. I always assumed that this place would belong to him someday. That's why I worked so hard to stay in the black. But if he doesn't want it, it's time for me to rethink my future here."

"But what would you do without this place?" Sister Agatha asked. "You've worked here almost your entire adult life. Be careful, Paul, I've seen this happen before. It's not easy for someone used to working hard to suddenly find himself with nothing to do. Having time on your hands may not turn out to be the blessing you think it is."

Paul nodded slowly. "I saw something like that happen to my dad. He talked and talked about retiring, then, when he finally did, he didn't know what to do with himself. He'd go fishing in the mornings then rattle around the house every afternoon. Before long, even fishing stopped being fun for him. Eight months later he passed away." He paused. "That's why I'm taking this slow. I need to make sure I'm doing the right thing. There are some decisions you just can't undo."

Sister Agatha thought of Sister Bernarda and how some choices came back to haunt people when they least expected it. "I'll say a prayer for you, Paul. I'm sure you'll do the right thing when the time comes to decide." She placed the gas hose back in its place, then noticed that he didn't have his writing pad. "Did you want me to sign for this inside so you can keep track of the donation?"

"You know where the sheets are, right?"

"Of course." She started to go into the small office, then stopped. "By the way, Paul, have you heard anything about our monastery having enemies in town? There's a rumor flying around, but I'm not sure how much weight to give it."

He rubbed the back of his neck with one hand. "When I heard what happened to the monastery's gate, I wondered if I should say something to you. Then I was told that Liz Leland and some other kids were responsible."

"We thought so at first, but that may not be the case after all."

Paul stared at his shoes, lost in thought. "I've never been much for gossip, but from what I hear, there's a group of people in this area who are ticked off at the sisters. It's because of the computer work the monastery's doing these days. When the NexCen contracts were awarded to the monastery, a local company, Computer Crue, took quite a hit. They laid off a lot of people. They even fired their janitorial services. Liz Leland's dad owned P.M. Janitorial, and he was suddenly forced to trim down his own staff. That caused him to lose other clients because he couldn't service them adequately anymore. Then his last major client, the mailing service that also lost their Nex-Cen contract to the monastery, ran into trouble. After that, P.M. Janitorial folded."

"So Mr. Leland was inadvertently hurt twice by our monastery," Sister Agatha observed, shaking her head slowly.

"Yeah. I think Dennis Leland works for a company in Rio Rancho now."

"I didn't know," she said, suddenly understanding why Mrs. Leland had been so bitter. If the cutbacks had created a ripple across the local economy, there was no telling how many other enemies they'd made, including the relatives of those who'd lost their jobs.

"I'm sorry to hear about this, but thanks for the information, Paul."

Then she remembered the photograph of Angie Sanchez in her pocket. Almost everyone in the area depended on private vehicles for transportation, and Paul had pumped gas for decades. "Before I go, will you take a look at a photo and see if you recognize the woman there? I've been trying to find her."

Paul studied the photo for several seconds, then handed it back to her. "I think she's stopped here for gas a few times over the last few months. She drives a silver Kia, or maybe it's a Toyota. Her face is a lot rounder now, like she's put on weight since that picture was taken."

"Her name is—or was—Angie Sanchez. Does that help?"

"I know several Angies, one of them with the last name of Sanchez. But this lady never introduced herself. Never even got out of the car."

"Did she pay with a credit card, maybe?" Sister Agatha asked, hoping to get a name.

"Not that I recall. Sorry."

"What else can you tell me about the woman?"

"Her face looks older now and her hair's lighter, too. But I see a lot of people, so I could be wrong about all this. I wish I could be more help."

Sister Agatha smiled. "You've done more than you realize."

After signing the donation sheet, Sister Agatha continued on to the station, glad to finally have a lead on Angie Sanchez. As she drove south down Camino Real, a prickly feeling touched the base of her spine. Uneasy, she looked around. A glance in the rearview mirror revealed a dark-green sedan several car lengths behind her. She wasn't exactly sure how long it had been there; her mind had been on Angie, but she kept an eye on the car now. It wasn't the sheriff this time, that was certain.

The vehicle stayed with her, not getting any closer or moving farther back, all the way into the heart of town. When she finally pulled into the sheriff's department parking lot, the sedan continued down the street, streaking by too quickly for her to get a good look at the driver or his plates.

Sister Agatha walked into the building, Pax at her side, and went directly to Tom's office. Maybe the sedan had also been on its way to town and she was reading too much into what had happened—or not. As she approached Tom's door, he glanced up.

"Come in, Sister. I've been waiting for you. What's up?"

She told him about the connection between Liz Leland's family and the monastery. "They could have a serious grudge against us."

"I'll look into it but, in all honesty, I think we've gotten all we're going to get out of that girl and her mother."

Sister Agatha relayed Reverend Mother's request for added protection, then continued. "At least the monastery's gate repairs should begin soon, thanks to the check we got from Mr. Gutierrez. And, of course, I'll still do my best to find Angie Sanchez quickly. Once I do, our financial problems will ease up considerably."

Just then Millie came in and placed a file on Tom's desk. "Angie Sanchez? I remember that name. It caused a lot of problems around here some time back." Seeing Sister Agatha looking expectantly at her, she continued. "A woman by that name testified against some major bad boy in an Albuquerque court. A murder case, I think it was. The reason it sticks in my mind is because an older woman here in town had the same name, and she started getting some heavy-duty threats. She was terrified, but before we could do much to help her, she moved away. I don't know where she went." She paused.

Sister Agatha brought out the photo of Angie, but Millie didn't recognize her. "You said that it was an Albuquerque case?" Sister Agatha pressed.

"Yeah . . . something fairly dramatic that got TV coverage a few years ago. But I can't recall the details. Sorry."

"Then my next stop is *The Chronicle*," Sister Agatha announced.

"What on earth could you possibly find there?" Tom said with a smile. "They have, what, one column of news? No, wait, that's their entire paper."

"Oh, be nice. So they're small," Sister Agatha said.

"Small? In newspaper terms, they're a pamphlet," Tom answered.

"They specialize in local news, but I'll bet they've got access to the archives of the Albuquerque dailies." She stood. "Oh, before I leave, one more thing. Maybe it's just a coincidence, but I thought a green sedan was following me earlier. He drove on past when I entered the parking lot here. I guess it's possible he was just traveling in the same direction, but I wanted to mention it to you," she said, giving him all the description she had.

"Did it have New Mexico plates?"

"No, the license plate wasn't yellow. It was whitish with a darker color at the top, like the ones from Texas or maybe even Colorado. That's all I know for sure."

"If you see it again, call."

"Will do."

As she walked outside, Pax at heel, Sister Agatha considered what she'd learned. She'd have to compare the photo John Gutierrez had given her with one of the witness as soon as possible. She was positive that the Albuquerque newspapers would have one archived. If the photos matched, then she'd have another talk with Gutierrez before she went any further. Angie Sanchez's safety would have to come first.

The sun was going down when she passed the feed store and the mercantile. A short time later, Sister Agatha pulled into the parking area beside *The Chronicle*. The old building had come a long way since Janice Bose had turned it into her newspaper's main office and printing facility. There was not much landscaping around it—mostly gravel and a few yuccas—but it beat the tangle of tumbleweeds that had once made it difficult to even reach the door.

As she walked in with Pax, Chuck Moody saw them and, with a wide grin, rushed up to greet them. "Sister Agatha, it's good to see you and Pax again! What brings you by here today?" Chuck was short and wiry, with long, dark hair that seemed to explode from his scalp in all directions.

"It's good to see you again, too, Chuck." He'd proved to be

a never-ending fountain of information for her. Chuck knew everyone in town and had his ear close to the ground. "Is Janice around?"

"No, she's already gone for the day. Is there anything I can help you with? It's slow right now, so I'd be happy to lend you a hand with anything you need."

His enthusiasm was irrepressible, so she decided to make the most of the opportunity. "I'm looking for information on a high-profile criminal trial that took place a few years ago in Albuquerque. One of the prosecution's witnesses was a woman by the name of Angie Sanchez."

"Janice has Internet access to all the major papers in the state from her desktop computer. Let's do a name search, put in the words 'trial' and 'prosecution witness,' then look at the hits we get." Chuck led her inside Janice's sparsely decorated office, and Pax followed them silently.

The desk was an old metal job that probably dated back to the 1950s, and the file cabinets looked as if they'd been salvaged from the dump. The only decoration on the wall was an old paint-by-numbers of a horse.

Chuck pulled out a wooden chair for her, then sat down behind Janice's state-of-the-art computer. This was where some serious money had been spent. The LED screen and graphics were sharper than anything she'd ever seen before. Once Chuck entered a username and password, they zoomed past the home page of a big local newspaper's Web site, ready to search the archives.

"Why are you interested in this particular story?" Chuck asked, entering the key search words in the proper box on the display. "If you tell me just a little more I might be able to help you find what you need faster."

"Keep it between us, Chuck?" Seeing him nod, she continued, leaving out the details concerning John Gutierrez. "I'm looking for an Angie Sanchez who's supposed to be in this area. There's a slim chance that it's the same Angie Sanchez who was involved in a big trial a few years ago. I want to compare the photo I have to one of the witness in the newspaper archives." She pulled the photo from her pocket. "By any chance do *you* know her?"

He studied the photo then shook his head. "She looks a little familiar, but that's about it. Sorry."

Chuck found several articles dealing with Angie Sanchez, then, as he clicked on one with the computer mouse, a phone in the other room started to ring.

"Sister, I've got to get that. Sometimes Janice calls when I'm on night duty to make sure I'm still holding down the fort, you know?"

"Go ahead. I can take it from here."

"Excuse me, Pax," Chuck said, edging by the dog, whose head had gone up as the phone began ringing.

Sister Agatha clicked the mouse again, enlarging the article enough to read the text without a magnifying glass. Several photos were included, including one identifying Angela Sanchez. It was a grainy snapshot taken at some outdoor event. Angie's face was so washed-out from the light it was impossible to match the image to the photo John had given her.

Sister Agatha leaned back in her chair, her gaze focused on the on-screen image. The only features that seemed somewhat clear in the photo were Angie's dark hair and expressive large eyes, but they weren't enough to make her recognizable. Before long Chuck came back into the room.

He studied the image on the screen. "Neither photo looks like anyone I know in town, and, all modesty aside, I *do* know everyone," he said.

"I think this is a dead end," she said, and stood. "I better be on my way then." Pax walked over and sat by her side, alert to the likelihood they'd be leaving.

"I was hoping you'd have some time to talk," he said, obviously disappointed.

"Is something wrong?" she asked, curious about his reaction.

"No. Well, maybe. Look it's almost dinnertime. How about I treat you to a roast beef sub? It's a foot-long, but I'm not that hungry."

"All right," she said, following him to the small break room at the back. Pax followed, a step behind them.

Chuck brought out a paper sack from the fridge, placed half of the sandwich on a paper napkin before her, and the other half on a napkin for himself. Then he brought out two cans of soda.

Sister Agatha bowed her head and said Grace, and Chuck added a quick "Amen" before taking a quick bite of his sandwich. "Janice has offered me a partnership in the business but, until now, I've never stayed anywhere longer than a few years. How do you do it, Sister? Doesn't it get boring, the same 'ole same 'ole?"

After allowing herself a moment to enjoy the beef and crisp lettuce, she answered his question. "Once you find the work that was meant to be yours—and you'll know in your heart when you do—you'll never worry about something like that again. You'll still have good and bad days, everyone does, but finding your niche also brings inner peace, which is a blessing all on its own," she said. "What I'm saying to you is this— if you love your work here, go for it."

Hearing a loud clank just outside the window, Chuck muttered a soft curse and set down his sandwich. "It's those punk kids again."

Pax stood, growling low, his ears up.

"I'll run them off, then come right back, Sister. We put bars on the windows to keep them from breaking in, but they still keep trying."

"I'm going with you, and so's Pax. I'm afraid the Harley might be their target."

"Okay. With Pax around, we can gang up on them," he said, grabbing a flashlight from a shelf, though there were bright floodlights around the building.

Sister Agatha followed Chuck and Pax out the front door. They checked the Harley and sidecar parked in front, along with Chuck's old pickup. Then she and Pax followed Chuck around to the rear of the building.

He swept the flashlight in a big circle, then directed the beam at the window. "The little dipsticks are gone now, but they've been fiddling with the bars on this window. I'd better take a closer look and make sure they haven't pried any loose. You might as well go back inside and finish your sandwich. I'll join you in a few minutes."

"Okay. I think I'll make a printout of the article with the photo, too, while I'm waiting. It may come in handy."

Sister Agatha and Pax went back to Janice's office. She'd just clicked on "print" when the lights suddenly went out. The soft glow of the computer monitor screen became the only source of illumination, and it cast a greenish aura around her.

Sister Agatha heard the beep that came from the computer's backup battery, and checked to make sure the article was being printed. Fortunately, the ink-jet printer was on battery power, too. The page was almost printed when she heard the front door click open. "Chuck?"

Pax's hackles rose, he growled, and a heartbeat later, the big white dog bolted out of the room. She heard him bark once, then there was the sound of a door slamming shut. After that, the sound of his barking suddenly became muted. He'd somehow become trapped in another room.

Her heart hammering at her throat, Sister Agatha reached for her cell phone, called Tom's direct line, and gave him a quick report. "I can hear Pax barking up a storm, so I think he must be okay. But I don't know who's out there. It's not Chuck. He would have answered my call, and Pax wouldn't have reacted like that."

"Lock yourself in Janice's office, or block the door," he instructed instantly. "One of us will be there in minutes. And don't worry about Pax. He can take care of himself."

She closed up the cell phone and inched toward the door, torn between following Tom's instructions and going to help her dog. Moving silently, Sister Agatha listened for the intruder, but all she could hear was Pax's furious barking.

The farther she got from the computer screen, the darker the room became, and she was forced to feel her way around the file cabinets. She was almost at the door when she felt a stirring in the air and the almost imperceptible warmth of another body slipping past her in the dark. Danger had now found her.

10

SISTER AGATHA HELD HER BREATH, THEN, GLANCING back, saw a figure cross in front of the computer. The illumination from the screen silhouetted him. Sister Agatha stepped silently out into the hall, suspecting from his actions that the intruder didn't have a fix on her position yet. Suddenly the shrill wail of sirens overwhelmed the sound of Pax's barking, which seemed to be coming from the next room.

Hearing it also, the intruder spun around, and, before she could take another step, they collided. The impact knocked her to the floor. Sister Agatha looked up as her assailant opened the rear exit and fled outside. He was visible for only a second as he ran past the glow of a streetlight, but she was almost certain it was a man. By the time she struggled to her feet and ran to the door, there was no sign of him.

Sister Agatha went back and opened the door next to Janice's office, releasing the dog. Excited and angry, Pax spotted the open exit door and shot toward it but, at her command, came to an abrupt stop.

The room lights were switched on again, and Sister Agatha squinted at the sudden brightness. Less than ten seconds later, Pax began to wag his tail and Chuck came in, the room lights giving his face a deathly pallor.

"Are you two okay in here?" Chuck asked quickly. "I got coldcocked by some jerk. He must have also turned off the lights at the outside panel. I flipped them back on as soon as I came to my senses again."

Before she could answer, an unmarked car with flashing red emergency lights slid to a stop in the gravel of the parking lot. Tom came running in, his hand on the butt of his pistol. "Where's the intruder?"

"He's gone," Sister Agatha said. "Ran off just before Chuck got the lights back on."

"So you never got a look at him?" Tom asked, moving his hand away from his weapon.

"From his outline in the glow of the computer monitor, and the brief glance I got when he ran outside, I got the impression that the intruder was a man, but that's all I can tell you. I'm not even sure of his height. When I was actually close to him, he was leaning over."

"Did he take anything?" Tom pressed.

"I have no idea," Sister Agatha said.

Tom glared at Chuck Moody. "Well?"

"Well, what, sheriff? I didn't see what went on in here. I was outside checking the bars on the windows when I got slugged from behind. Knocked me out cold. We've been having trouble with kids, so when we heard a noise outside. . . ."

"You think this was the work of a kid?" Tom asked, looking at Sister Agatha, then back at Chuck.

"No way," Sister Agatha replied first. "I mean, I suppose it's possible, but then we'd be talking about a kid who's adult size, strong, and very cool under pressure. Pax isn't fooled easily as you know, and he somehow managed to trick the dog and shut him inside that room," Sister Agatha said, pointing.

Tom checked it out. "He must have thrown something in there. The dog went after the sound and got locked in."

Chuck retrieved a can of cola out of the fridge and held it up to the back of his head. "I'd offer you one, Sister, but this is the last of the batch, and my head's going to explode without it. Wish we had some ice trays in there."

"You should get that looked at, Moody," Tom said.

"Nah. It'll be fine once the swelling goes down. I've taken worse knocks."

"Okay. Then let's take a look around. I need to know what—if anything—was taken," Tom said.

Chuck led the way through the remaining rooms, then at long last shook his head. The gesture made him wince. "He didn't take anything important or I'd have noticed. I don't think he had time, and, remember, he was operating in the dark when he sneaked in."

"Wait." Sister Agatha walked to the printer beside Janice's computer. The output tray was empty. Ducking quickly beneath the desk and finding nothing there, or anywhere on the floor, she stood back up. "He grabbed the printout of an article I'd found with Angie Sanchez's photo. I can print another one so it's no big deal, but that sure seems like an odd thing to take."

"No one touch the machines. Maybe he left some prints,"

Tom said quickly, then in a thoughtful voice added, "But this really doesn't add up. He went to all the trouble of breaking in here just so he could take a printout of an article he could have dug up at, say, the library?"

"It takes a subscription fee and a password, but, yes, anyone could have accessed the information," Chuck said. "Maybe he thought you were printing out something really important, Sister, so he grabbed it."

"Maybe he followed me here wanting to know what I was up to," Sister Agatha suggested.

"Did you see someone tailing you again?" Tom asked.

"No, but the Harley was parked out in front. It's bright red and hard to miss under the floodlights."

"I'm going to have my deputies do a little digging and see what they can turn up on the monastery's enemies."

After she gave him her statement, Tom began a search for prints. Knowing she was no longer needed, Sister Agatha said good-bye and drove down the road to the Siesta Inn. She needed to talk to John Gutierrez.

After parking, she motioned to Pax. "Okay, boy. Out. We have to make this a quick visit, so let's get a move on."

Less than five minutes after leaving *The Chronicle*, Sister Agatha sat on a chair facing John's bed while Pax remained at "sit and stay" near the door. Ralph Simpson, who'd let her in, sat back in a corner chair, not taking part in the exchange.

Sister Agatha told her ailing client what she'd learned about Angie Sanchez—the trial witness. John sat up, very interested, nodding his head with each new detail. When she finished her report, he leaned back against the pillows and closed his eyes for several moments.

At long last he opened them again. "It's the same Angie, Sister. When that story broke it made all the regional newspapers," he admitted slowly. "I tried desperately to contact Angie back then, but I wasn't able to do it. The private investigators I hired couldn't track her down, either. I let it go, figuring law enforcement people would be keeping her safe." He paused, then reluctantly added, "I was also convinced that she'd eventually call and ask for my help. But she never did. Then, when I learned that my time was running out, I knew I had to find her. Only by that time, the trail was stone cold."

"The problem is that she may not *want* anyone to find her, and that's going to make it a lot tougher. She's been covering her trail, no doubt, and is probably using an alias," Sister Agatha answered.

"That's why you're the best person for the job. She's more likely to trust a nun than some private detective," he said, then in a strong voice added, "Find her for me, Sister Agatha, so I can die in peace."

"I'll stay on it," she said, standing up. "But you should have mentioned the criminal trial to me before. Is there anything *else* you're holding back?"

"No," he said softly. "You know everything I do now."

"Then we'll talk again soon."

Pondering all the recent events, she and Pax returned to the monastery. Sister Agatha unlocked the parlor door, and, as she stepped inside, saw Sister Bernarda placing a small thermos on the desk.

"It's past seven and we're all at recreation," Sister Bernarda said, "but Sister Clothilde wanted to make sure you ate something. She saved some hot soup for you."

"I'll be sure to thank her. I'm freezing." Sister Agatha poured the creamy tomato soup into the cup and sipped it gratefully. Nights were getting cold now, and riding in the motorcycle after dark just seemed to drain the heat from her body.

"While you're warming up, I'll take Pax into the kitchen for his supper," Sister Bernarda said, signaling the dog.

Sister Agatha had just finished her soup when Sister de Lourdes walked past the parlor's grille, saw her, and came out of the enclosure to talk. "We've had more problems in the scriptorium."

"What's going on?"

"When Merilee compared our e-mail files with NexCen's invoices to verify that all the orders were getting through now, she found the messages from 'Wilder.' The name immediately caught her eye. It's one of the characters in a role-playing computer game that NexCen has been involved with recently."

"What's the game about?"

"A pig in battle gear who goes on quests. But it's not for young children. I saw parts of the game, and it was very violent. Merilee told me that the earlier versions of Wilder's Quest had some bugs in it, and that a lot of people got angry with NexCen. Some of the users had to buy new video cards in order to play the game."

"Interesting. Anything else?"

"She also told me in confidence that NexCen is very focused on their bottom line, and unless things start running more smoothly for us, they'll give the mail-order contract to another company after our trial period is over."

"That's hardly fair! If we're getting outside interference from one of NexCen's disgruntled customers, the monastery's not to blame."

"I pointed that out myself, but she said that if we couldn't fix the problem—meaning her and us—we'd both suffer. Her job's at stake, too, so she'll be checking with us periodically."

Still annoyed at the news from NexCen, Sister Agatha

went to the kitchen, rinsed out the thermos, and left a thank-you note for Sister Clothilde. The small, unselfish acts, like making sure an extern had something warm waiting for her after she returned from town, helped define their monastery and what they stood for. Here, time wasn't measured in dollars and cents. It was measured in good deeds and blessings. When everything was done for God's glory, life all of a sudden became easier.

As she walked outside past the kitchen into the garden, Sister Agatha saw Sister Bernarda sitting alone on the bench near the statue of St. Joseph and went to join her.

"Are you all right?" Sister Agatha asked her softly.

"Of course," Sister Bernarda replied, too quickly to be convincing. Realizing it, she shook her head. "No, not really. I've spoken to Reverend Mother, and after Compline I'm going to stay in chapel for as long as it takes. I know that becoming a bride of Christ was the right decision for me. I chose God and continue to choose Him. Yet I still can't get this sadness out of my head."

"So Reverend Mother knows what's been bothering you?"

Sister Bernarda nodded. "She said to give it time, and to not be afraid to discuss my feelings with the sisters who have already gone through the change." She paused for a long moment. "The worst part of all this is the feeling deep in my gut that I'm falling short of what He expects of me."

"No, you're falling short of what *you* expect of yourself. But every day is a new day. And, if you fail to master your feelings today—and remember a lot of those are based on your body's chemistry, not your heart—there's always tomorrow. A contemplative's life is all about patience."

Hearing the bell announcing Compline, Sister Agatha bowed her head and followed Sister Bernarda inside to chapel.

Sister Agatha remained with Sister Bernarda in chapel long after Compline and the start of the Great Silence. In the quiet that surrounded and protected them, she joined her prayers to those of her fellow extern.

It was around ten when the dull throbbing in her joints reminded Sister Agatha that she'd forgotten to take her arthritis medication again. She closed her eyes in prayer, trying to shut out the pain, and reached out to her Lord, asking for His help for both herself and Sister Bernarda.

Then she felt a hand on her shoulder. Sister Agatha looked up and saw Sister Eugenia motioning for her to follow. Sister Agatha went with her, knowing Sister Eugenia would have her pills close by. Just as she stepped out of the stall, Reverend Mother came in to take her place. Sister Bernarda wouldn't be alone tonight. The spirit of the monastery would enfold her gently and lead her into the arms of God.

11

AFTER MASS AND MORNING PRAYERS, SISTER AGATHA went straight to the parlor and found it more crowded than usual. Sister Bernarda was there wearing a leather tool belt, sitting on the floor working on one of the outlets. Sister de Lourdes was manning the parlor's desk, her breviary open before her.

"Reverend Mother told us that your work for the monastery will require you to be away for irregular periods of time these next few days," Sister de Lourdes said, looking up. "I'll be taking your place as portress so you can be free to come and go."

"Will you be able to handle both scriptorium work and parlor duties?"

She nodded. "So far today, everything's running smoothly. The computer records and saves the orders, and I can process them later and print out the invoices and labels. And if I get into a jam, Sister Bernarda will help me."

"We've got it covered," Sister Bernarda said.

"We've got some good news, too," Sister de Lourdes added. "The workmen arrived early and are making great progress on our wall."

"That's wonderful!" Sister Agatha said, taking a quick look out the front window. "Everyone's hard at work, so it's time for me to do the same. I'll see you two later."

Sister Agatha stepped out of the parlor and whistled for Pax, who came running immediately. Sister Agatha smiled. The dog took the job of escorting her to town very seriously.

A short time later, Sister Agatha drove out of the monastery, passing the repair crew at the wall. Step by step, God would help them find solutions to all the challenges they were facing. Holding on to that thought, Sister Agatha drove on to Bernalillo and the Catholic Charities office, praying all the way there for guidance.

An idea had come to her late last night after night prayers. She'd been trying to remember who in town drove a silver Toyota or a Kia. That's when she'd recalled Terri Montoya, the caseworker at Catholic Charities. A silver Toyota had been parked in one of the staff slots when she'd visited with Terri there a few days ago.

The more she considered it, the more convinced she'd grown that it was a lead worth pursuing. Even if Angie Sanchez had put on a lot of weight and dyed her hair, one thing would have remained constant—the shape of her eyes. That slightly oriental tilt was striking, and unusual in a Hispanic woman. Now, Sister Agatha prayed that she was tracking down Angie, not just the woman Paul remembered stopping by for gas.

When they arrived at the Catholic Charities tiny office, Sister Agatha was disappointed to see that the silver Toyota had been replaced by another vehicle in the staff parking spot. Father Rick Mahoney, the monastery's chaplain, was standing in front of a desk talking to Lucinda Gomez, one of the caseworkers, as she walked in. Before becoming a priest, Father Rick had been a pro wrestler who used the stage name "Apocalypse Now." Although that had been at least ten years ago, Father Rick still retained his bulging muscles and heavy frame. He worked out daily because, as he said, a priest needed to remain fit to do God's work.

"Hey, Sister Agatha." He greeted her.

"Hay is for horses, Father. Good morning," she said cheerfully.

"Hello, Sister," Lucinda said with a bright smile. "What can I do for you this morning?"

"I was looking for Terri. Do you know where I can find her?"

"She's visiting Mrs. Griego this morning," she answered. "Is there something I could help you with?"

"No, I really needed to talk to her," Sister Agatha answered. "When will she be back in the office?"

"Probably not until tomorrow. She has several other stops to make after Mrs. Griego's. Today's her turn to be out in the field. We alternate manning the office and going on calls. You want her to call you when she checks in?"

"No, I'd rather talk to her in person. If you'll give me her address, I'll try to meet her there at lunch or after work."

The woman hesitated, then shook her head. "I can't. We have a very strict policy against giving out employee information. I'm sorry."

"It's okay," Sister Agatha said, and managed a smile. "If there's anyone who can understand adherence to a rule, it's a nun. I'll just keep a look out for her silver Toyota and catch her here when she returns."

"That would be fine," Lucinda responded.

"I've always felt that rules should be tempered by common sense," Father Mahoney said, giving Lucinda an engaging smile.

Lucinda shook her head. "Father, if God had given the ten commandments to you instead of Moses, you'd have negotiated Him down to five."

Father Mahoney laughed, then, his own business apparently completed, walked back outside with Sister Agatha. "You look worried about something, Sister. Is there something I can do?"

"I'm not sure," she said slowly. "Maybe you can," she added, then explained in confidence why she'd come, wishing aloud that she had a copy of the newspaper article to show him.

"I have an online subscription to that paper. Come over to the rectory and let's use my computer."

Sister Agatha followed Father Rick to the small rectory that stood beside the tall adobe-and-brick church near the center of old Bernalillo, along Camino del Pueblo.

Sister Agatha pulled up beside him, parking in the graveled parking area. She was just taking off her helmet when Pax made a beeline to the door, anxious to go collect his usual treats. As Frances opened it, he slid to a stop at "sit."

"At least he's too well trained to knock someone down," Frances said, bending over to pet him.

Frances, in her sixties, had been the rectory's housekeeper for as long as anyone could remember. Her faded brown hair in a bun, she held the door open for all of them.

"Sister Agatha, with your permission I'll take Pax into the kitchen with me. I've been saving some cookies for him."

"Sure, go ahead, but make him 'sit' or 'down' before you give him any treats."

"Of course," Frances said, then glanced down at Pax and gave him a wink.

Sister Agatha sighed, knowing in her gut that Frances had no intention of requiring Pax to do anything except eat.

"Don't worry," Father Mahoney said, chuckling. "Pax isn't going to get spoiled that quickly."

"Are you kidding? Did you see him racing to the door? He *knows*."

Father Rick led the way to his office, then went to his desk and began the computer search. It took them several minutes to find the article with Angie's photo. Father Rick saved the image to a photo-editing program, then enlarged and studied it for several moments. "There are physical similarities—the shape of her eyes, as you said—but the rest. . . ." He shook his head.

"I never claimed that it was an identical match . . . but what do you think?"

"Terri's a good hundred pounds heavier, and look at the hair. The woman in the newspaper photo has short, dark hair. Terri's hair is light brown and past her shoulders."

"You can change hair color in less than an hour, and weight gain . . . well, it happens. The shape of her eyes, though . . . that's impossible to fake."

"Okay, so it *could* be Angie Sanchez. What next?" Father Rick asked.

"I thought I'd confront her and see what she has to say. Unless I miss my guess, she'll be getting a substantial inheritance from her uncle. If Terri and Angie *are* the same person, she may end up thanking me."

"You know it's really strange how things work out," he said after a moment. "You're interested in learning about Terri, and Terri's *always* been curious about the monastery . . . to the point of being annoying sometimes."

"What do you mean?"

"Food or clothing donations for St. Francis's Pantry sometimes get dropped off at the Charities office. Usually I go pick those up and deliver them to the monastery, but when Terri's at the office, she always insists on coming along. Yet instead of helping, all she does is drive me crazy. She floods me with questions about the nuns and the monastery. Her curiosity is insatiable—and sometimes she crosses the line."

"How so?"

"Well, one day when we were there I got a call on my cell phone. I became distracted and by the time I hung up, I couldn't find Terri anywhere. Sister de Lourdes was helping put the food away in the pantry, and went with me to look for her. After several frantic minutes, we finally found Terri over by the cemetery."

"That's *way* off limits," Sister Agatha said firmly. "It's part of our cloistered grounds."

"I know. I chewed her out like crazy but she said that it was so peaceful at the monastery she'd been unable to resist going for a short walk. She apologized repeatedly but, after that, I always kept a closer eye on her. Come to think about it. . . ." He held up his hand, then checked the small screen on his pocket messenger. "I almost forgot. I'm scheduled to meet with her at the pantry today. One of our parishioners made a canned-food donation and Terri offered to pick it up at the woman's house and meet me at the monastery a half hour from now. I made a note to call you—but I guess in person's okay," he added with a sheepish smile.

"I'll go get Pax, drive back to the monastery, and wait for you there."

As she stood, the phone began to ring. Father Mahoney picked up the receiver and, after a second or two, his face grew somber. Sister Agatha slipped out of his office discreetly, giving him some privacy, and went into the kitchen. Pax was there gnawing contentedly on a rawhide bone.

"What's this? Cookies *and* rawhide?"

"He wasn't too excited about the cookies. They're my sister's recipe. She's been trying to create the perfect eggless cookies, but so far it's been a disaster. These were flavorless—even to the dog."

Before Frances could say anything more, Father Rick came into the kitchen. "Sister Agatha, I wonder if I can impose on you."

"Certainly, Father. What do you need?" she asked.

"There's been a serious auto accident and I've got to go anoint the injured. Can you meet Terri at the pantry for me and handle things?"

"Of course, Father. Is there anything else I can do?"

He glanced around. "I need to find my keys."

"On your desk, Father. You set them down by the keyboard." Sister Agatha said.

"Oh, yes! I remember." He hurried out of the room.

"Anointing has to be one of the most difficult of all duties," Sister Agatha said.

Frances nodded and remained silent for a moment. "When he comes back, he's always very quiet, and tends to spend quite a bit of time alone in the chapel," she said. "Mortality isn't an easy thing for anyone to face."

As Sister Agatha drove home those words stayed in her mind, reminding her of John Gutierrez's predicament. The prospect of dying alone had to be one of the most frightening things any human being could experience. She said a prayer that she'd be able to help him find his niece and also that the injured people Father Rick was going to see would feel the comfort of God's ever present love.

As Sister Agatha drove through the monastery's partially restored entrance, she saw Terri's silver Toyota parked by the front of Saint Francis's Pantry, a red-beaded rosary dangling from the rearview mirror. No one was inside the car, and neither of the other externs were in sight. Remembering Father Rick's warning that Terri liked to wander, she glanced around quickly.

Unable to spot her, Sister Agatha parked in front of the pantry and climbed off the bike. Pax jumped out and, anticipating her routine, ran to the pantry door. It was always kept locked because of its proximity to the street, so wherever Terri was, it wasn't inside this building.

Sister Agatha hurried to the west side of the grounds, where their cemetery was located. She'd just passed the circular rose garden that bordered the statue of the Blessed Virgin when she saw Terri standing beside the eight-foot-high block wall near the *banco*.

"Terri," Sister Agatha called out.

Terri jumped, startled, then waved. "Hi, Sister Agatha. I've been waiting for Father Mahoney. He's due any moment, which is why I didn't go to the monastery's front door. No sense in bothering anyone there until he arrives."

"This whole section is off-limits—cloistered. Father's told you that before, and there's also a sign on the gate."

"Oh, but the gate wasn't locked. I thought it meant that the cloister was up ahead—you know, inside the building."

Rather than argue, Sister Agatha led her quickly away to St. Francis's Pantry. "Father has been detained, so he sent me to meet you."

"You have such a beautiful place. Does your monastery host retreats?"

"No, we're not that type of religious order. The only facility we have that can house outsiders is an area we've set up inside the pantry for overnight guests. It'll be used mostly by family members who come to visit the sisters."

After Sister Agatha unlocked the pantry door, they worked together to carry the boxes of canned goods from Terri's trunk to the small building.

"I've been wanting to talk to you, Terri," Sister Agatha said. "One of our benefactors approached me recently and asked me to find his niece, Angela Sanchez."

At the mention of the name, Terri suddenly stiffened.

Pretending not to notice, Sister Agatha continued. "Angela used to live in this area and ended up testifying against some criminals at an Albuquerque trial. Her uncle, John Gutierrez, is dying and wants desperately to find her."

Although there'd been a gleam of recognition in Terri's eyes when she'd heard John's name, her expression quickly became neutral. "Why are you telling me this?" she asked casually.

"I think you know," Sister Agatha said softly.

"We've unloaded everything, Sister Agatha, so I should be leaving now. I have other stops," Terri said, heading back to her car.

"John Gutierrez is a sad, lonely man, dying from cancer. He's got no other family. Finding Angie will help him die in peace. And Angie might end up getting a sizeable inheritance in exchange for that act of kindness, too. Her uncle became a very successful businessman in the Denver area. If you're who I think you are, that money could give you a financial cushion that'll help you stay under the radar for as long as you want."

Terri sat down on a wooden stool that had been moved over against the wall and remained silent for a while, staring at the floor. Finally she spoke. "Sister Agatha, I don't know how you figured it out, but by exposing my new identity you may have turned me into a target. Who else besides you knows who I really am—was?"

"I only shared my suspicions with Father Mahoney and Sheriff Green, nobody else. And it'll stay that way if you wish."

"It's absolutely vital that it's kept confidential, Sister Agatha. The man looking for me won't stop searching until one of us is dead. I don't know how much you've learned, but a few years ago I witnessed a man burying someone he'd just murdered. The killer was convicted, but later he escaped from jail and came looking for me. I was lucky, and managed to get away—just barely. To this day James Garza is still at large."

"We don't have a television or subscribe to local newspapers at the monastery. Can you fill me in a bit more?"

"Garza was involved in a multistate land-fraud deal, which is why the Feds were involved and why I was offered a chance to become part of the Witness Relocation Program. But life in hiding, so far away from everything I know, was tougher than I ever dreamed. I put on close to ninety pounds thanks to the pits of a depression. One day, realizing that my looks had changed drastically, I decided to leave the program. I was betting that Jimmy wouldn't be able to recognize me even if he saw me on the street."

"But if Garza's still at large, why on earth did you come back to *this* area? That's got to be the worst strategy in the world!"

"It depends on your viewpoint, Sister. The fact is I seriously doubted that *he* would ever come back here. He grew up in this town, and tons of people knew him. This *is* the safest place for me."

"Hiding in plain sight—more or less," Sister Agatha commented thoughtfully.

"Yeah, but I hadn't really planned to move here for good. It just worked out that way. After leaving Phoenix, where I'd been relocated, I decided to stop by Bernalillo—to see it one last time, you know? I took a side road near the river and passed by a beautiful little adobe *casita* for sale by owner. I fell in love with the place and the price couldn't be beat, so I bought it. At first, I thought I'd fix it up and use it as income property. But after I moved in and made the repairs, it really felt like home to me, and I just didn't want to leave." She paused. "But that's a whole other story. Let's get back to what you were saying about my uncle John. The last time I saw him he was a hunting guide at some mountain lodge, but that was years and years ago. How did he know I was back in town?"

"Apparently a business associate of his saw you at one of the local malls."

"And recognized me right off the bat?" she asked, surprised. "Who?"

"I'm not sure."

Terri pursed her lips, lost in thought for several moments before speaking. "Uncle John has—or had—black hair with a little gray on the sides, a rough complexion, and some scars on the side of his face. He's lived a hard life and looks it. He's around five-nine, taller than me."

"That fits the general description of the John Gutierrez I'm working for. But I can't verify his height. He's bedridden, confined to his room at the Siesta Inn. All I can tell you is that he very much wants to see you before he dies."

"Understand, Sister, that this is a tough call for me. I really don't want to come out into the open. It would be stupid for me to point a finger at myself. What if Jimmy Garza's watching my uncle?"

"That's a good point, and since these are special circumstances, I suggest that we notify Sheriff Green and let him handle the security details for us."

"That plan sounds okay, but give me a chance to think this through. I have to make a few more stops, but we might be able to get together later today. Why don't you give me a call on my cell this evening and we'll settle things then." She brought out a Catholic Charities business card, wrote a telephone number on the back, then handed it to Sister Agatha.

Sister Agatha placed the card into her pocket. "All right."

"I don't want there to be any misunderstandings, Sister Agatha. If what my uncle's looking for is a relative to take over his business, he's going to be disappointed. I want that clear up front. I don't care if he's a banker instead of a backpacker now. If he leaves me an inheritance, I intend on cashing it out."

"His company, I think, is in Denver. Maybe you could stay in hiding and let people he trusts continue to run things on your behalf."

She shook her head. "That business means something to *him*, not to me. I have my own life to live, Sister. Angie Sanchez died. I'm Terri now, two hundred pounds and all, and I have a new way of looking at things. I have to take care of good old number one. If I take this risk and come out into the open, I want cash, not headaches."

The lack of emotion behind Terri's words and her simple, matter-of-fact tone was like a cold wintry blast. She'd heard people Terri's age referred to as part of the "Me Generation" and at least in this case, the label seemed to fit.

"You disapprove of me, Sister Agatha?" she asked softly.

"I think that your world is a lot colder than the one I left behind when I became a nun."

12

SISTER AGATHA FINISHED HELPING SISTER CLOTHILDE clean up in the kitchen after their main meal of the day. It was nearly two now. Sister Agatha stopped by the scriptorium to check on things once more before heading into town, and found Sister Ignatius sitting in front of one of the computers. Surprised, she went up to her. "Is everything all right here? Where's Sister de Lourdes?"

"She's been running back and forth between here and the parlor. Sister Bernarda has been working on the outlets, and we've had several visitors, mostly workmen with questions concerning the gate and wall repairs. Since I'd finished mopping, I offered to come into the scriptorium and help. My job is to print out each order and update the report for NexCen so they'll be able to track which products are selling. I can handle that just fine. But we've also received some odd correspondence," she said, pointing. "I'm not at all sure what to do with those."

She groaned. "Not Wilder again."

"Yes, that's his name."

Sister Agatha picked up the two e-mails Sister Ignatius had printed and set aside. The first one read:

LOOK BEHIND YOU 'CAUSE I'LL BE THERE!

Along with Wilder's computer-generated signature at the bottom was a crude stick figure looking over a wall. The graphic was repeated in the other e-mail as well. On the second letter, Wilder had waxed poetic.

ROSES ARE RED

VIOLETS ARE BLUE.

WILDER'S AT WAR

AND COMING FOR YOU.

Sister Agatha stared at that last post. She had a bad feeling about this not-so-veiled threat. "Have you had any computer problems since you took over today?"

"No, but all I basically do is hit 'print' and keep a running count of the merchandise that'll have to be shipped out. After Sister de Lourdes returns from the parlor, Sister Eugenia, Sister Gertrude, and I will package up the orders, stick on the address labels, then get them ready to ship."

Sister de Lourdes came in just then, portable phone in hand. Her face was reddened and she looked out of breath. "I'm sorry I stayed away so long, Sister Ignatius." Seeing Sister Agatha, she added, "Is everything okay?"

Sister Agatha and Sister Ignatius nodded. "We're fine," Sister Ignatius answered for both of them.

"Catch your breath, Your Charity," Sister Agatha said. "I know it's been difficult handling both posts today. Why don't I postpone my visit into town and give you a break?"

"No, please don't. You have other important work to do for our monastery," Sister de Lourdes said. "Sister Bernarda will be taking over portress duty in another half hour and that'll help. She's making great progress with the wiring, but she doesn't want to do much more until Mr. Fiorino checks out the work she's already done."

"Sounds like you've got things under control," Sister Agatha said with an approving nod.

Another order came in and Sister Ignatius printed out the combination form, which included label and invoice as well. "I better get back to the packing room," Sister Ignatius said. "Today's orders have to be ready to go in an hour when the parcel express man comes."

"I'll be in town for a while this afternoon," Sister Agatha told Sister de Lourdes, "but if there's a crisis here, don't hesitate to call me back."

Sister Ignatius picked up the order sheets from the desk, then froze in place. Smiling broadly, her eyes lighting up as if by an inner fire, she pointed a watermark left on the surface of the desk by its previous owner. "My heavens, look!"

"Is something wrong?" Sister Agatha asked, leaning over.

"Don't you see it? It's an angel!" Using her index finger Sister Ignatius traced the vague outline of what could have been wings.

Sister Agatha moved closer, then leaned to one side, but the blob looked more like an amoeba to her.

"It's a sign, Sisters. We'll come through this present trouble just fine. Our angels are watching over us," Sister Ignatius said with a big smile.

Sister Agatha remembered the visitor they'd had a year ago and the incident that had convinced even the most skeptical among them that God had given their monastery a special angel to keep them safe. Yet the only proof the water stain before them held was that wood and water couldn't coexist without casualties.

"It's not that I ever doubted we'd be fine," Sister Ignatius added quickly. "It's just so nice to see little signs like these."

As she left, Sister de Lourdes glanced at Sister Agatha. "Do *you* see an angel?" she whispered.

"No, but she did," Sister Agatha replied. "Maybe that's enough."

A short time later Sister Agatha headed to the sheriff's office to meet Tom. She'd be calling Terri soon, and, by then, she wanted to have all the security details worked out. Deep in her heart she prayed that it would turn out to be a real family reunion—that once they got together, Terri would realize the value of what she'd been given a chance to reclaim.

She and Pax arrived at the local station in less than fifteen minutes. Sister Agatha waved to the desk sergeant, then, keeping Pax with her, continued down the hall. Tom was behind his desk, muttering curses as he checked the computer's connections.

"I recognize that M.O.," Sister Agatha said, shaking her head as she looked at his monitor. "Oh, no—the blue screen of death. I believe that's what the techies call it."

"This antique, worthless pile of junk just locked up on me for no reason at all. Everything I've entered since my last save is probably gone to data limbo."

"Maybe not all's lost. Do you have an auto-save feature?"

"You're asking me? I have no idea. I'll have Millie handle this," he said, looking over at the blue screen again and scowling. "But first, what's up? I can always tell when you've got something on your mind," he said, his attention exclusively on her now.

She told him about Terri and John Gutierrez. "If she comes forward as Angie, I want to make sure no one's waiting in the sidelines. Terri thought that Garza might be keeping watch on her relatives in case she decided to contact them one day."

"That's a valid concern. Let's go to Terri Montoya's place and work this out together in detail."

Sister Agatha called Terri's number but had to leave a cryptic message. "Drat. I can't get hold of her and I didn't get her address—come to think of it, she didn't offer it. I was supposed to call first and arrange for us to meet."

"I can get it," he said, then glanced at his computer and scowled. "On the way out, that is. Millie's computer is nice to her."

Sister Agatha, with Pax in the sidecar, followed Tom south through town. Just before the fence indicating the beginning of pueblo land, he turned down a gravel road. At the far end of the cul-de-sac sat five small pueblo-style adobe homes in a half circle. According to the house numbers, Terri's home was the one farthest back, in the center.

Sister Agatha parked and walked with Pax and Tom to the front door. The low adobe home had been plastered in natural sand tones, and the wood trim on the windows and doors was painted in a familiar, distinctive shade called Taos blue. Tom knocked loudly, but only silence echoed back.

"Let's take a look 'round back," he said.

Pax led the way, walking a few feet ahead of them. As they

walked along the left side of the house, a woman who'd been on her knees working in a flower bed next door stood and came into full view. Seeing Sister Agatha, she placed a small hand trowel into the pouch of her apron and waved.

"Hi, Sister!" she said, moving closer to the hedge.

Sister Agatha recognized Cindy Mason immediately. The young brunette volunteered at the rectory whenever Father Mahoney needed yard work done.

"If you're looking for Terri, you just missed her. She drove away less than a half hour ago," Cindy said.

Tom glanced at Sister Agatha, then back at Cindy. "Did she say where she was going?"

"We didn't talk," Cindy answered. "I came out front looking for my cat and noticed a suitcase beside her car. It looked like she was going on a trip, so I waved. But I guess she didn't see me. About then, my phone rang, so I ran back inside. By the time I got back outside Terri's car was halfway down the street."

Sister Agatha took a look through one of the windows into a bedroom. Terri had obviously packed in a hurry. Half-empty drawers were open, and clothes hangers were scattered all over the floor.

"Looks like you're right, Cindy. She's gone," Sister Agatha said, stepping aside so Tom could take a look for himself. After saying good-bye to Cindy, they walked back to the driveway.

"My guess is that Terri decided to take off before anyone else found out her real identity," Tom said.

"Let me give her a call," Sister Agatha replied, bringing out her cell phone. She punched the number but got an out-of-service message. "Can't get her. Something must have frightened Terri if she left in such a hurry. I'll call Catholic Charities when I get back to the monastery just in case Lucinda's heard from her. But I think I should go talk to John Gutierrez next."

"Your client isn't going to like this very much, but it wasn't your fault," Tom said.

Yet the truth was that she *had* failed. Maybe if she'd handled Terri differently. . . . "I wish she'd given John a chance—for her own sake and ours. Without that buffer zone, we could be facing a very rough time with our future neighbors. The outside world is really bearing down on us."

"Everyone feels that way at one time or another. Just do the best you can with each day. That's how I define a win."

Sister Agatha watched Tom as he drove away. No matter how difficult things got, Tom and she had been blessed. Their course in life was defined by purpose and a love for the work they did. The ones like Terri, who'd lost their way, traveled the most painful road of all.

Sister Agatha drove from Terri Montoya's home straight to the Siesta Inn. Mustering the courage it would take to deliver the bad news, she and Pax went down the hall to John Gutierrez's room and knocked. After being ushered in by Ralph, she went directly to John's bedside.

"I've got some news," Sister Agatha said, taking an offered seat and silently noting that her client's breathing seemed better today. Hopefully, what she was about to tell him wouldn't bring on a relapse.

John was sitting up, resting on several pillows, obviously anticipating her report. "Have you found my niece?" he asked hopefully.

Sister Agatha filled him in without emotion, then concluded. "I can't speak for her, but one possibility is that she decided meeting you is too much of a risk—for both of you."

"Sister, I'm very disappointed," John said slowly. "I hired

you because of your knowledge of this area and because people trust you. I expected more from you."

His words stung, but she tried not to show it. "I warned you from the start that I couldn't guarantee results. When someone wants to stay lost, finding them often makes them want to burrow even deeper than before."

He made an impatient gesture with his hand. "Let's move on. I need you to find her again, Sister Agatha. Only this time, just tell me where she is. We'll do the rest. If you succeed, then you'll still get the rest of the money and the land, as promised. If Angie is afraid for her life, I have the financial resources to take her somewhere safe and hire people to protect her. From what I can see, it's more important than ever that we get together."

"She may not be in the area anymore," Sister Agatha warned. "I have no idea where she went, either, except that she took a suitcase."

"Then check with those who knew her. See if you can find out where she might have gone. That alone is still worth something to me. Angie obviously needs me now as much as I need her. There's no stronger bond than blood."

She heard the determination in his voice and knew that John meant every word. "All right. I'll see what I can do."

"Sister Agatha, I know Angie," John said. "She's too stubborn to cut and run that easily. My guess is that she's still in the area, checking things out on her own while she tries to decide what to do next. If I can talk to her face-to-face, I can make her see that she's better off taking the protection my corporation and my resources can offer her."

A cell phone on the dresser rang, Ralph answered it, then approached the bed with the device in hand. "You'll have to excuse John for a minute, Sister," Ralph said, handing his employer the small phone.

"We're done for now," she said, nodding to John. "I'll be in touch." As she moved away, she saw the label attached to the side of one of the medical devices John was using. It read PRIORITY ONE HOME CARE.

As she left the room, with John in the background speaking on the phone, she couldn't help but notice that his breathing was almost normal. Gone, too, was the sickly pallor he'd exhibited before on her earlier visits. Today, John didn't seem like a dying man—more like someone on the road to recovery after a bad respiratory infection. Even the bad news she'd brought him concerning Angie hadn't impacted his condition in any noticeable way.

As she walked out to the parking lot with Pax, she saw the blue van Ralph had been driving earlier. It was a rental with New Mexico plates. Maybe that meant something, maybe not, but she knew what her next step should be. It was time she learned more about their benefactor—John Gutierrez.

13

ER NEXT STOP WAS PRIORITY ONE HOME CARE.
she'd get some answers there. When Sister Gertrude
had needed oxygen, Michelle Zamora, the owner, had
loaned them the equipment. She was a staunch friend of the
monastery.

As Sister Agatha pulled into a parking slot in front of Priority One, Pax's tail began to wag. Although they hadn't been here recently, Pax wasn't about to forget anyone who always had a box of doggy treats ready.

"Hey, pal, she may not have anything for you today, so don't get your hopes up."

Pax jumped out of the sidecar and gave her a haughty look that told her he was sure he'd score something.

Sister Agatha passed through the front entrance a moment later.

Michelle looked up and beamed her a smile. "Sister Agatha and Pax, what a pleasant surprise!"

Pax hurried across the room and sat in front of Michelle, who promptly reached into the desk drawer and brought out a dog treat. Pax gulped the green-colored biscuit down in an instant, then placed his massive head on the edge of her desk so Michelle would pet him.

"How's Sister Gertrude doing?" Michelle asked, her hand on Pax.

Sister Agatha took a seat and glanced absently out the plate-glass window. A dark-green sedan, like the one that had followed her before, drove by and continued down the road.

"Sister Gertrude's doing fine," Sister Agatha answered. "I just can't tell you how much all of us appreciated the medical equipment you loaned us."

"My pleasure. Besides, the monastery's prayers are good for business," she added with a smile.

"So things are going well here?" Seeing her nod, Sister Agatha continued. "I met a new client of yours, a man staying at the Siesta Inn in Bernalillo. He's one of our monastery benefactors."

"Ah, Mr. Gutierrez," Michelle said in a low, thoughtful voice. "That whole business is a bit on the strange side," she said, then stopped speaking abruptly. "I'm sorry. It was inappropriate of me to make a comment like that."

"Don't worry. I've noticed that our out-of-state visitor is a bit odd, too. In fact, if you know *anything* that'll help me understand Mr. Gutierrez or Ralph Simpson a little better, I'd sure appreciate you sharing. I'll keep whatever you tell me confidential."

After a brief, thoughtful pause, Michelle continued. "The way they handled the equipment rental was really peculiar, that's all. Ralph Simpson insisted that there was no need for me to consult with the patient's health-care people or even arrange for set-up and monitoring. He said they'd handle all that themselves. This equipment is expensive and requires expertise to set up properly, so I insisted. But he never gave an inch. Legally, we *can* rent oxygen equipment and heart monitors directly to a patient, so I went along with them, but I charged them a hefty deposit."

"Maybe they're used to handling medical machines and didn't want to wait."

"Yeah, but here's the thing. I can't understand why Gutierrez would travel by car all the way down from Denver without portable equipment if he was so ill. If he *had* brought down his own equipment, he also wouldn't have had to rent it here. There was plenty of room for it in the big van, after all."

"Those are good points." After thanking her, Sister Agatha walked back out to the Harley with Pax.

She was pulling out of Priority One when she saw the dark-green sedan again. This time it passed by quickly—much too fast, in fact, for a thirty-five-mile-per-hour zone. She was trying to decide whether to follow it or not when the driver left the main road and parked in the driveway of one of the smaller houses in the adjacent subdivision. The car had yellow New Mexico plates.

She *was* getting paranoid. That was all there was to it. Some poor man was trying to get home after work and she'd been sure it was a tail. She took a deep breath then let it out slowly. What she needed now were a few hard facts to go with all her vague suspicions.

Sister Agatha drove back into Bernalillo to the *Chronicle*'s office. As she pulled up, she saw Chuck sitting on the front step, sipping a can of cola.

"Hey, Sister! It's good to see you, and Pax, too. Janice is off covering some harvest festival, and I'm dying of boredom. Any more excitement come your way?" He reached over and scratched Pax atop the head.

"In a way. Actually, I came hoping you'd help me do some more research. But I'll still have to ask you to keep it confidential."

"Sure, but if there's a story in this, will you make sure *The Chronicle* gets it first?"

"Deal."

Chuck took her to Janice's office and slid a chair across from her while Pax lay down in a sunny spot. "Good thing you've been coming when Janice is gone," he said with a grin. "She wouldn't be as easy to deal with as I am."

"I appreciate this, Chuck. I really do."

"Okay, then let's get started. What do you need, more on that murder witness, Angie what's-her-face?"

"No, actually, I need anything you can get me on John Gutierrez, the current owner of Luz del Cielo Vineyards and Winery. He's from Denver, so that's probably where his headquarters are located."

"Ah, you're worried that his check will bounce?" he asked. "People who put on a good show claiming to have money all too often do that to get extra perks. No one knows they're flat broke until it's too late to collect on outstanding bills."

"In this case it's not that clear-cut," she said. "I just need to get a better handle on the kind of person the monastery's dealing with."

"Sure, Sister Agatha. I'll help you. I can get anything on anybody on the Internet."

"I probably don't have to say this, but keep it legal, okay?"

He scoffed. "Of course. Legal is my middle name. But what you need is going to take more than an article search. We're going to have to get creative. I'll begin by using the *Chronicle's* business status to get a credit report for the vineyard," he said then, after a moment, added, "Looks like they're solid. I can't check on his tax status, of course, but all his bills are paid up. Gutierrez does business under the banner of Moxom Corporation. Weird name, huh?" He did a search on them, then continued. "Moxom owns several other enterprises, too."

Sister Agatha looked at the screen, standing behind Chuck. "I need all you can dig up on Moxom."

"Good thing this is a company that trades publicly. That means that we've got a huge repertoire of reports we can tap into—from the Securities and Exchange Commission to state corporation ones. Most of that is public domain."

He typed a password that led him to another database, then glanced up at her. "For the last two quarters, Moxom Corporation has shown a steady rise in profits. They look very healthy." He leaned back in his chair.

"So John Gutierrez is doing well?"

"According to these corporate numbers, you bet he is."

Sister Agatha considered what she'd learned. John had mentioned wanting top dollar for the vineyard, which was why he hadn't wanted to sell to Eric Barclay, the former owner and now caretaker of the vineyard. He could undoubtedly afford to sell it for less, but maybe that was part of what made him so successful—getting the most out of every deal.

From what she'd just learned, John Gutierrez appeared to be pretty much as he'd presented himself—all except for some inconsistencies pertaining to his medical condition. Of course, maybe his symptoms were highly variable at this stage, with good days as well as bad. Maybe he'd traveled down in another vehicle, or by air, then had Ralph rent the van and the medical equipment just in case of an emergency.

"Can you find anything on a Ralph Simpson? He's Gutierrez's assistant," she asked Chuck after a brief pause.

That request turned out to be harder to fulfill. They needed more than just his name to continue a credit check. Unlike his employer, who had many business assets, Ralph was scarcely a blip on the radar. All they could find out was that he worked for Moxom Corporation. "I can get more for you, but I'm going to need more time."

"Okay," she said, then added, "But for now, can you just track down a good close-up photo of John Gutierrez for me? I need something that'll verify we've been researching the right John Gutierrez—bank account notwithstanding."

Chuck worked all the newspaper archives and even tapped into other regional papers, but came up empty. "I guess he's just not newsworthy," he said, "at least visually so."

"Well, all things considered, that may not be a bad thing," Sister Agatha said, but before she could go on, her cell phone rang. It was Sister Bernarda.

"Sister Gertrude's doctor called in a prescription for her, and we need you to pick it up. Sister de Lourdes can't leave because the computer crashed again. Merilee from NexCen is here working with her. Since the lights have been flickering more than normal, we're not sure if our computer troubles are the work of Wilder or due to our electrical system. We may have a problem with the main electrical line coming into the monastery. Merilee's running diagnostics on the computer right now. In the meantime, I'm checking out the circuits with a volt-ohm meter."

"I'll go by the drugstore. It's no problem," she said, then closed up the phone.

"I've got to go, Chuck. Something's come up," she said.

"Okay, Sister. I'll keep digging and see what else I can get for you."

Sister Agatha went outside and was putting on her helmet when she saw the outline of a person standing in the shadows across the street. Pax noticed at almost the same moment, and growled softly, teeth bared.

By the time she lifted off her helmet for a good look, the person had vanished.

The knowledge that she was still being watched made her uneasy. Maybe someone besides John was using her to find Terri—perhaps Jimmy Garza. The thought frightened her, but she had no time to indulge in those emotions now. She had work to do.

Sister Agatha went to the pharmacy just down the street and waited for the prescription. A moment later, the pharmacist, who was also covering customers at the drive-up window, hurried back to the counter. "It's almost ready, Sister, but I just spotted someone outside taking a real close look at your Harley. Maybe you should go and introduce him to Pax," he said only half-jokingly.

Sister Agatha moved to the front door and looked through the glass. A man in a green jacket, sunglasses, and a baseball cap was next to the bike, his face shaded by the bill. Almost as if sensing her eyes on him, he turned and walked away briskly in the opposite direction. "Well, he's no threat now," she said.

A few minutes later, prescription in hand, Sister Agatha went outside with Pax. The man in the green jacket was long gone, but she still wanted to check the bike carefully.

Sister Agatha walked around the Harley, verifying that all the connections were still intact on the wiring and twin V engine. Then, as she glanced inside the sidecar, she spotted a small note on the seat. Handling it only by the edges, she brought it out and read it.

YOU'RE IN DANGER. WATCH YOUR BACK.

Sister Agatha stared at it in surprise, then took the bottle of pills out of the paper sack and placed the note there instead. She'd drop the bag by the sheriff's station, then continue to the monastery.

14

NINE O'CLOCK THE FOLLOWING MORNING FOUND most of the nuns busy with their work assignments. Sister Bernarda was moving from cell to cell—their bedrooms—adding copper wiring and special wire nuts, then reconnecting each outlet.

The electrician, Mr. Fiorino, had come and inspected her work earlier that day and pronounced it "excellent." Sister Bernarda had practically beamed when Reverend Mother had thanked her publicly during Chapter.

Sister de Lourdes, with Merilee's help, had managed to get their computer server up and running again and had untangled a mess with the orders.

For now, things were blessedly peaceful. Then it occurred to Sister Agatha that it shouldn't have been quite that quiet. The gate repairs should have created a certain amount of chaos.

Sister Agatha glanced outside the parlor window and saw that work on the partially restored gate had come to a stop. Worried, she tried to telephone the contractor to find out why they'd left, but the company's line was busy.

Sister Bernarda came in then, brushing off her long skirt. "I can take over for you here at the parlor now. I'm out of supplies, so I'll need to wait for Mr. Fiorino before I continue. Do you need to go into town?"

"Yes, actually I do. I'm very worried about Terri," she said and explained. "I'm hoping that Mr. Gutierrez is right, and she's still around, just lying low for the time being."

"So do I, though my reasons are selfish ones. Did you know that work on the gate has stopped?"

"Yes, and I just tried to call the contractor to see what's going on, but I haven't been able to get through."

"That was a blessing to you straight from God. Lou Curtis, the owner, is *really* angry with us," Sister Bernarda said, then in a whisper-thin voice added, "Our check bounced."

"*What?* That can't be."

"It happened. Apparently there was a misunderstanding between Sister Gertrude and Sister Maria Victoria. She took funds out of the checking account and put them into the savings instead of vice versa."

"Oh, no!"

"Maria Victoria is a world-class seamstress, but she's a disaster as the assistant cellarer," Sister Bernarda said, shaking her head. "I think I could do a better job, and I intend to approach Reverend Mother about it soon."

"But your schedule is so full already."

"I'm needed."

Her response was as simple as it was indicative of the Rule of the Monastery, which required them to put the good of the community ahead of their own. But, in this particular case, she suspected that Sister Bernarda had more than one reason for wanting to keep busy—she didn't want time to think about the crisis she was facing.

"But I don't understand why Mr. Curtis stopped working on our wall. If it's just a matter of transferring funds, that's easy enough to fix. The money *is* there."

"Yes, but since the check bounced, Mr. Curtis has now demanded that we pay the full amount up front. We can't do that, not even with the money from John Gutierrez."

"No, I don't suppose we can," she said softly. "But if I manage to find Angie Sanchez and earn the rest of the money he promised us. . . ."

"Then you'd better get busy with that," Sister Bernarda said, sitting down at the parlor desk. "I'll start a novena asking that you find a quick resolution to Mr. Gutierrez's problem."

With Sister Bernarda's words still ringing in her ears, Sister Agatha stepped out the parlor door and onto the small porch. Hearing a songbird up in one of the cottonwood trees, she smiled and glanced up. The enjoyment that respite gave her served as a reminder that the quiet and seclusion they now enjoyed could come to an abrupt end if the land adjacent to theirs was developed.

Sister Agatha walked toward the motorcycle, whistling for Pax, but then noticed he was already in the sidecar. He leaned across the side of the cockpit, and, resting one huge paw on the motorcycle seat, stared at her impatiently.

"I'm coming," Sister Agatha said. She had no idea where to start her search—a motel? They were as common as silver sedans, even Toyotas. She said a prayer as she started the bike, and by the time she passed through the entrance where the gates had been, an idea came to her.

She'd go see Cindy, Terri's neighbor. She had a strong feeling that she'd find answers there—providing she asked the right questions. Knowing that it was willingness to listen with the heart that often allowed God's unerring guidance to come through clearly, she headed south toward Bernalillo.

Less than twenty minutes later, she parked in front of Cindy's home and found her working in the garden.

Having heard the distinctive sound of the motorcycle, Cindy waved and motioned for Sister Agatha and Pax to join her. "I'm glad you came by again, Sister Agatha," she said brightly, brushing the dirt off her jeans. "I was going to call you about Terri. I've remembered something that may be important."

Thanking God for his help, Sister Agatha waited.

"When Terri first moved in, she asked me to keep an eye on her place. She told me that if I ever saw anyone just hanging around, I should call her at work. From what she said . . . or maybe the way she said it . . . I got the impression that she wanted to avoid an ex-husband or ex-boyfriend, not just bill collectors. And, yesterday, not long before she left, I saw a guy wearing a blue baseball cap and olive-green windbreaker hanging around behind her house. I just caught a glimpse of him, but he was wearing sunglasses."

"Did you tell Terri?" Sister Agatha asked.

"No, she left shortly after that so I never had a chance to mention it to her."

"Show me where the guy was," Sister Agatha said.

Cindy led her to the back of the property. "He was standing here, looking at her house."

Sister Agatha studied the gravel-lined road. The man she'd seen in the pharmacy's parking lot, the one who'd tried to warn her off the case, had been wearing the same thing, down to the sunglasses. It was the same person, she was sure of it. And, by now, Tom might have his fingerprints.

"Were the sunglasses the man was wearing black-framed?" Sister Agatha asked.

Cindy thought about it. "I think so. Yes, come to think of it, I'm sure they were. How did you know?"

"I've seen him around. One more thing. Are you sure it was Terri who drove away in her car?"

"It looked like her, but all I saw was the back of her head. "What's going on, Sister?"

"She may have been followed—or worse. I'm not sure yet, but I'll let you know as soon as I find out more."

Sister Agatha hurried to Tom's office. Traffic was light this morning, and she made good time. With a quick wave to those busy behind the front desk, she and Pax walked down the hall.

Tom was standing outside his office talking to someone in a suit when he saw her coming. With a casual wave, he motioned for her to go into his office.

Sister Agatha and Pax made themselves comfortable, and Tom came in a few moments later. "Before I get sidetracked," he said, easing down into his chair. "I wanted to tell you that we weren't able to lift any prints from that note you dropped off yesterday."

Disappointed, she told him about her visit to Cindy and what she'd learned about the man who'd probably been watching Terri as well as her. "If he's been tailing me all along, he's skilled at it, Tom. I'm worried that he may have followed Terri when she left—maybe even caught up to her."

"We've got an APB out on Terri. Keep a sharp eye out, and call me immediately if you spot that guy or his car again. I'll give the description to our patrol officers, but without a plate number or vehicle model, I doubt we'll get far."

"I'll try her cell phone again," she offered. Once again, she got a message that the call couldn't be completed. "No luck, Tom. How about I give you the number?"

"Good idea. I can get a location if she makes a call."

Before she could write it down, her cell phone rang. Sister Bernarda sounded tense. "Sister Agatha, we've received a call from NexCen. Their local warehouse was vandalized last night. It's mostly spray paint, but the warehouse supervisor, a Mr. Orem, would like you to meet him there as soon as possible."

"He needs to talk to the sheriff, not me."

"A deputy is already there."

"Did the supervisor say why he needs *me*, then?"

"Merilee suggested it. That's all I know."

"Okay, thanks." Sister Agatha hung up quickly, then filled Tom in.

"If someone is messing with your Internet mail orders, there are federal agencies that can become involved, but, as far as the vandalism goes, that's generally a misdemeanor. I can also tell you right off the bat that it's unlikely we'll be able to do anything more than file a report unless we get a name. We don't have the manpower to follow that up unless there were major damages."

"I guess I better go talk to Mr. Orem."

Sister Agatha gave him Terri's cell phone number, then left the station. She drove southwest until she almost reached the city of Rio Rancho, then turned onto the side street that led to the warehouse. She'd been here once before, right after they'd taken on the NexCen account.

She pulled up to the gunmetal gray building with a large wooden sign that read NEXCEN. A wide, concrete loading dock about four feet off the ground extended the width of all three doors, each the size of a garage bay. The center door was raised, and she could see Merilee Brown speaking to a man she didn't recognize.

Sister Agatha parked in a visitor space, removed her helmet, then walked up the steps at the end of the dock with Pax at her side.

Merilee, having watched her arrival, gave her an uncertain smile. "I'm glad you're here, Sister Agatha. This is Dean Orem."

Sister Agatha shook his hand. His eyes were a soft blue and his face was gently weathered and lined. Orem was in his midsixties and in good physical shape.

"Pleased to meet you, Sister," he said in a surprisingly gentle voice.

"The second I read the report Dean faxed us, I thought I'd come take a look for myself," Merilee said. "Now I need your corroboration, Sister Agatha. Remember the e-mails the monastery received from that Wilder crank and the funny little graphics attached to them?"

"Of course," Sister Agatha said.

"I want you to look at the spray-painted drawings inside. See if you agree with me that we're dealing with the same artist."

"Has the sheriff's deputy already finished?" she asked. "I didn't see a vehicle in the lot."

Merilee nodded. "He took photos, our statement, then left."

Sister Agatha followed her into the warehouse. On the inside of the closed doors someone had spray painted a figure that resembled a kid peering over a wall.

"It's the same drawing," Sister Agatha said with a nod. "Just on a bigger scale."

Taunts like FRY YOUR MOTHERBOARDS had also been spray

painted everywhere—on packing crates, the walls, and even the concrete floor.

"It looks like the person responsible has a grudge against NexCen, not the monastery," Sister Agatha added.

"Maybe so," Merilee agreed. "The e-mails you get pass through our Web page, and this warehouse has the same zip code as the post office box NexCen uses for its orders."

The news and the possibilities it opened changed everything. She'd have to reevaluate her theories now. If the network problems had been caused by someone with a grudge against NexCen, then they were dealing with two separate sets of people. One person was clearly out to harass the monastery, and had been watching them with binoculars. The other was focusing its hatred on the company, and their scriptorium was just caught in the middle.

Sister Agatha left the warehouse with more questions than when she'd arrived. She thought of going back home, but everyone at the monastery was depending on her to find answers.

She needed to figure out what to do next, but no ideas came to her. Sister Agatha pulled off the road into a rest area, suddenly aware that she'd forgotten to do the most important thing of all. Bowing her head, she prayed with all her heart. "Lord, I'm so sorry. I did it again. I know You don't go where You're not invited, and here I was thinking that I could do something without You. Show me what I have to do, where I should go."

As she finished her prayer and looked over, she saw Pax sitting up, looking at her expectantly. She reached out and stroked his massive neck.

Sister Agatha noted the rapidly gathering clouds and felt

the wind rising ever so slightly. They'd have a storm later today for sure. Seeing a piece of trash blowing past her and into the adjacent field, she glanced at it absently. The torn newspaper page had a photo of one of the local public high schools. Slowly an idea formed in her mind.

"I've got it, Pax. Let's go to St. Charles," she said, speaking of the local parochial school. "Maybe we can find out something helpful about Liz and her family. And while we're there, I'll ask around and see if anyone on staff remembers Jimmy Garza or fell victim to him. Our town is small, so there's a good chance we might get lucky."

Whispering a prayer of thanks, she drove north into Bernalillo. The school parking lot was almost empty by the time she got there, suggesting that the students and most of the staff were gone for the day. Sister Agatha parked in a visitor's space, then walked to the office with Pax at her side. Mary Wagner, the younger of the two school secretaries, looked up from her desk and smiled as they walked in.

"Hey, Sister Agatha! It's good to see you and Pax. What can I do for you today?"

"I was hoping to use the school administration's computer to get some information on a former student—Elizabeth Leland."

"You're on our substitute staff, so you're authorized, but you won't be able to print out any of her records, of course," she said, then added, "But isn't Liz in public school now?"

Sister Agatha nodded. "Liz is in a bit of trouble, and I need some information."

"Then go for it," she said.

Sister Agatha read Liz's file, but there was nothing there that she didn't already know. "I guess I struck out."

"Maybe you should talk to Kasey Gordon, our librarian.

The students got out early today because of a teacher conference in Albuquerque, but she's still around. Liz worked as her student aide for a semester, I think."

Sister Agatha walked down the hall to the library, now labeled the "media" center, and went in. The blinds were closed, and the only light came from the fixtures and through a half-opened window. A young woman barely out of her twenties was shelving books from a wheeled cart, unaware that she had company. Sister Agatha cleared her throat, and the woman jumped and spun around.

"Sister, I didn't hear you come in!" she said with an embarrassed smile.

"I'm Sister Agatha," she said, extending her hand.

"Mrs. Gordon—Kasey. I recognized you the instant I saw your dog. You're practically a legend around here." She gestured toward her office, a room within the library. "Can I get something for you to drink? I've got some soft drinks in there today, with the children gone."

Sister Agatha shook her head. "I just wanted to talk to you for a few moments about Liz Leland."

"Liz is attending public school now, and I can tell you that I was sure sorry to see her go. She's one of those kids who's poised on a fence and can go either direction. I think she would have had a better chance of staying out of trouble if she'd remained at St. Charles. But it wasn't meant to be, I guess. Liz still comes by to visit from time to time though."

"She got under your skin, did she?" Sister Agatha observed.

"Yeah, she did, mostly because I've been in her shoes. My parents lost all their savings in a land-fraud deal a con man ran a few years back. All of a sudden my college fund was gone. I ended up living at home, working part-time, and taking night classes."

The mention of a land fraud scam got Sister Agatha's immediate attention. "Your parents didn't get caught up in that scheme run by James Garza, did they?"

Kasey nodded. "You remember? So many families around here lost everything. Garza and his cronies literally got away with murder." Kasey led Sister Agatha to a low desk that held a sign reading CHECK OUT MATERIALS HERE. On the desk was a small computer terminal, which the librarian quickly accessed. "I've kept a personal folder filled with links to articles about him—like a scrapbook—so I don't ever forget how he almost wiped out my future. Garza broke out of jail, and they never caught him. But I intend to remember the man. If he ever comes back, I'll know him and I'll have the cops down on him in a flash. I'd love to see that man in prison where he belongs."

Judging from the number at the bottom of the file, Sister Agatha could see it was several pages long. "It may take me some time to get through this but I'd like to see it. Would you mind?"

"I have to go meet a potential guest speaker for my students, but you can stay and take as much time as you want. When you finish, exit back to the main screen and leave the terminal on. Also, be sure to ask the custodian to lock up this office and the media center. She's around somewhere, cleaning rooms."

"Not a problem."

"I'll catch you later, Sister," she said, walking to the main door, and turning off all the library lights except the one above the desk. "Do you mind, Sister? We're trying to save on the electric bill."

"That's fine."

Kasey waved, pulled the library door shut, then disappeared. Sister Agatha got down to work right away. Finding a grainy press photo of James Garza, she zoomed in and cleaned up the distortion created by the newsprint as much as she could.

Studying the results moments later, she noted that Garza was a dark-haired, handsome man. He looked the part of the quintessential con artist. Although it was impossible for her to make a positive ID from the photo, there *were* similarities between Gutierrez and Garza, particularly the scarred face that bore evidence of a harsh life. To be fair, however, Garza also bore some resemblance to Ralph, particularly around his eyes, but the similarity between those two ended there.

Sister Agatha leaned back in her chair and looked up, hearing a thunderstorm brewing outside. With all but one of the blinds completely lowered and only one of the room lights on, it was now darker in the library than outside. As a strong gust of wind blew across the desk, rattling the window blinds, Sister Agatha dove forward to catch the papers before they ended up on the floor. After securing everything, she ran to close the window, then lowered the last blind before returning to the desk.

Except for the intermittent rumbling of thunder, the school was eerily silent. Then, inexplicably, she heard a door click shut, followed by shuffling footsteps inside the library. Pax's hackles rose and he began to growl—a low, menacing sound that left her covered with goosebumps.

Gathering her courage, Sister Agatha peered across the large room toward the main door. "Who's there?" she called out, but there was no answer. Then the remaining light went off, plunging the library into darkness.

15

THE ONLY LIGHT INSIDE THE LIBRARY NOW WAS WHAT managed to filter in from around the edges of the blinds. It made for a muted, dim glow that barely revealed the location of the tall bookshelves.

"I think you should know that I have a very large dog with me—one who's attack-trained. What you're doing is not only foolish—it's suicidal."

Pax growling intensified, sparked by the tone in her voice.

For a moment, silence stretched out. Opposing wills clashed, then she heard the library door opening and, seconds later, footsteps running down the hall.

"Easy, boy," Sister Agatha said as Pax began to bark. "It was probably just a kid." Sister Agatha sent Pax over to the door to stand guard, then reached for her cell phone and called Tom. "I think he's gone now, but you might want to come check things out."

"Stay in the library. I'll call the school number and warn the office staff. Expect me or a deputy in a few minutes."

Sister Agatha looked in the desk for a flashlight, but there wasn't one. Moving slowly, she worked her way across the library to the light switch, near where Pax was sitting at "stay." She could see his white outline even in the subdued light.

Suddenly Pax gave off a sharp bark and stood, his attention on the closed door. Following his gaze, Sister Agatha saw the trickle of smoke coming in from beneath the door leading into the hall. A heartbeat later, the fire alarm sounded and the strobe light attached to the alarm began to blink to alert the hearing impaired.

Sister Agatha flipped on the light switch and looked around the library to verify nobody else was in sight. After making sure the door wasn't hot and she wouldn't create a bigger problem by opening it, she took Pax and hurried out.

As she emerged from the library, she discovered a smoldering trash can in the hall about four feet from the closest wall. The fire, mostly paper ignited with a match or cigarette, was already starting to burn out, judging from the absence of flames and dwindling smoke. Spotting a tripped fire alarm on the closest wall, she reached up and closed the lever. The shrill sound stopped at once.

Sister Agatha looked beyond the smoldering four-foot-high container, searching for the closest exit. There was a student restroom opposite the trash can, but she didn't know if it had an exit, except possibly through a window. This time of day, with no students on campus, it was probably locked anyway.

She was walking past the restroom when a hand suddenly snaked out and grabbed her by the arm, yanking her into the gap between wall and partially opened door. Pax, a half step ahead of her, whirled around, but got entangled in the leash. With her body blocking the entrance, he couldn't get at the person holding her in an iron grip.

"Don't let the dog get past you, and keep him quiet, or you and he are both dead," a deep, obviously disguised, voice warned. "I've got a gun," he added, shoving the barrel in front of her nose.

"Pax, quiet!"

Pax continued struggling, but he stopped barking.

"What do you want?" Sister Agatha demanded, trying to find a way to slam the steel door shut on her assailant. He must have been blocking the door with his foot, since it didn't budge when she managed to grab the handle and push.

"Don't mess with me, Sister. I make a bad enemy," he said in a sharp whisper. "Go back to the monastery and stick to praying."

As sirens pierced the evening air, she felt the pressure of his grip ease. Seizing the moment, she jerked away and the bathroom door slammed shut.

Sister Agatha instantly reached down to uncoil the leash from Pax's neck and body, but the effort was complicated by his pawing at the door.

"No, stay!" she ordered. The dog's loyalty and sense of duty were admirable and commendable, but neither of them had a chance against a gunman. She leaned against the door, hoping her weight would keep the man from opening the door again once he realized he was trapped.

A heartbeat later, Tom came around the hall corner, running in their direction. Seeing Pax barking frantically and scratching at the door, he drew his weapon.

"What's going on?"

"There's a man with a gun inside the restroom. He grabbed me by the arm and threatened me. He might still be there—he didn't come out this way."

"Stand back and keep a firm hold on Pax."

Tom waited until she was flat against the wall, closer to the library. He then yanked open the door, keeping his body clear, but taking a quick glance inside.

"Crap. There's a door on the other side. He went out onto the grounds." Tom ran into the restroom, disappearing as the door closed behind him.

Sister Agatha kept a firm grip on Pax, who wanted to follow. He was wired and angry, and wanted nothing more than the chance to turn their assailant into hamburger.

"You're a *monastery* dog, Pax. Stop that."

A few minutes later Tom came down the hall, short of breath. "I circled the building, but saw no one except for the office staff and the custodian. They'd all gone to the staff parking area," he said. "My deputies are checking the neighborhood and school grounds now."

Minutes later, the fire chief, a dark-haired, portly man, joined them, carrying a large fire extinguisher.

"Hey, Tom, Sister. I smelled the smoke all the way from the main door." He spotted the trash can immediately, and went to look inside. "Doggone, kids. Either of you two see who did it?"

"Sister Agatha got a glimpse of the perp—an adult. But it was more than just a prank, Bob. I'll be taking it from here. I'll need to save the contents of the trash can as evidence and dust the area for prints. If we need your expertise on the fire itself I'll give you a call."

"It's all yours, Tom," he said with a wave of his hand.

As the fireman left, Sister Agatha looked at Tom. "I don't

think you'll find prints. Remember the note? This was probably the same guy."

"I'll check anyway. Maybe we can get a print from the bathroom door. Was the guy who grabbed you wearing gloves?"

"I'm not sure. All I saw clearly was the barrel of his gun. But you might also want to check the light switch inside the library, and the door handles leading in and out," Sister Agatha said, quickly recounting the scary moments in the library.

"Which brings me to my next question. What were you doing here that generated all this attention?"

She told him what she'd found out about Jimmy Garza, pointing out the potential risk to Angie Sanchez if Garza was really back in the area. "But all I've got is coincidence, supposition, and a lot of guesswork. My next stop's Luz del Cielo. We still don't know who has been hanging around the vineyard and watching the monastery. If Garza found out that I've been trying to find Angie for her uncle, he might be the one staking us out. If so, maybe Eric has seen the guy up close and can give me a lead, or at least a description of his vehicle."

"Good thinking. Let me know what you find out."

Sister Agatha drove down the road to the vineyard, then entered the property through the open gates. Eric was seldom home these days, it seemed.

Sister Agatha parked, then heard her name being called from across one of the fields. Eric was waving at her from beside what appeared to be a pseudo golf cart. Sister Agatha walked down the pathway between the vines and went to meet him. Pax maneuvered through the vines instead of going around and reached Eric first.

"You two didn't have to come over. I was just waving so

you'd see me and wait," he said. "But since you're here, take a ride with me. I'd like to show you something very special!" He motioned for her to step up onto the cart. Sister Agatha sat beside him on the front bench while Pax made himself comfortable in the back.

Several minutes later they arrived at the now-gentle slopes of a long, narrow mesa that had been sculpted over time for farming. They climbed off the cart and Eric proudly showed Sister Agatha the sturdy vines growing there.

"You can't see these fields from the monastery, except maybe from the roof, but these vines are my pride and joy. They're descendants of the original Mission grapes that the Franciscans brought over with them in the 1600s. I found them at an old vineyard farther south, but they never produced more than a few bunches of grapes no matter how I babied them.

"Then, shortly after my wife passed away, I had a dream where she told me to come take another look. When I came, I saw that the vines were really thriving. Before long, they became my best producers."

"They're small grapes," Sister Agatha commented.

"Only table grapes are big. I stress our vines so that the fruit will have a more concentrated flavor. I also snip off many of the bunches, so that the ones we *do* pick are of the highest quality. I've now developed a special, deep-colored, long-lasting red wine by mixing these with Tempranillo grapes. I call it San Miguel Rojo, after the archangel, the warrior. I'll need his fighting spirit if I want Luz del Cielo to make it. So far St. Michael's been on our side. Our wine has won every competition around."

"That's great."

"My wife's medical bills forced me to sell the vineyard, but

I'm now in the process of finding backers so I can buy Luz del Cielo back."

Watching Eric, Sister Agatha realized that the heavy weight of mourning had been lifted off his shoulders. The vines he'd so loved had called him back to life.

"I've entered San Miguel Rojo in a major national competition this year. Luz del Cielo Vineyards has been quiet for too long. If it wins, maybe John Gutierrez will change his mind about selling to the developers and give me a chance to buy him out."

They drove back to the main house and Eric invited her inside. Once in the kitchen, he poured two mugs of coffee, then placed one before her without asking. "Help yourself to sugar, if you like. I also have cream in the fridge."

"No cream, thanks. Sugar's all I need," she said, then waited for him to continue.

"When I sold him Luz del Cielo, John Gutierrez agreed to give me first refusal rights if he ever decided to sell the place. He assured me that he'd set the price at market value—no more. Then a month ago he suddenly changed the terms and put the land up for sale."

"You mean he raised the price?"

"Considerably," Eric answered. "Yesterday he told me he's received an offer that's ten percent above mine. I can't match that." He paused, his voice unsteady now. "I *never* would have sold this winery to Gutierrez if I'd known he wouldn't honor his word. I should have insisted he put it all down in writing. But at the time I really needed the money—not more lawyer fees. I thought our word was sufficient."

"In this day and age, if it isn't in the contract. . . ."

"I know that now. Honor all too often takes a backseat to profits."

"I don't have any pull with John," Sister Agatha said in a heavy voice. "But I'll talk to him for you anyway and see what I can do. Believe me, the monastery doesn't want to see a developer stacking up houses beside our walls, either."

"I appreciate your help. I still believe he should honor his word."

"So do I," Sister Agatha said. "Have you tried to work something out with him—like maybe tacking on a percentage of the winery profits in addition to the sale price?" she suggested.

He nodded. "I tried several things, even sending him a sample bottle of our newly developed wine."

"Does it look like the sale to the developer will go through?"

"From what I've heard, yes," he said. "I spoke to his assistant a little while ago and Ralph said it was all in the hands of the attorneys—a matter of dotting the i's and crossing the t's. Once the paperwork's ready, John intends to sign."

Sister Agatha considered the news. Since she still hadn't found Terri, the monastery probably wouldn't get the allotment of land he'd initially offered them, either. The news was as bad as it could get. "I better talk to Reverend Mother. This will have serious repercussions on our monastery. But before I go, I need to ask if you've seen anyone hanging around near our common wall. We've spotted a man watching us two or three times now, but when we approach, he disappears."

"No, I haven't seen anyone, but I haven't been outside much lately. Manipulating the fermentation process is the key to making wine, and that takes careful monitoring. I've been spending most of my time in the winery."

"Okay then. Thanks. Pax and I better be on our way. Take care of yourself, Eric."

Sister Agatha arrived at the monastery as the bell for Vespers rang. She'd missed most of the liturgical hours and, more than anything else, she felt the very real need to reaffirm the spiritual connection that made her His. Sister Agatha entered the chapel as the choir nuns filed into the cloistered section and took a seat in their respective stalls.

After Vespers they went into the refectory for collation, their simple dinner meal. They ate in silence except for the daily reading. Tonight, Sister Eugenia stood behind the lectern and read from the life of St. Isidore. Afterward, Sister Agatha helped Sister Clothilde clean up. Once done, they both joined the others outside. Pax was already there, walking with Sister Gertrude. The dog seemed to understand that the elderly nun needed encouragement to continue her exercise walks and would nuzzle her hand, trying to spur her on.

Reverend Mother had returned to chapel to leave some flowers by the altar but would soon join them again. Sister Agatha made up her mind to speak to her about the sale of Luz del Cielo Winery as soon as she did. Aware of soft footsteps behind her, Sister Agatha turned her head and saw Sister Ignatius approaching.

The elderly nun smiled broadly. "I've got wonderful news. The monastery's peace will soon be restored. I received a sign today."

Sister Agatha waited, understanding that Sister Ignatius' signs were usually ordinary things that lent themselves to a dozen other rational explanations.

Sister Ignatius smiled, her expression filled with understanding. "Knowing how much comfort a clear sign would bring to the sisters, I asked for something more difficult this time. Do you remember that rose bush by the cemetery—the one that died all the way to the ground, and then came back up? It hasn't flowered since."

"Sister Ignatius, I'm not even sure that's still a rose. Something came up in its place, but it could just as easily be a tall, hardy weed or a shoot from one of our other plants."

"Come take a look." Sister Ignatius led her to the bush, then parting the branches in the middle, called her attention to the two small red roses in its center. "I asked for two roses. One is a sign our peace will be restored; the other, that Sister Bernarda will soon find comfort in God's gentle hands."

As Sister Ignatius walked away, Sister Agatha stared in stunned silence at the roses. Then she heard Reverend Mother's voice behind her.

"She showed you the roses, I see," Reverend Mother said. "Her faith is really quite extraordinary."

"It is, isn't it," Sister Agatha agreed, amazed. "But, despite all this, I have some bad news," she said, and told Reverend Mother about the impending sale of the vineyard.

"We'll have to cling to God and the promise His roses hold out to us," Reverend Mother said.

As the bells for Compline rang, Reverend Mother bowed her head and silently headed back inside. Sister Agatha followed, answering the summons that made them a part of Our Lady of Hope Monastery.

Shortly after morning prayers, they each left for their work stations. Sister Agatha and Sister Bernarda met in the parlor.

"Are you getting any closer to finding answers for Mr. Gutierrez?" Sister Bernarda asked. "We sure could use another of his checks right now. We haven't been able to get Mr. Curtis to change his mind about fixing the gate on credit," she added. "He still insists we pay in advance."

"The woman I found has disappeared again and nobody

knows where she's gone. I'm having to start from the beginning again, almost."

"Then we'll continue praying," Sister Bernarda said.

"*Benedicite*, Sister," Sister Agatha said and stepped out into the cool morning air. As she glanced around for Pax she found him beside the Harley, anticipating a trip.

Sister Agatha drove slowly down the graveled road to the main highway, her final destination the sheriff's office. She'd traveled less than a mile when her skin began to prickle. She was being watched. She could *feel* it. Knowing instinct was often the result of an unconscious observation, she glanced around.

Sister Agatha studied the waist-high vegetation on both sides of the road, but saw nothing. Trusting her gut, she rounded a long curve, alert to her surroundings, and caught a glimpse of a figure standing in the shadows of an old cottonwood. Sister Agatha slowed quickly, turned around, and headed back to confront the person. She was tired of cat-and-mouse games.

Pax sat bolt upright, hackles raised, though it was impossible for her to say if he was sensing danger or simply reacting to her own fears.

It took her less than thirty seconds to reach the spot where she'd last seen the figure. Pulling off the road, she drove up beneath the tree, but no one was there anymore. As she got off the bike she heard the rumble of a vehicle pulling away. There was a dirt road alongside an old orchard ahead and she spotted the cloud of dust the passing vehicle left in its wake.

"Pax, stay," she ordered, intending to go check for footprints.

The ground was strewn with plant debris and underbrush but she managed to find two footprints beside the road next to a set of fresh tire tracks. The footprints could have belonged to just about anyone in the area—except for one thing. They were a size reminiscent of Bigfoot. Surely there weren't many people with *that* shoe size around. If her suspicions were correct, the man she'd seen today was the same one who'd crashed into the monastery gates.

Sister Agatha called Tom on her cell phone and reported the incident. "If I'm being watched this closely, I must be making someone very nervous."

"Yeah, me," he snapped. "By turning up the heat, you're placing your life in danger. Let me have one of my deputies take a look around the back roads near the monastery. Maybe we'll get lucky and he'll spot whoever's been lurking around."

"I appreciate it. I'm on my way to your office, so expect me within fifteen minutes," Sister Agatha said.

"Better give me a few hours. I've got my hands full here right now."

Sister Agatha placed the phone back in her habit's deep pocket. Discovering someone was still keeping her under surveillance had unsettled her. Terri was gone, so there was no reason for it.

The unexplained always made her nervous. "We might as well go home, Pax. Maybe visiting the chapel and asking Our Lord for help is the best thing to do now."

16

SISTER AGATHA WAS WALKING DOWN THE LONG HALL-way when Reverend Mother came out of her office and motioned to her. A moment later they entered her office.

"Do you think there's any way for you to dissuade Mr. Gutierrez from selling the vineyard to the developer? If not, can you convince him to donate the land he offered us adjacent to the grounds? You *did* find his niece. It's not your fault she didn't want to see him."

"I'm pretty sure he'll continue to insist that I find his niece again first, Mother. He's results-oriented. Our problems don't concern him."

"The world is such a hard place these days," Reverend Mother said.

Sister Agatha could hear the weariness in Reverend Mother's voice. Shouldering the responsibility for the monastery took a heavy toll on her. The darkened circles under her eyes attested to more than one sleepless night.

"Mother, forgive me, but you look exhausted. Have you been getting enough rest?"

Reverend Mother brushed the question aside with a wave of her hand. "I'm fine. Please don't worry, child."

Sister Agatha walked out of Mother's office feeling help-less and detesting her own inadequacy. Somehow she had to find a lead to Terri. Taking a deep breath, she forced herself to view the case dispassionately. What she lacked was informa-tion. Maybe this was a good time for her to dig into the details of the case that had driven Angela to assume a new identity.

An idea formed in her mind, and, inspired once again, she hurried out the side door and to the Harley. Leaving Pax be-hind this time, Sister Agatha headed to the downtown Albu-querque library, more than a half hour's travel time away.

After an extensive periodical search, Sister Agatha got the court date and the name of the presiding judge in James Garza's trial. She then headed to the county courthouse, a few blocks away. Case files were sealed, but court records were pub-lic record, available to anyone. Though she'd never be able to get specific information about the witnesses, the court's tran-script would shed more light on Angie's enemy.

It was lunchtime now, and most of the office staff at the courthouse was gone. Only one young woman remained at her desk behind the high counter, eating a sandwich. Seeing Sister Agatha, she stood up immediately. Sister Agatha knew then that she was undoubtedly a former Catholic school student.

"I'm Emily Gomez, Sister. How may I help you?"

With a smile, Sister Agatha told her what she needed.

Emily disappeared into a back room. About five minutes

later she returned with a small folder. "The records are saved on microfiche. I'll put the sheet on a viewer and show you how to use it. You'll have to scroll through the records until you find the right file number. If you find a page you'd like to copy, just push the print page button. Copies are ten cents a sheet."

Familiar with the technology, Sister Agatha located the documents quickly and skimmed the materials. The man Angie had testified against, James Garza, had used a real-estate office as a front and brokered fraudulent land deals in three states. After the murder of his partner, Mark Rio, Rio's family had testified against Garza. They'd claimed that Rio had been an unknowing accomplice and, in actuality, just another of Garza's many victims. Garza's accomplices had all disappeared by then, but Garza himself was arrested and convicted of murder, mostly on Angie's testimony. She'd been on the office staff of his front business. Garza had loudly protested his innocence, pointing his finger at others, Angie included, but the jury had quickly brought in a guilty verdict.

The illegal profits from the scam—what had turned out to be an indecently large sum of money—were never recovered. The money had been withdrawn from several banks, but the trail stopped there. Garza was offered a sentencing deal if he'd agree to return the money he'd stolen, but, to the very end, he'd claimed not to know what had become of it. On the last page of the file Sister Agatha found a police addendum stating that Garza had escaped custody while awaiting transfer to the state penitentiary.

Sister Agatha leaned back in her chair, lost in thought. Would Jimmy Garza have risked capture by returning to the area just for the sake of revenge? Or maybe the cash was an even more powerful incentive. It was possible he'd never had time to recover the money—his priority being to make a clean getaway. Maybe the possibility of reclaiming that cash and exacting revenge at the same time had become a temptation too powerful to resist, and that was why he'd returned to town.

Sister Agatha made a note of the men and women who'd handled the case. Although she didn't recognize any of them, she was sure Tom would know at least a few. She then removed the microfiche sheet from the viewer and returned it to Emily. "Thank you so much. Please don't let me interrupt your lunch any more than I already have."

"Actually, Sister, it's lonely in here right now. Would you like a tuna sandwich? I brought two, but I sneaked a couple of doughnuts earlier and I'm not that hungry anymore."

"Thanks. I'd love a sandwich," Sister Agatha said, going around the counter at Emily's invitation.

They ate in silence for a while, then Emily looked at her. "If you don't mind my asking, what's your interest in the Garza case, Sister?"

"I'm looking into it on behalf of someone else. Are you familiar with it?"

She nodded. "I remember the events because I knew Mark Rio. I was really surprised to see him tied into that mess. He was a Lobo football star before then. Though he never knew I was alive, we both went to UNM at the same time and I had a major thing for him."

"So what do you think—did Rio go bad, or was he just another victim of Garza's scam, as his relatives claimed?"

"Both," she answered after a brief pause. Seeing the confusion on Sister Agatha's face, she continued. "Mark always assumed that he'd be playing pro ball one day. But he was injured his last year and that was that. I think he had a tough time adjusting to that change in his career plans, and Garza hooked him by promising to make him rich, you know?"

"Was Mark the gullible sort?"

"No, not really, but to understand how Garza reeled people in, you would have had to see him in action. He was super smooth. When you looked at him you just *wanted* to believe him. He might have gotten off if it hadn't been for that woman's testimony—an employee of his, I think." She paused for several long moments, lost in thought, then added, "But after all was said and done, Garza escaped through an identification mix-up at the county jail. Personally, I think he just conned his way out."

"Charm and money can be a powerful combination," Sister Agatha answered.

"But, you know, it's the missing money that intrigues people most. Garza had cleaned out all his bank accounts by the time he was arrested—around a million dollars worth of cash. With the cops on his tail, Garza had to make a fast run for it, so a lot of people believe the cash is still hidden around here someplace."

"Interesting theory . . . a million dollars just waiting to be found."

Sister Agatha thanked the woman, then returned to the Harley, glad to be leaving the city behind. The incident at the school and the fear she'd felt was still fresh in her mind. It was undermining her courage and the resolve she needed now to continue to push for answers.

Sister Agatha turned wholeheartedly to God, knowing no one could help her now except Him. "Forgive me, Lord. By being afraid, all I'm really doing is saying that I don't trust You to handle the situation. You're in control, not me. I'll find whatever answers You want me to find. You're with me, inside my heart, and that means I already have all the help that's necessary."

It was then that moment she began to understand a little more about what Sister Bernarda was going through. They all strived for perfection, but their humanity meant that they'd often fail. The only sure gift they could bring to the Lord daily in exchange for all His sacrifices was the determination to try and do better.

And that is enough for God, her inner voice assured her, giving her peace.

When she reached the monastery, Sister de Lourdes was sitting behind the desk in the parlor. Looking up from her breviary, she smiled at Sister Agatha. "Welcome home."

"How is our scriptorium work going? Any more problems?" Sister Agatha asked.

Sister de Lourdes shook her head. "No, things have been running smoothly. Sister Ignatius found out that St. Isidore of Seville is the patron saint of computer workers, so she asked him to pray to the Lord for her," she said. "And it's working, too, because, so far, we haven't had any more glitches."

Sister Agatha nodded. Prayer in the hands of Sister Ignatius could move mountains.

"You look like you've had a very hard day," Sister de Lourdes commented after a moment.

"The case I'm working is . . . difficult," she said at last. "I have a strong feeling that I'm missing something important—a crucial bit of information that's probably right in front of my eyes." The sudden ringing of the parlor phone made Sister Agatha jump.

Sister de Lourdes took the call, then handed the phone to Sister Agatha. "It's the sheriff."

"Can you come to the station? We've got to talk," Tom said gruffly.

"I'll be there shortly," she said. Tom was always curt when something was troubling him, and right now, judging by his tone, something major was brewing.

17

SISTER AGATHA FOUND PAX, AND, THIS TIME, THEY SET
out together in the Antichrysler. The weather had turned
too damp and cold for a ride in the Harley. When they
arrived at the station she headed directly to Tom's office. The
door was open and Tom Green was standing by the window,
looking outside.

"Sheriff?"

"Come in, Sister, and have a seat." Tom returned to his
desk and sat down. "I've had an APB out on Terri, and someone matching her description checked in at an Albuquerque
motel yesterday. I went over there myself and found suitcases
with her tags on them, but the room was empty."

"Was her purse there?" Sister Agatha asked.

"No. Her car was still parked outside, though, so I know
she didn't drive off, at least in that vehicle. No calls were made

from her room, so I'm hoping she just went for a walk. I have an officer watching the motel in case she comes back."

"Any chance she was abducted? She could have been grabbed outside, maybe by that guy Cindy saw lurking around her property."

"It's possible. The circumstances convinced me that we should search her home, motel room, and car, and a judge agreed. I've already been through the two suitcases left in the motel room, and deputies are searching her car as we speak. If we find evidence that she was kidnapped, I'll notify the FBI and the Albuquerque police."

"Either she dropped out of sight completely or Garza nabbed her. Maybe Garza thinks Angie knows where the money is. Assistant District Attorney Mercedes Castillo prosecuted the case. She might know more. I think we should talk to her. Do you know where she lives?"

"Sure. She's retired and lives right here in town off of Calle Bonita," he said, then checking in his computer, gave her the house number. "She's listed in the phone book, so it's not a secret."

Sister Agatha was acquainted with the area. Rows of new, upscale southwestern-style houses had sprung up near the river where apple orchards had once thrived. "Why don't we go over there right now?"

"I'm waiting for some calls and have my hands full here. You go ahead and let me know what you find out."

"All right. Afterward, I'll visit Lucinda at Catholic Charities. Maybe if I ask the right questions I can get her to tell me something about Terri I don't already know."

"Both are good ideas. People speak to you much more freely than to me or one of my deputies."

"It's one of the advantages of being a nun."

Sister Agatha drove down a newly paved road that bisected a large apple orchard. Soon she pulled into the driveway of an adobe-style hacienda. The sprawling one-story home was elegant but not flashy, with well-shaped piñon trees and chamisa adding to the simple landscaping.

As she let off on the gas and hit the brake, the car backfired so loudly it made Pax bark in protest.

A woman in her late sixties came to the door and glanced out. Seeing them, her frown changed to a smile, and she waved.

"I think our fame—or maybe that of the Antichrysler—precedes us," Sister Agatha whispered to Pax, rolling down the window to give him plenty of air while he waited in the car.

As Sister Agatha went up the flagstone walk to meet Mercedes, the former prosecutor was gracious enough to meet her halfway. Mrs. Castillo was wearing jeans and a freshly pressed white cotton shirt.

"Hello, Sister. Why don't you bring the dog, too? I've heard so much about him."

"That's very kind of you, Mrs. Castillo. Thank you." Sister Agatha walked back to the station wagon. "She wants you to come in, too, Pax. Be on your best behavior now."

Moments later she and Pax followed Mercedes inside.

"Your timing is perfect," Mercedes said. "I was just fixing myself a cup of decaf mocha latte. I like a leisurely cup of flavored coffee in the evening. Will you have some with me?"

Knowing how most people relaxed over coffee, Sister Agatha agreed. "I'd love some," she answered.

"Wonderful. Why don't you join me in the kitchen?" she invited.

Sister Agatha followed her through the spacious house, noting the simplicity of the furnishings and the beauty of the dark log *vigas* and crossed *latillas* that comprised the traditional ceiling. The few pieces of Spanish-style furniture that were there seemed unusually large.

Soft guitar music was playing from hidden speakers as they entered the kitchen/dining area, which was decorated in rich earth tones. The backsplash was composed of colorful Mexican tile.

Mercedes set out two cups, filled them with steaming liquid, then brought them to the table. "It's my own blend of instant coffee powders, mind you, but I add a bit of cream and evaporated milk and it really sparks up the flavor."

Sister Agatha tasted it and nodded. "It's wonderful," she said.

Mercedes took a sip and smiled at Pax, who was lying on the cool redbrick floor by Sister Agatha's feet. "So what can I do for you today, Sister?" she asked.

Sister Agatha took a deep breath. "I need to ask you about a case you prosecuted several years ago before you retired."

"The Garza thing?"

"How did you know?"

"Sheriff Green called a short while ago," she admitted. "But that would have been my first guess anyway. That case has persistently followed me, mostly because Garza is a fugitive and so much money is still unaccounted for."

"The uncle of a prosecution witness who chose to leave the Witness Protection Program came to us for help locating his niece."

"Ah—that would be John Gutierrez, which means you're looking for Angie," Mercedes said. "It was amazing to me that she actually left the program. There was no doubt that Garza blamed her for his conviction. He swore she'd pay for her lies, yelling almost those exact words in the courtroom when the verdict was handed down."

"It sounds like it was a difficult case from start to finish."

"That's the thing. I don't consider it finished." Mercedes stared at some indeterminate spot across the room. "I remember the case as if it happened yesterday. Angie had seen Garza burying Rio's body near a ditch bank and was able to take us to where it was. She had no idea what he'd done with the gun, but her testimony helped us get Garza convicted," she said, then added. "We worked really hard back then to keep the location of Rio's body out of the papers. We were worried that people would dig up the whole area looking for the money and destroy the flood protection along the river in the process."

"You were right to be concerned," Sister Agatha agreed. "A large sum of money like that would make people a little crazy."

"Angie was an invaluable witness, providing us with details of the fraudulent deals and the friction between Rio and Garza, but there were times . . ." Mercedes grew silent and shook her head.

"You can speak freely, Mercedes. Whatever you say will stay between us."

"I was the ADA back then, and Angie handed me that case on a silver platter. But Angie's story *never* deviated by more than a few words—as if she'd memorized it. That's what made me suspect that Angie had something to hide. I speculated for a while that she and Garza had been partners in the beginning and that she'd turned on him later, killing Rio and framing Garza. But I never had enough to prove it. The murder weapon was never found, you know."

Sister Agatha leaned back in her chair. "If you're right,

Angie may know exactly where that money is. That would explain why she eventually left the Witness Protection Program. She couldn't go get it until then."

"That's possible."

After saying good-bye to their hostess, Sister Agatha walked back to the Antichrysler with Pax and slipped behind the driver's seat. She'd stop by Catholic Charities next. Although it was already close to five, maybe Lucinda would still be there working late.

When she arrived, however, the office was locked up for the night. Fortunately, Sister Agatha knew where Lucinda lived. She and her terminally ill mother shared an old farmhouse near the monastery.

Sister Agatha arrived at the Gomezes' home less than ten minutes later. Lucinda was outside feeding the chickens.

Seeing the Antichrysler, Lucinda waved, finished her work, and came over. "Sister, what a surprise! What brings you out here?"

"I needed to ask you a few questions, Lucinda. Do you have a couple of minutes to spare?" Sister Agatha asked, getting right to the point.

"Sure. Let's go inside, but be very quiet, okay? Mom's asleep."

As they approached the house Lucinda glanced down at Pax, then back at Sister Agatha. "Don't let him bark."

Sister Agatha looked at the dog, and held up one finger—a signal that he should be very quiet. The dog understood and padded silently by her side.

Lucinda invited them into the den, offered Sister Agatha a seat on a comfortable-looking sofa, then closed the heavy wooden door.

"We can talk freely here," Lucinda said. "With the door

shut, sound doesn't carry to her part of the house easily." Lucinda sat down across from them. "So what can I do for you?"

"Tell me about Terri Montoya. What's she like?" Sister Agatha asked. "I'll keep whatever you say strictly between us."

"If it was up to me, Terri would have been fired weeks ago," she said honestly.

"Why?" Sister Agatha asked, leaning forward.

"She's completely unreliable. She'll make a field visit to one of the families we're working with, then take off on personal business. That leaves me stuck in the office, and all too often ends up making me late for my own appointments," she said.

"Have you talked to her about that?"

"Yeah, more than once. I even tried befriending her, thinking it would help us work together better. But it was a disaster. I've met women who like to protect their privacy, but Terri's on a level all her own."

"How so?" Sister Agatha pressed.

"Let me give you an example. I told her that I grew up near Colorado Springs, where my dad and mom managed a small resort. Then when I asked her where she was from, she gave me this really hard look and told me it wasn't any of my business. Every once in a while I ask her again, just to bug her," she added with a mischievous grin. "The marine in me doesn't give up that easily."

Sister Agatha smiled. "Sounds like Sister Bernarda."

"Another ex-marine, naturally. But I'm telling you, Sister Agatha, Terri gives new meaning to close-mouthed. I asked her once what she liked most about Bernalillo and why she'd chosen to live here. She never answered me. She just glared at me like I was asking for her deepest secret. In my opinion, there's some heavy-duty stuff in that woman's past—something she's determined to keep hidden. Everything about Terri is off-center somehow."

Hearing the sound of a bell, Lucinda stood up. "That's Mom. She needs me."

"Can I help?" Sister Agatha asked.

"No, it's all right. About now her pain pills are starting to wear off. She doesn't like to take the next batch right away because they zone her out, so when she wakes up we visit and talk until the pain gets bad again. Then she takes the next batch and drifts back to sleep," she said, then added, "Is there anything else I can do for you?"

"No, and thanks for helping," Sister Agatha said. "If you need anything, call the monastery. We *are* neighbors."

"Thanks. I appreciate that. And say hello to Sister Bernarda for me, will you?.

Sister Agatha and Pax returned to the Antichrysler but, this time, when she turned the key, the motor flat-out refused to start. With a sigh, Sister Agatha pulled the hood-release lever below the dashboard, rolled up her sleeves, and grabbed a big screwdriver from out of the glove box. The lessons she'd taken from her brother, a car mechanic, had come in handy lately. "Stay, Pax."

"I worked in the motor pool back in the Corps," Lucinda called out, stepping onto the porch. "Can I help?"

It took five minutes for them to determine that an in-line fuel filter was clogged, and another five to clear the obstruction and reattach the part.

Soon after that Sister Agatha was on her way, but she hadn't gone far when she noticed that she'd picked up a tail, a faded gray Mustang. Not wanting the driver to know she was on to him, she picked up the cell phone, called Tom, and filled him in.

"Are you on the way to the monastery?" he asked.

"I was," Sister Agatha answered, "but I'm not sure I should go there now."

"Head for the station, staying on the main highway. I'm sending a deputy to meet you. Any idea who's following you?"

"No, not yet. I haven't been able to see his face," Sister Agatha answered.

Placing the phone down, Sister Agatha slowed, looking for a place to turn. Suddenly the Mustang behind her whipped around the Antichrysler and cut in front of her.

Sister Agatha slammed on the brakes to avoid a collision, but the Antichrysler's brakes locked on the driver's side. The station wagon spun around on the loose gravel, coming to a jarring stop facing the wrong way, the engine dead.

Before Sister Agatha could even take a breath, a dark-haired man built like a refrigerator with arms suddenly appeared at her window, knife in hand.

Seeing the weapon, Pax lunged at him, but the angle was wrong and he missed the man's hand by inches. Startled, the man flinched, and Sister Agatha took the opening. She threw open her door, slamming him backward onto the road.

More angry than afraid now, Sister Agatha dove out of the car and kicked away the knife, which her assailant had dropped. Pax jumped over the seat and out the front door, attacking the man before he could stand up.

Once she was sure the knife was well out of his reach, she gave Pax the command to stop. "Pax, out!"

The dog obeyed reluctantly, and remained less than three feet from the man, snarling and baring his teeth.

Sister Agatha grasped Pax's collar, and held him. "If you give me the slightest reason, I'll release the dog. And, just so you know, you can't run fast enough to evade him."

"Okay, okay!"

"Who are you and what do you want?" she demanded.

"Are you crazy? I was having car trouble. I came to ask for help but you and that dog attacked *me*!" The man was looking in every direction, trying to find the means to escape.

"Your defense is that you got jumped by a middle-aged nun and her dog? The knife will have *your* prints on it, pea brain."

Before he could reply, she heard sirens. The help Tom had sent would soon arrive. "You may not realize it, but God smiled on you today. This dog is trained to take out an armed opponent. It's a miracle you're still in one piece."

18

WHATEVER YOU WERE PAID—IT WASN'T ENOUGH," sister Agatha called out to the assailant as Tom's deputy led him away.

"No kidding," he grumbled as the deputy placed him in the back of the squad car.

"Nice work," Tom said, giving Sister Agatha a thumb's up and scratching Pax behind the ears. "We'll find out what he knows and who hired him. Follow me to the station. We'll have your official statement typed up and then you can sign it."

"You already know all I know, Tom. Could we finish the paperwork tomorrow?" Sister Agatha asked, trying to suppress the shivers. Anger, after being cut off the road, had given her momentary courage. Now only a lingering, bone-chilling fear remained. "I'd like to go home. I have a feeling Sister de Lourdes will need me to pitch in with the scriptorium work after recreation."

"I thought that no one spoke at night over there," he said.

"We don't, not after Compline, but we can work in silence in the scriptorium," she replied. "And write notes."

"Okay, go ahead. I'll see you tomorrow."

The following morning, after Terce, which commemorated the Third Hour, when the Holy Spirit descended on the apostles, Sister Agatha set out to town once again in the Harley with Pax. It was eight-fifteen, and Sister Bernarda was acting portress this morning while Sister de Lourdes handled their scriptorium work.

So far, they'd had no more problems with either the computers or the orders. Wilder's identity, and that of the person who'd vandalized NexCen's warehouse, remained a mystery.

Sister Agatha arrived at the station a short time later and saw Tom coming out of the bull pen. "Good morning," she greeted as he came out to see her.

"I'm glad you're here. I have news," he said, leading the way down the hall. Tom didn't say anything more until they were inside his office and the door was shut. "Have a seat."

Sister Agatha made herself comfortable as Pax lay by her feet.

"The guy you two ran into last night is a lowlife by the name of Benny Kowalski. Benny claims that Garza contacted him through the mail and hired him to scare you off. He didn't want you meddling in his business. Garza refused to meet Benny face-to-face and that made Benny curious, since they'd been friends and all. So Benny did some checking and heard that Garza had cosmetic surgery to alter his appearance. Apparently, he doesn't want anyone to connect his new face with his old identity."

"What exactly was Benny supposed to do to me and Pax?" Sister Agatha asked, her voice taut.

"He was told to scare you—the method was left up to him. He got five hundred bucks for the job."

"They're both creeps," she said softly, then lapsed into a long silence. "Tom, I'd really like a look at the Garza case file."

"Since the man remains at large, it's considered an active case—off-limits to those outside of law enforcement."

"Garza may be in this community right now and I really need to know everything I can about him. Come on. If you can't trust a nun, who can you trust?"

He smiled. "I'll leave the file on my desk while I go get myself a Coke—which shouldn't take me more than five minutes. Got it?" He went to the cabinet near his desk and pulled the file out. "Want a Coke?"

"Split one with me?"

"I'll bring two cups and a Coke . . . in five minutes," he said, and left.

Sister Agatha leafed through the pages quickly, skimming the investigator's reports. She'd already gathered most of what was in there from the papers and other sources, including transcripts of the hearing. Then, as she read the report from the medical investigator, her blood turned to ice.

She'd known that Mark Rio's body had been found not far from their monastery, but she'd never realized how close. By her estimate, Rio had been buried in a shallow grave just a few hundred yards from their walls.

By the time Tom walked back into the office, she was sitting bolt upright in her chair, one hand on her rosary.

He placed a foam cup filled with cola in front of her. "What's on your mind?"

"Mark Rio's body was found pretty close to our monastery.

Put that together with the fact that we had someone crash through our gate, taking part of the wall with it, and that someone's been watching our monastery recently. There's a circumstantial case building here."

"What exactly are you thinking?"

"Maybe Terri *does* know where the money's hidden. In fact, she might have been the one who crashed through our wall to make sure she had access to the grounds at night. She's always been interested in the monastery. So let's say that the killer hid the money near Rio's body—someplace where it was bound to be safe—like on our grounds. Maybe *that's* where the money is and why we've had so many problems lately."

"Even if I buy that theory—which is filled with lots of speculation and very little evidence, I might add—why did Terri decide to come back *now?* She could have recovered the cash a long time ago."

"No, not really. She was in protective custody, and when she left the program, she had to watch out for Garza," Sister Agatha said, then after a thoughtful pause, continued. "When she came back to town, she discovered that a lot of things had changed, too. We'd had a new wall put up, for one. When that was compromised, we began using Pax to guard us so there was still no way for her to get in. Now with the threat of developers coming into the area, she may have been scared that the sudden influx of people would guarantee that the money would stay out of her reach forever. Or even worse, it could have ended up in some lucky heavy equipment operator's pocket."

"It's a *theory*, but that's all it is."

"It also has a few holes in it," Sister Agatha admitted reluctantly. "Terri's not tall enough to have required the SUV seat to be pushed all the way back, which is where it was after the crash," she said. "And I'm convinced that I saw a man running away, not a woman."

"If Garza has Terri, her life is hanging by a thread. Her cell phone is still out of service, but I'll check out Terri's computer today. That's usually a treasure trove of information."

"Have you searched Terri's computer at work?"

"I can't—not unless Catholic Charities gives me permission."

"I don't think you'll have a problem with that under the circumstances. She's a missing employee, and the computer records aren't *her* property," Sister Agatha said. "While you're busy with all that, I'm going to dig a little deeper into John Gutierrez's past. I have an idea I want to check."

"Okay, but be careful."

Once outside, Pax jumped gracefully into the Harley's sidecar. "We're going to the rectory, Pax," she said, and the dog barked almost as if in approval.

A short time later, as she pulled up behind the church, she spotted Father Mahoney up on a ladder. He was trimming some cottonwood branches that were right above a utility wire. Seeing the ladder sway, Sister Agatha ran to steady it. "Father, what on earth are you doing?"

Frances came out just then. "Father, you *told* me that you were only going to cut a few low branches!"

"I finally got the hang of this tree cutter thingie so I wanted to keep going," he said.

"The diocese doesn't need an injured priest, Father," Frances said sternly. "My cousin's got a crane with a bucket on the end. He'll be by later to take care of those branches." She glanced at Sister Agatha. "Thank God you pulled up when you did. I heard the motorcycle, looked outside, and that's when I saw what Father was up to!"

Father Mahoney looked at Frances, then at Sister Agatha. "I'm perfectly capable of doing this. But, if it'll make you both feel better, I'll wait for Frances's cousin."

"Good," Frances said.

Father Mahoney smiled at Sister Agatha. "So what can I do for you and your trusty sidekick today?"

"I really need your help. Can we go into your study?"

"Of course, Sister Agatha."

As they reached his office, he gestured for her to make herself comfortable, then closed the door behind them. "Tell me what's troubling you, Sister."

She told him how she'd found, then lost, Terri—really Angie Sanchez. "If John Gutierrez's search for his niece stems from the best of motives, then I should continue to work for him. Heaven knows the monastery needs that buffer zone and the extra money for our gate. But what if there's more to it than that? What if we're both being used by Terri's most dangerous enemy—Jimmy Garza?"

"I'm not sure how to advise you on this, Sister Agatha," he said slowly. "I know you've discussed the criminal aspects with the sheriff, but there's much more than that to consider here."

"Father, you've got access to something that might help me decide what I should do next. Father Anselm kept files with bios and information on benefactors who could be counted on to help financially whenever the need arose."

He nodded. "Yes, that file's still in the computer. Let's go have a look." He typed a few commands, then called up the file. "And here's a John Gutierrez—date of birth is December 10, 1940. There's no Social Security number listed. But he hasn't made a donation since 1991. Here's a note saying that he began making donations to the monastery instead. It's dated a year before Father Anselm died."

Sister Agatha nodded, then did some quick math in her head. "From the birth date, that would make him sixty-seven. It can't be the same man. The John Gutierrez I'm dealing with doesn't look anywhere near that age."

Father Mahoney shrugged. "Have you ever looked at Dick Clark? A face lift—okay, several—some hair dye, and it's hard to figure out anyone's age."

Sister Agatha nodded. "Good point."

"The more I think about Terri, the more I wish I'd been more alert right from the beginning," Father said. "I should have realized that there was something weird going on. Remember I told you how interested she always was in the monastery?" Seeing her nod, he continued. "One time I even found her taking photos of the grounds when my back was turned. I was furious. I asked her for her camera, one of those digital ones, so I could erase the images. But then we got distracted by a delivery. I went back to help Sister Bernarda. And you know what? I never did get the camera from her."

"What was she photographing, do you remember?"

"Come to think of it, she was taking photos of the grounds, not the buildings."

The phone rang and Father answered it. After exchanging a few quick words with the party at the other end, he glanced at Sister Agatha. "One of our parishioners needs me. He's been very sick, and his daughter has been pressuring him to request an anointing. He wouldn't hear of it because, in his day, anointing the sick was called Last Rites. But now he's asking me to come, so things must be really bad. I better hurry. I should be back in a few hours, if you want to talk again," he said, then hurried out.

Alone, Sister Agatha walked to the kitchen. As she'd expected, Frances had a box of dog treats open and was chatting with Pax as if he were human.

Seeing her, Frances smiled. "Can I offer you a cup of coffee, Sister, or maybe a glass of iced tea and a sandwich? It's nearly lunchtime and I bet you haven't eaten anything. Isn't lunch the big meal of the day at the monastery?"

She nodded. "It is."

Frances pulled out some French rolls from the canister. "I made these earlier today," she said, beaming. "Came out great, too, if I say so myself." She then began to layer several different kinds of cheese, tomatoes, lettuce leaves, and turkey slices. "Wait until you taste this, Sister."

"I didn't mean for you to go through so much trouble," she said. "I would have been happy with peanut butter and jelly."

"Not if this is going to be your main meal today," she said, piling it on. "Take a taste while I get you some iced tea."

Sister Agatha took a bite and smiled. "This is truly beyond good, Frances."

Frances picked up a glass from the dishwasher, looked at it with a critical eye, then washed it again in the sink. "I'll get your drink in a jiffy, Sister. Just let me rinse this glass."

A second later, Frances placed a glass of iced tea in front of her. "I think I got all of the marks."

"Forget it. It's fine," Sister Agatha picked up the glass, took a swallow, then, as she set it back down, saw the clear imprint of her finger on the glass. Slowly an idea began to form in her mind.

Finishing lunch quickly and thanking Frances, she hurried out with Pax to the Harley. She knew exactly what she had to do next.

19

SISTER AGATHA ARRIVED AT THE SIESTA INN A SHORT
while later and parked in the back lot where the staff left
their cars.

Using the side door, she went inside the building, the dog
at her side. All she needed was some trash—John Gutierrez's to
be specific.

If she could get something John had handled and then
take it in for fingerprints, she'd know once and for all who she
was dealing with. The discrepancy between his appearance
and the age stated on his records still bothered her.

Sister Agatha walked down the hall leading to John's
room, trying to think of a way to get what she needed. It promised to be tricky, because she'd have to do it without his knowledge. As she drew closer, she heard the sound of angry voices,
and, a second later, Ralph stepped out of John's room.

Seeing her, he smiled stiffly. "Hello, Sister. What brings you here?"

"I came to update John and assure him that I'm still working." She heard the sound of hurried footsteps, a pace that was too fast to belong to an invalid, and tried to look inside the room, but Ralph blocked her, closing the door behind him.

"John's had a hard morning, Sister Agatha. I'll tell him you're here and see if he feels well enough to meet with you."

Still curious, she tried to look past him as Ralph opened the door and stepped inside. Nothing out of the ordinary caught her eye before the door closed once again. Seconds later Ralph returned.

"He's ready for you, Sister Agatha. You can bring the dog, too."

She went inside and saw John in bed, a breathing therapy machine close by but not in use at the moment.

"I suspect from the expression on your face that you've had no luck finding my niece again, am I right?" Seeing her nod, John continued before she could speak. "Then we've reached the end of the road, and I'm wasting my time here. I'm leaving for home tomorrow morning. This trip has been too hard on me." He began to cough, a deep rumbling sound reminiscent of bronchitis, though in his case it could have indicated something more serious.

"Can I get you something to drink?" she asked quickly.

"Water," he said, on his side, leaning forward and gasping for air as he pointed to the nightstand.

"Here you go," she said, picking up the plastic bottle, a common local brand, and holding it out to him.

He took several long sips, emptying the container, then lay back against the pillow.

Sister Agatha kept the water bottle in her hand. It was too bulky to stick it into her habit's pocket, but she wasn't walking out without it.

"Sister, let me take that from you," Ralph said, suddenly appearing beside her, though she hadn't heard him approach.

She had no choice but to hand it over. Then, out of the corner of her eye, she saw him drop the bottle into the waste bucket by the dresser.

As John began coughing again, Ralph led her out of the room. "John needs to rest now."

Ralph said good-bye, but, even after he'd closed the door, Sister Agatha remained in the hall. While she'd been speaking to Ralph, she'd definitely heard someone in the room moving about quickly. Yet no one except Ralph and John had been inside. Something wasn't right.

As she stood there, wondering how to get the contents of the waste basket still in the room, she heard a familiar voice behind her. "Pax is so terrific. Someday, for sure, I'm getting a dog just like him."

Sister Agatha turned around and saw Liz Leland coming up the hall pushing a housekeeping cart filled with linens and cleaning supplies.

"What on earth are you doing here? Shouldn't you be in school?" Sister Agatha asked.

"We had a half day today, a teacher in-service for the public schools, so I decided to put in a few extra hours at work," she said. "I'm trying to save up some money. College tuition is expensive."

"Will you be going to UNM?"

"That's my plan. I want to study computer programming. I'm hoping to get a scholarship, too. That's why I've been working so hard to get my grades back up." She met Sister Agatha's steady gaze. "Did you ever find the person who framed me and my friends?"

"No, but I will."

"Cool." When Sister Agatha didn't move, she added, "Is something wrong?"

"I need your help, Liz," she answered. "Can you empty the trash basket in the Chamisa room and bring me the empty water bottle that's there? Just don't touch it, or let the people inside suspect anything."

"Fingerprints, huh? Done deal, Sister. Where do we meet afterward?"

"How about by the ice machine?" she suggested.

As Liz went to John's door, Sister Agatha took Pax back outside. After standing by the ice machine for twenty minutes, she began to get worried. What if Liz had tipped them off? Sister Agatha brought out her rosary and began praying. Before she'd finished the fifth Hail Mary, she saw Liz pushing the utility cart out the door, humming, a bright smile on her face.

"I've got it!" she said and pointed to a trash bag on the bottom shelf of the cart. "I kept it separate from the rest of the trash."

"Thanks a million, Liz."

"Tell me as soon as you can what this was all about, okay, Sister? I'm dying of curiosity!"

"I will. Promise."

Sister Agatha hurried out to the Harley, white trash bag in hand. After placing it in the nose of the sidecar where it would be out of Pax's way, the two of them drove back to the sheriff's station. Sister Agatha parked near the main entrance and hurried inside.

Tom, who was talking to the desk sergeant, came over immediately. "I didn't expect to see you back here today. What's up?"

She motioned him to one side, then, whispering, told him what she'd done. "The bottle won't prove anything in a court of law, but I want to know whose prints are on it, besides my own. I just have to know who I've been dealing with."

"I'll have it processed," he said. "In the meantime, I've asked one of my people to check out Gutierrez, using the birth date you got. We have access to several databases and might be able to find a good photo."

It took over forty minutes for the print comparisons to be finished. When Tom returned to join her, he had a somber look on his face. "One set of prints belongs to Jimmy Garza. And there's more. Millie did a search on John Gutierrez, Angela Sanchez's uncle. It turns out he owns a lodge up in southern Colorado, and spends most of the year backpacking in hunters and fishermen. Millie got him on the phone, and he says he hasn't heard from Angie or any of his relatives in years. The man you've been dealing with isn't Angie's uncle, though it's clear he's really done his homework, maybe even including plastic surgery, to pass as Gutierrez. The way I see it, either he or Ralph Simpson is actually Jimmy Garza, or maybe Garza's been to see them very recently. I'm hauling both those guys in here right now."

"But what if they're mixed up in Terri's disappearance? By bringing both those men in, you could be condemning her to death."

Tom pursed his lips, then nodded. "I'll stake out the Siesta Inn for the next twenty-four hours and make sure we tail them if either goes anywhere. But, after that, I'm moving in on them."

"Let me help. I could keep an eye on Gutierrez while you focus on his assistant."

"No way. Too dangerous." He picked up the phone and made arrangements to have an officer watching the motel effective immediately. "Go home. I'll be in touch."

Sister Agatha left the station in a dark mood. She tried to come up with a plan that would allow her to get actively involved but, before she could work out the details, her cell phone rang. It was Sister Bernarda.

Sister Agatha pulled the motorcycle over to the side of the road and removed her helmet so she could take the call. "I'm here," she said at last.

"We have a problem," Sister Bernarda said. "Merilee, from NexCen, has been in the scriptorium for nearly an hour. She consulted with some of the other techs and she has a theory about our hacker. She asked to talk to you."

Sister Agatha hurried back to the monastery and arrived just as the bells were ringing for None. As she entered the parlor, she heard the soft chanting coming from the chapel. Sister Bernarda acknowledged her with a nod, then began whispering Pater Nosters, the Our Fathers.

Sister Agatha joined her in prayer. In the silence of her mind and heart, she reached up to the Lord, asking for a resolution to their problems. Despite all her good intentions, she'd muddled things badly and now it was possible Terri was in mortal danger.

After None, Sister Agatha walked directly to the scriptorium and met with Merilee. "I'm here," Sister Agatha said. "Are you closer to finding our hacker?"

"You're actually our best hope of finding him or her, Sister Agatha. I've been thinking a lot about this, and you know almost everyone in town. Who loves computer games and has the know-how to pull a stunt like this?"

"I don't generally talk to people in town about computers, Merilee. I'm sorry, but I don't think I can help you."

"Will you look through the e-mails NexCen received complaining about the graphics card needed for the Wilder game? I've got the folder with me. See if there's a name in here that catches your eye."

Sister Agatha did as Merilee asked. "Nothing, I'm sorry," she said after about fifteen minutes. At the bottom of the stack of printouts, she found copies of the e-mails the monastery had received. She studied them as well. "Wilder's letters have gotten progressively nastier. But it makes no sense. Does he want to shut down NexCen, or us, or both of us?"

Merilee shrugged. "With cranks, who knows?"

Sister Agatha focused back on the e-mails. "Did you notice that there's a pattern here? The last three e-mails were sent at around 12:30 P.M., give or take five minutes, and they're from a different ISP, though they're all signed by Wilder."

"I didn't realize that. Let's see if we can use that to track it back to the sender. I know that the earlier e-mails were rerouted from special Internet sites designed by hackers and spammers to hide the originating computer. But maybe now that he's using a different server we'll get lucky."

After about fifteen minutes on the phone with NexCen's techs, Merilee finally hung up. "I've requested some special software for the monastery's computer. According to one of our techs, the ISP on the last three e-mails is for the library network at the public high school. Do you know any kids who attend that school?"

"Had it been St. Charles, I would have been able to help you a lot more, but public school is a different world. We could go talk to their media specialist. We've got the time the kid logged on, so if their system is like the one at St. Charles where kids have to sign in, the media specialist will know who was using the computers at the time."

Sister Agatha rode into town with Merilee. Her sedan, a luxury model, seemed to have every imaginable amenity. With the windows up, road noises simply vanished. "It's like a magic carpet ride," she muttered in awe.

"It is, isn't it? This car set me back some, but since I drive quite a bit and get mileage from NexCen, I decided to go for it. What kind of car does the monastery have? All I've seen parked outside is an old station wagon. Does that belong to the gardener?"

Sister Agatha laughed. "Gardener? *We're* the gardeners. That old bucket of bolts is our mass-transportation system. And let me tell you a secret, we don't call it the Antichrysler for nothing."

Shortly afterward, they pulled up to the area high school, a large complex of cinder block and metal beside an enormous gymnasium. As they parked, Sister Agatha noted the large stylized bird of prey painted on the four-story wall of the field house. "Their athletic teams are the Falcons," she said for Merilee's benefit.

She'd run into Liz earlier, so she knew today had been a half day. But in-service days, if the meetings were held on campus, usually meant that teachers would still be required to put in regular hours. They walked into the main building and eventually found their way to the library. A tall, thin woman in her fifties and a petite brunette in her late twenties were standing beside a big, U-shaped counter. The older woman glanced at them as they came though the door.

"I'm Mrs. Dale, the media specialist. May I help you?" she asked.

Sister Agatha introduced herself and Merilee, then proceeded to explain the problem. "These last e-mails were sent at 12:30 P.M. and I was wondering if you used a sign-in system," Sister Agatha said, handing her the printout. Mrs. Dale looked at the letters, then handed them to the other woman with her. "Check the logbook and see who was here at the time."

"This really disturbs me," Mrs. Dale said. "I can't believe one of our kids is using our computers to hack into a company's system and send harassing e-mails."

The younger woman introduced herself as she came back up. "I'm Holly Finney. I'm normally on duty here when Mrs. Dale has her lunch. The student you want is Ernie Rowe—the kids call him Macho. He's the one logged in, but I don't think he'd know how to hack into anyone's system. He's just not that good with computers."

"Maybe he's working with someone else," Mrs. Dale said. "Give me a chance to talk to Ernie's friends, and I'll get back to you."

Sister Agatha and Merilee thanked both women, then left and headed for the main entrance. Halfway there, Sister Agatha suddenly stopped in midstride. "Wait a minute. I've got an idea. Let's drop by the office before we leave."

As they reached the busy administration office, Sister Agatha recognized one of the staff and smiled. Maria Paiz came to Mass at the monastery on a regular basis.

"Hello, Sister Agatha," the middle-aged, portly woman greeted. "What a surprise to see you here."

"I need to talk to Leeann Karon. Is there any chance she's around school, maybe at basketball practice or a club meeting?"

"Probably not—though she does have an absolute gift for landing school detention. Let me check," she said, then typed in some information on a computer screen. "You got lucky," she said after a moment. "She's here, or at least *supposed* to be. Do you want me to call the detention room and have the teacher on duty send her to the office?"

"We'd appreciate it if you would," Sister Agatha said.

Sister Agatha explained the connection between Leeann and Macho to Merilee. "From what Liz said, Macho has a thing for her, so let's see what she can tell us about him."

A few minutes later, a worried Leeann came into the room, then, seeing Sister Agatha, gave her a shaky smile. "Am I in trouble again?"

"Not with us. Just relax, Leeann," Sister Agatha said.

"What's going on?" she asked, looking at Merilee. "You're not a cop . . . policewoman, are you?"

Merilee laughed, shaking her head.

"We've been having some problems with a hacker," Sister Agatha said, giving Leeann a quick summary of what they'd learned from the media specialist. "Do you think Macho would do that to us?"

"Macho?" Leeann burst out laughing. "Oh, Sister, he still types with two fingers! He won't even play computer games. Macho's into cars. Whenever a student's ride won't start, Macho's your go-to guy. He can get anyone back on the road. He's great with a screwdriver, but he's totally hopeless with a mouse."

"I'm looking for someone who could hack into a corporate server," Sister Agatha said. "Does anyone come to mind?"

Leeann grew quiet, considering the possibilities. "There are only a few kids who could pull off something like that."

"Is there one in particular who has the ability *and* a grudge against Macho?"

"Macho makes a lot of enemies, Sister," Leeann answered

slowly. "He likes to push people around—but the schoolboys get the worst of it."

"You mean the nerds?" Sister Agatha asked.

"Yeah, 'schoolboys.' That's what the tough guys around here call them. Macho has it in for them . . . maybe because they make him look stupid in class."

Merilee pulled out a computer printout from her bag. "This is a list of local people who've e-mailed NexCen in the recent past. Do any of the names match the 'schoolboys' you mentioned?"

Leeann looked the list over. "Two names fit—Joey Weaver and Eva Stanley. Macho's not too bad with Eva. She's, well, unfortunate looking, and he doesn't pay too much attention to her."

"What about Joey Weaver?"

"Macho shoves Joey every chance he gets, or knocks books out of his arms, just stuff like that. He doesn't hurt him, not really."

"Are either of those kids capable of some serious hacking?" Merilee asked.

"Oh, yeah. They're *really* into computers."

"Thanks, Leeann," Sister Agatha said.

As Leeann headed back to detention, Sister Agatha glanced at Merilee. "We've now got it narrowed down to two kids, so we're making progress. But which one should we focus on first, Joey or Eva?"

"Research shows that more boys play computer games, but that's hardly conclusive. Why don't we make sure we're around the media center tomorrow at noon and check things out?" Merilee suggested.

"As long as we're here, let's go talk to the kids' teachers

first." Sister Agatha approached Maria again. "I hate to bother you, but how about one more favor?"

"Shoot."

"Are there any advanced computer classes offered in the curriculum here?"

She nodded. "Computer Graphics. They learn how to use advanced software and design Web sites."

"Who teaches that class, and are Joey Weaver and Eva Stanley enrolled?"

"I'll check," she said, calling up the right screen. A moment later, she nodded. "They're both in Mr. Lopez's fourth-period class. Most of the teaching staff is probably gone by now, but I'd be willing to bet he's still here. He's always at the keyboard. You'll find him in the last room down this hall to your left."

"Thanks!"

"Those kids aren't in any serious trouble, are they?" Maria asked.

"I'm not sure yet," Sister Agatha answered honestly.

They walked to the classroom Maria had indicated, then knocked on the open door. A man in his early thirties looked up from his computer terminal and smiled. "Can I help you?"

Sister Agatha made the introductions. "We're looking into the work of a hacker. Does the name 'Wilder' mean anything to you?"

"*Wilder?* Sure. It's a very popular role-playing game. What about it?"

"Do any of your students have a particular interest in the game? Maybe even an obsession?" Sister Agatha pressed.

"Only one name comes to mind," he said without hesitation. "Liz Leland. She's competing for the scholarship Nex-Cen's offering in conjunction with Los Angeles Animation

Studios, and the software company that produces the game. She's altered the Wilder character and turned him from a pig into a woman superhero. Her version is really creative. She's already got a script for her game and has been working on the animation."

"A game designer in the making," Merilee said thoughtfully.

Shocked, Sister Agatha said nothing. Had Liz been playing her all along?

"Do you happen to know Liz, Sister? She used to go to St. Charles," Mr. Lopez said.

"Yes, I do. What about Eva Stanley? Is she interested in that game, too?"

"I don't think so. She has plans to go into computer engineering. Says that games are for kids and those just interested in programming will be working for *her* someday." He chuckled.

Sister Agatha filled Mr. Lopez in on what she knew. "Have you seen anything that might indicate Liz was doing something illegal?"

"Sister, that kid's really turned her life around. No way I'll believe she hacked into the monastery's computers. She wouldn't jeopardize any shot she might have at that scholarship, and I don't think she has the hacking skills. Her creativity goes in a whole different direction."

"What about Joey Weaver? Is he a Wilder fan, too?" Sister Agatha asked.

"More of a Liz Leland fan, from what I've seen around school. Joey would do anything for Liz and has helped her quite a bit on her project. They hang together after school, too, I gather. Joey's skilled with computers, but a little strange—in a good way. Unfortunately, he's not really motivated, not like Liz. But there's no way I'm going to believe Liz is doing anything to bite the hand of the companies she hopes will pay her way into college. She's much too smart for that. That would blow her career before it got started," Lopez said flatly.

After thanking him, Merilee and Sister Agatha left for the parking area. "At least we know we're on the right track," Merilee said.

"But there's more to this than we're seeing. I can feel it in my bones," Sister Agatha said slowly. "Let's go talk to Liz."

20

A FTER A QUICK DRIVE ACROSS TOWN, THEY ARRIVED at the Leland home. Sister Agatha knocked on the door and Mrs. Leland answered.

"Now what, Sister Agatha?" Margot asked wearily. "Just when things were starting to look up a bit, here you are again."

After introducing Merilee, Sister Agatha added, "We'd hoped to catch Liz at home. Is she here? We'd like to talk to her for a few minutes."

"She's in her room with a friend. Is this about the scholarship she's been working on?" Her voice finally sounded upbeat, and she looked at Merilee with a hesitant smile.

"I'm not on that particular NexCen committee, Mrs. Leland," Merilee replied. "But this *is* computer related."

Margot looked worried as she called out to her daughter. "Liz, someone wants to talk to you. Get out here. Now!" she added sharply.

Hearing her tone, Sister Agatha cringed. She'd hoped to ease into the matter quietly and privately with Liz.

Almost immediately, a door opened and Liz came down a short hall into the living room. "Mo-o-o-om, I'm trying to work. What?"

"Sister Agatha is back, and she has someone with her," Margot said in a tense voice. "You haven't done anything illegal with that computer of yours, have you?"

Sister Agatha's heart went out to her. "Mrs. Leland, really, there may not be a problem at all. I'm not accusing anyone. I just need to have a few words with your daughter."

Sister Agatha caught a glimpse of a boy peering out from a doorway farther down the hall. *Could that be Joey?* He looked vaguely familiar, but before she could get a good look at him, he ducked back in.

"Then let's sort this out," Mrs. Leland said, and glancing at Pax, added, "Bring your dog in, too, if you want, Sister."

Following Margot's lead, they stepped into the living room.

"Do you know why we're here, Liz?" Sister Agatha asked gently, taking a seat on the sofa beside Merilee. "Mrs. Brown is from NexCen."

Liz beamed them a hopeful smile. "Is NexCen interested in my version of Wilder? That would be so terrific! But I'm surprised that you'd actually come over to talk to me about it. When I had some problems with NexCen a few weeks ago, nobody would even answer my e-mails!"

Sister Agatha stared at her for a moment. What she was seeing in Liz's eyes was hope, not fear. Maybe she'd made a mistake. "Let's take this one step at a time. What problem did you have with NexCen?"

"I bought a graphics card from them with money I made

from my after-school job. I really needed it to power the version of Wilder I was using as a reference to generate my own spin on the game. But the card started crashing on me. I tried *everything* to make it work right. Then I found out that I'd need an upgrade in order to continue running the game. I wrote a letter to NexCen and asked them to make good on their offer to give customers an upgraded version or their money back. At first I didn't hear anything, then I got an e-mail saying I was ineligible because I didn't have my receipt. The thing is I *really* needed that new card. It was the only way I could stay in the scholarship competition. But there was no way I could earn enough money to buy another in time to finish my program."

A slender boy with hair styled in tiny spikes that stuck out vertically peered into the living room. Mrs. Leland gave him a bored look. "Joey, Liz is busy. Maybe you can come back tomorrow?"

"Mom!" Liz looked at her mother and then gave Joey a thin smile.

"Tell them the rest, Liz. If she's from NexCen, maybe she'll fix it."

Sister Agatha looked at the boy and suddenly remembered where she'd seen him before. Joey was the boy Macho had been intimidating the day she'd talked to him and Liz at Burger Biggins. A picture was starting to come together in her mind.

"Joey, why don't you join us? You can tell us the rest of the story yourself." Sister Agatha said.

"Yeah, well, okay," he said.

He was like compressed energy, too wound up to stay still for even a second. Joey moved around even when he stood in place, and Pax watched him carefully. "Strange, but in a good way," Sister Agatha recalled Mr. Lopez saying when he'd described Joey.

"Look, Liz has talent, but she needed the attention of the right people," Joey said. "She wanted to enter her game in the contest for that NexCen scholarship, but without the proper hardware, she had no chance—I mean zero."

He looked at Merilee, then continued. "Liz had done everything right. She worked hard, saved her money, and bought the game and the NexCen video card the Wilder people recommended. But then it turned out the crummy card wasn't good enough. NexCen refused to replace the card because Liz had lost her receipt. The Wilder people refused to help her, too. They told Liz that the game wasn't defective, so they could only refund her money if the game hadn't been taken out of the package. It was a con. I mean, come on. Who finds out a game won't work right *before* they try to use it?"

"You expect life to be fair, Joey?" Mrs. Leland said with a groan. "Ask me about that sometime."

"Neither one of us could afford a lawyer, so all we could do was find a way to make noise until we got the right people's attention," he answered. "We didn't start this, but I made up my mind not to quit until I got justice."

The girl's eyes widened. "Oh, God! What did you do, Joey?"

Mrs. Leland glowered at him. "Joey, if you got Liz in trouble, I'm going to . . . I don't know, but it's going to involve your parents and the police, that's for sure."

Margot looked over at Sister Agatha. "They pulled some stunt with those computers, didn't they?" Without waiting for an answer, she glared at Liz. "You can kiss your keyboard good-bye, lady. I'm taking it all out of your room *permanently.* From now on your computer will be in the den where I can keep an eye on you. And I'm keeping that modem locked up. No Internet."

"No, Mom! You *can't!*" Liz cried out. "I'll lose the chance to get my scholarship. You didn't already blow it for me, Joey, did you?" She turned to look at him, tears welling in her eyes.

"No, no. They can't blame *you* for a thing." Joey looked directly at Merilee. "Her version of Wilder is nothing short of amazing. Liz is a *genius.* She turned the pig into this really cool babe that gets even for people who can't get justice for themselves."

"Is that what you did for Liz? Got even with NexCen?" Sister Agatha pressed him.

His eyes narrowed as he turned to look at her. "What does a nun have to do with NexCen? I mean I can guess why *she's* here," he said glancing at Merilee, "but you?"

"The computers that were hacked into are at the monastery. We process and fill NexCen's Internet and mail orders. Nuns are at the keyboards there. We work for a living, too."

"Oh, crap." His face grew pale. "NexCen outsourced its order department to the Vatican's minions?" he asked, his voice going shrill. "I'm going to hell now for sure."

Sister Agatha struggled to keep a straight face. "You're the ones who hacked into our system and left those messages signed 'Wilder,' right?" Sister Agatha pressed.

Before Joey could reply, Mrs Leland cursed, and then hastily apologized to Sister Agatha and Merilee. Without drawing a breath, she glared at her daughter. "Look at Joey very carefully now, Liz, so you'll remember who to avoid at school. You're not to talk or see Joey ever again. I'll speak to your teachers and maybe you can get transferred to another class. And don't think I'm changing my mind about *your* computer use at home."

Liz tried to speak but all she could produce were tears.

"No, Mrs. Leland, this isn't Liz's fault," Joey said, his voice strained. "I just wanted NexCen to suffer a little for what they'd done to Liz. We're kids and they took advantage of us. But I was planning to make them a deal in a day or so. For real. I'd show them how I'd hacked into their system *if* they gave me a decent video card for Liz. I figured they'd go for it just to get me out of their hair. And if things went down right, I might have even scored a part-time job there myself, too. Computer companies sometimes hire hackers in order to have somebody on their side. It's a way of improving their own security, right?" Joey looked at Merilee, who nodded.

Seeing Liz's face covered with tears, Merilee gave her a gentle smile. "I'm familiar with the hardware problem you had, Liz," Merilee said. "I can't condone what Joey did, but I can understand why you were both so upset. We had a lot of angry customers."

"I never heard about the problem—not until much later," Liz said, wiping away her tears with a tissue Sister Agatha handed her.

"So tell me, what kind of game *did* you create without the upgraded video card?" Merilee asked.

"It looks pretty stone-age on my own computer with its pitiful graphics. I knew I'd never win with that. Then Joey lent me his laptop because it has a much faster graphics card. The screen's way too small, and his sound card isn't as good as mine, but it's still an improvement."

"Show me what you've got," Merilee said. "I know someone who's working with the scholarship committee."

"Are they going to need a lawyer?" Mrs. Leland asked. "I'm starting to worry about copyright now."

"That's not a problem," Merilee answered. "Scholarship rules clearly state that the rights to any winning project belong to NexCen and the software company that created Wilder." She then smiled at Liz. "Let's go see it."

They all went into Liz's room and she started up the program. After a run-through, Merilee smiled at Liz. "The graphics need refining, but you've done a fantastic job, Liz."

Leaning back in her chair, Merilee looked at Liz then Joey. "Hacking into our Web site took a lot of skill, Joey. I don't approve of what you did, but I respect the talent it took to accomplish that. But vandalizing our warehouse . . . ," she said, shaking her head. "That's where you really screwed up."

Liz's eyes grew wide. *"What?"*

Joey stared at his shoes. "Well, NexCen wasn't paying attention. But I didn't break anything—except a padlock I cut off. And the spray paint can be removed. I used the cheap stuff."

Mrs. Leland put her hand on Liz's shoulder, then looked at Merilee. "You can throw the book at Joey, but leave Liz out of it. It wouldn't be right to drop her from the scholarship competition because of what one of her loyal—*but stupid*—friends did."

"I agree," Merilee said, looking at both kids. "I've come up with a much better option for both of you. You're both bright and imaginative, and we can always use fresh ideas. Come and work in our training department after school using our state-of-the-art hardware. But this offer's good *only* after Joey cleans up the warehouse on his own time and at his own expense. He'll also have to work with our techs to seal the back door you found into our business software. What do you say?"

Liz looked at Joey and they both nodded. "That sounds great," Liz said. "I'll help Joey clean up the warehouse, too. He may be an idiot, but he was doing it for me."

"Mrs. Leland, is this all right with you?" Merilee asked, noting her silence.

"Yeah, that sounds fine. I'll talk to Joey's parents about this and let them know what happened. And Liz, your computer's still going into the living room. I'm going to be watching everything that appears on that screen from now on."

"Mom, I have *private* e-mail. You can't read that!" Liz wailed.

"If I choose to, I will. And the rest of your grades better keep coming up."

"But . . ." Liz started, but when she saw the look on her mother's face, her voice faded.

"You both could have been in a world of trouble. Consider yourselves lucky," Margot said, then turned to Merilee. "I appreciate you giving the kids a break. They haven't got any common sense, but they're both pretty smart."

"And when they grow up, they'll be even smarter, and hopefully wiser with their choices. NexCen can always use creative people like Liz and Joey," Merilee answered.

Sister Agatha looked at the two teens. "Next time, *before* you act, say a prayer. Our Lord will show you the right way to go—but you have to *ask* first."

"You make it sound so simple," Liz said, "but prayers aren't always answered," she added, glancing at her mom.

"Yes, they are," Sister Agatha said resolutely. "It's just that sometimes God's answer isn't the one we'd hoped to get."

After having coffee with Mrs. Leland in the kitchen, Sister Agatha, Pax, and Merilee headed back to the monastery.

"You've done our company a good turn, Sister Agatha. Things worked out far better than I ever dreamed they would."

"So our contract will be renewed at the end of the trial period?"

"It's not entirely my call, but I can almost guarantee it," Merilee answered.

Merilee dropped Sister Agatha and Pax off by the parlor door, and they slipped inside as quietly as possible moments later. Neither extern was at the desk, but she found a note on the desk: Bowl of soup in kitchen by microwave. It wasn't signed, but she recognized Sister Bernarda's handwriting.

Pax hurried through the door of the enclosure and headed to the kitchen, where his kibbles would be waiting. Sister Agatha was hungry, too. She'd missed collation, their dinner.

The monastery was now in the midst of the Great Silence, so she shut and locked the door behind her as quietly as possible. In the kitchen she found the promised bowl of soup, still warm, so she didn't bother with the microwave. Pax was already there, eating, so she sat down, said Grace, and had dinner.

The stillness of the monastery encircled her protectively as she finished her eating. Today, God had blessed all of them. Their contract would be renewed and their hacker problems were now a thing of the past. Yet a very serious matter still remained before them, waiting for a resolution.

The kids hadn't been involved in the incident with the gate. The person responsible for that remained couched in shadows and out of her reach. Although she was tempted to call Tom and find out if his stakeouts had turned up anything new, she wouldn't break Silence for something that could wait until tomorrow. Instead, she'd take the advice she'd given the kids and spend some time in prayer.

As she stepped inside the chapel, the gentle glow of the votive candles by the statues of the Blessed Virgin Mary and St. Joseph soothed her. Two sisters were already there praying— Sister Bernarda and Sister Clothilde. Sister Bernarda's long vigils had received the prayerful support of all the sisters, and one or more of them were always there by her side.

Sister Agatha smiled at Sister Clothilde and bowed her head once, signaling that she'd remain. Sister Clothilde stood, then, moving as silently as only a nun could, slipped out of the chapel.

Sister Agatha knelt down and crossed herself. God's spiritual presence filled the chapel and, here, with her heart open to His whispers, she found peace.

21

THE FOLLOWING MORNING SISTER AGATHA JOINED the others for Matins, Lauds, Mass, and morning prayers, praising God and asking for his blessing on the day. Afterward, she felt strengthened, much like an athlete whose muscles needed to be properly exercised before running the course set before him.

As soon as the Great Silence ended, she reported to Reverend Mother's office and updated her on her progress. "But Angie's fate is still in question," Sister Agatha said, finishing.

"I can see that you still blame yourself. But that's a sign of pride. There is no 'you,' child. Here, there is only 'us.'"

Sister Agatha nodded. In more traditional monasteries, the words 'I' or 'you' were never to be used. There was really no such thing since, in community, that self of sense was given up and left behind.

"With your permission, Mother, I'd like to check with the

sheriff's office this morning and see if anything new has turned up concerning Terri and the fugitive, James Garza."

"All right. We'll pray that God blesses your efforts on behalf of all of us, and that things will be set right again."

Sister Agatha bowed her head respectfully, then left Reverend Mother's office and headed directly to the parlor. Once there, she called Tom. The news wasn't good.

"Last night I had round-the-clock coverage on that motel, but neither man left, and they had no visitors. This morning most of my people are out diverting traffic and keeping people away from a huge chemical spill near the interstate. It's a major health hazard. It could take hours."

"Are any deputies available to continue watching the Siesta Inn?"

"Just me. I'll be there alone. I called the state police for help, and they'll keep an officer in the area in case I need backup. But I doubt anything will happen this morning. People who are up to no good, especially escaped felons, prefer the cover of night."

"What John said about returning to Colorado was probably just an excuse to get rid of me. If they're involved with the disappearance of Terri, they'll hang around for a while longer. But you can't cover two men if they split up," she answered flatly. "You need me."

Before he could argue, she muttered a quick good-bye and hung up. By then, Sister Bernarda had come into the parlor to take the first shift. "Thanks for staying with me in chapel last night," she said.

"I needed time there, too, Your Charity. I had a few things to work out."

"We've all been praying for you, also. We know you've been trying hard to locate Terri Montoya."

"I'm grateful for the prayers," she said. "That means a lot

to me." And it did. On the outside, the words "I'll pray for you" were often used in lieu of "good luck." Here, those words were laced with the strength that came from an abiding faith that wouldn't falter.

"When this is over," Sister Agatha announced, "I'm going to take over all your shifts in parlor for a week. Then you can go to chapel in peace without worrying about being portress."

"I'm fine, Your Charity," Sister Bernarda said, taking her seat. "Duty gives us purpose."

Sister Agatha stopped by the parlor door and glanced back. "I'll be taking Pax with me today in the Antichrysler, not the Harley."

"Good idea. It looks like it might rain," Sister Bernarda said, glancing out the window.

After placing Pax in the backseat, Sister Agatha drove into town. The dog didn't seem to care which vehicle he rode in as long as he got to go along. She smiled, feeling a touch of envy. To him, life was one great adventure. Pax played, worked, and enjoyed life from moment to moment. They could all learn a thing or two from the dog.

"Good boy, Pax." The dog, hearing his name, wagged his tail enthusiastically, then stuck his massive head out the window again.

As Sister Agatha approached the Inn, she spotted Tom's unmarked unit. He'd picked a good location since, from his rear- and side-view mirrors, he could see the main parking area and the two exits.

Slowing down slightly, Sister Agatha checked out the cars. John Gutierrez had a rental van, but if she was right and he wasn't as sick as he'd made himself out to be, then it was possible that they also had another, less-conspicuous, vehicle close by for clandestine trips.

Driving down the road adjacent to the Siesta Inn, she studied the cars parked by the curb. Eventually, she spotted a dark-green sedan that had Colorado plates and a Denver Broncos sticker.

Sister Agatha telephoned Tom and filled him in. "I'm going to ask people up and down the street and see if the sedan belongs to anyone around here. If I can't find its owner, then I'm going to park close by and keep an eye on it."

"I'll run the plates and let you know what I find out as soon as possible."

Sister Agatha went to the first house, Pax at her side. The woman there recognized her, and her toddler instantly gave the big dog a hug. As usual, Pax loved the attention, and gave Sister Agatha a huge panting grin.

She was going up to the next house, trying to keep her veil from whipping around in the strong wind that preceded a storm, when a young woman came hurrying out the front door. Seeing Sister Agatha coming toward her, she stopped and gave her a harried smile.

"Hi, Sister Agatha. I'm late for work. Did you need something?"

Sister Agatha pointed to the sedan across the road. "I'm trying to find the owner of that car," she said.

"I don't know who he is, but I noticed him walking to the Siesta Inn a few days ago. I had the late shift that night, so it was around midnight. I figured he was probably just a sleaze who's having an affair with someone. He was acting sneaky—at least that's what it looked like to me. The car has been there, off and on, for several days."

"Can you give me a description of the man you saw?" Sister Agatha asked, then realized that still probably wouldn't tell her if it was Ralph or John.

"At a distance, I really couldn't see his features. He was broad shouldered and kind of tall, with dark hair."

"Was he walking fast, or slow, like he might be weak or disabled?"

"Not disabled. He walked like he was in a hurry."

"Okay, thanks. I appreciate the information."

"I've read lots about you in the papers before, Sister. Are you investigating someone again?"

"Kind of. But don't tell anyone what's going on yet. We wouldn't want to embarrass an innocent person, would we?"

"No way, Sister. People get sued for that nowadays."

As the young woman hurried off, Sister Agatha phoned Tom and filled him in.

"I just ran the plates," he answered. "The car is leased to the Three Clovers Corporation. I'm trying to check if that's one of Gutierrez's companies—or, more to the point, one of the companies established under John Gutierrez's name. The van, by the way, was rented under Simpson's name."

"It figures. Pax and I are going to stay put right here and keep an eye on the car. I'll let you know if anyone comes for it."

"Good."

Hours passed uneventfully. Since it was a windy, cool day, opening the windows was enough to keep the temperature inside the Antichrysler comfortable. Twice, Sister Agatha took Pax for a walk.

As noon came, she heard the sound of the monastery's bells ringing in the distance. No matter where she was, Our Lady of Hope Monastery was right there with her. Sister Agatha prayed the Angelus, joining her sisters in spirit.

When her cell phone rang sometime later, she picked it up quickly. "We're getting nowhere and wasting time," Tom said, his tone betraying his frustration.

"Maybe we can force John into taking action," Sister Agatha said. "I've got an idea."

After receiving the news that Three Clovers Corporation was a subsidiary of Gutierrez's corporate holdings, they set Sister Agatha's plan in motion. It was nearly four o'clock, and they were in the midst of one of New Mexico's rare but violent thunderstorms.

Sister Agatha, in position and over the rattle of raindrops atop the roof of the car, made the call from her cell phone. The static was bad, and the rain was coming down so heavy it was nearly dark around her, but somehow she managed to get a connection.

"This is Sister Agatha, Ralph," she said. "Let me speak to John. I've got some news for him."

A moment later John got on the phone. He sounded distant, but not short of breath.

"We're in the middle of packing up everything here. We'll be leaving tonight. Is there something I can do for you?" John asked.

"I just heard from Sheriff Green. A woman he believes is Angie Sanchez was found walking down a Bernalillo side street, dazed and frightened. All the deputy could get from her was a muddled story about being kidnapped. I'm on my way to see her now. If she's the woman who also goes by the name of Terri Montoya, I think she'll talk to me."

"Where's she at?" he asked quickly.

"The sheriff asked me not to disclose her location for security reasons," she said. "But I'll stay in touch."

"Let me know immediately if it's my niece," John said. "It's very important to me, but of course you know that already."

Sister Agatha called Tom back. "The bait's set. If they've got Angie, they'll have to go check and make sure she didn't escape."

"We better hope that there's no third player they can call, or that they haven't killed her already. But we've checked and they've had no visitors, so that supports our theory that either John or Ralph is Garza."

"If Angie was already dead, they wouldn't have stuck around. We just have to sit tight and be ready. At least the rain is letting up, so they can't sneak out without us spotting them."

"I have department backup on the way now, too, so if you see either man reach that sedan, tell me. A second deputy will be in position shortly, and he'll take over for you and tail our suspect if need be."

"If this is going to work at all, we shouldn't have long to wait," she said, disappointed that she wouldn't be able to take a more active part in the final part of the operation.

"Heads up!" Tom said suddenly. "One of the pair is coming out now, but I can't see his face clearly enough to ID. He's wearing jeans and a baseball cap." A few seconds passed. "He just got into the van. I'll tail him myself."

Sister Agatha remained where she was. The man Tom had seen leaving could turn out to be a decoy. Less than five minutes later, her hunch paid off. John Gutierrez came down the sidewalk wearing a jogging suit and climbed into the car.

Sister Agatha contacted Tom on the phone immediately. "He wasn't in any hurry, but Ralph's boss is certainly more mobile than he's been pretending. He just walked up and ducked into the sedan."

"My deputy's caught in traffic. Can you follow Gutierrez? Don't get too close, but don't lose him until my officer can catch up to you."

Sister Agatha smiled broadly. Alleluia! "I'm on it."

She started the Antichrysler, which backfired as soon as she let off the gas. The ear-shattering sound was quickly disguised by the roll of thunder that followed immediately. Saying a prayer of thanks, she waited, and once the sedan was halfway down the block, Sister Agatha followed.

She'd just pulled out into traffic when the Antichrysler began losing power. She pressed on the accelerator, but there was no response. The engine stuttered and appeared about to die, then, miraculously, began chugging forward.

"Thank you, Lord," she whispered. "If this was a high-speed chase, we'd be lost, but so far so good."

Tom called back just then. "Keep the line open between us."

As they moved through the waterlogged streets in a southerly direction, Sister Agatha periodically reported her position.

They soon entered a neighborhood that bordered one of the main irrigation canals. The homes became fewer in number here. Traffic was very light, and half the lots, most of them at least an acre in size, contained fields or orchards.

Forced to stay farther away because the country was more open here, she almost lost sight of Gutierrez's car when he turned a corner filled with tall tumbleweeds. Finally, when his sedan came to a stop, so did she, pulling to the side of the road by a ditch bank overgrown with sunflowers.

"He went into a house in the middle of what looks like an old cornfield, Tom. There was a fire there at one time from what I can see. There's smoke damage on the side and the windows are covered with sheets of plywood, but the front door works."

"Do not get out of the car. The deputy's ETA's less than a minute. Sit tight."

Sister Agatha placed the phone down, rolled down her window halfway to let in some fresh air and clear the traces of fog from the windshield, then turned the ignition off. But before the car wheezed its last breath, it backfired. This time there was no thunder to obscure the sound.

Less than ten seconds later, John appeared on the front porch, pistol in hand. She ducked down, then remembered Pax was beside her in the front seat. When she looked up again, Gutierrez was walking straight toward the Antichrysler.

"Oh-oh, Pax. We're leaving," she said, reaching for the ignition. As she turned the key, the Antichrysler coughed and died with a rattle and a whine.

As he drew near, Pax spotted the gun in John's hand. Responding to his training, he barked furiously, and tried to squeeze through her partially open driver's side window.

"Pax, no, stay!" she ordered, knowing he'd be no match for a firearm. She fought the ignition system, trying to will the Antichrysler to start. If John got much closer, Pax would smash through the glass and attack. But in the process, he'd certainly lose his life.

"Come on, car, start!"

John was less than twenty feet away when the Antichrysler roared to life. As John raised the pistol, Sister Agatha slammed on the accelerator, but instead of flying forward, the engine suddenly died.

Sister Agatha saw John smile. At this distance he couldn't miss and the glass would be no protection. Pax was doing his best to squeeze through the window, but in a few seconds they'd both be dead.

"Oh, Lord, help!" The plea came from the depths of her heart. She grabbed Pax, trying to pull him down out of view, and placed both their lives in God's hands.

22

You CAN SIT UP, SISTER AGATHA. I'M SURRENDERING to you. It's over for me now."

She raised her head to look. John took the pistol by the barrel with his other hand, bent down, and placed the weapon on the ground. Then he stood and raised both hands in the air. His face was pale, and she suddenly realized how just old and tired he looked—burned out.

"I almost lost you on the drive over here. If you're going to continue playing detective, you should find a more reliable car. But let me warn you about Angie Sanchez before you go inside. I'm a thief, that's true enough, but she's a liar and a killer. I had Ralph leave you a message in the Harley warning you to watch your back because of her. She's dangerous.

"Unfortunately, I've run out of time. You and the sheriff caught on too quickly—and I'm out of options now. I've had a relapse." He began coughing, and Sister Agatha saw the blood on the handkerchief he held up to his mouth. "I'll go to jail, but I'll be dead in a few months anyway, so that doesn't matter to me anymore," he said. Holding her gaze, he continued. "Sister Agatha, grant a dying man's last request and don't let Angie get away with what she's done. I tried to get a confession from her, but she's held out and I've got nothing. She'll walk away free as a bird and rich to boot, unless you can figure out how to stop her."

Sister Agatha stared at him, still uncertain what was going on.

"Don't move!"

Sister Agatha turned and saw an armed deputy standing about ten feet from John, just beyond the ditch bank.

John obeyed, and the deputy advanced, gun pointed steadily at him. "Okay, facedown on the street."

Working quickly, the female officer quickly handcuffed Gutierrez. "I'm Deputy Sims. Are you all right, Sister?" she shouted, glancing toward the Antichrysler.

Sister Agatha nodded, then managed to speak. "We're fine," she answered weakly.

"Good." Deputy Sims took her prisoner to her unit and placed him in the backseat of the white squad car, which had been parked beside the ditch. She then walked back to the Antichrysler. "Are you sure you're all right, Sister?"

Sister Agatha nodded, though she'd been trembling for several minutes now and couldn't make herself stop. John's abrupt surrender had taken her by complete surprise. "I think there's a kidnap victim in that house," she said, her voice still very shaky. She started to open the car door, but Pax pushed his way in front of her again. "Pax, stay!"

The dog obeyed but his ears remained pricked forward, his

eyes on the house. "You've seen or sensed something, haven't you?" She studied the animal, then grasped his leash firmly and opened the door all the way, sliding out first. "Heel!"

"Let me call this in," Deputy Sims said. "There might be another perp in there."

Sister Agatha, with Pax alongside her, approached the house from the side, keeping an eye out for any sign that would indicate someone was inside. Once she was close enough, she called out from behind cover, hoping her voice would carry through what she suspected was an open bathroom window. "Hello? Anyone there?"

"Yes, I'm here!" came a muted cry.

She recognized Terri's voice instantly. "Terri, it's Sister Agatha. Are you alone?"

"Yes. Jimmy Garza was here, but he left a few minutes ago. I'm handcuffed to the pipes in a bathroom."

Her voice seemed thick, but Sister Agatha was certain it was Terri. Sister Agatha hurried to the front door, then released Pax. "Search!"

Following the dog as he raced down a narrow hallway, Sister Agatha and Deputy Sims, who'd followed them in, quickly discovered Terri handcuffed to a drainpipe below the sink in a small bathroom. Her face was bruised, as were her arms, and her left eye was almost swollen shut.

Pax sat about three feet from Terri and waited for a command. Sister Agatha called him back to her so that the deputy could work to free Terri.

"Take it easy, Terri. You're going to be okay," Sister Agatha reassured as the woman began to cry.

The scene became one of orderly chaos as the paramedics arrived and Terri was freed, then taken by ambulance to the hospital.

Sister Agatha and Pax waited by the Antichrysler. The sun had come out, and the warmth felt wonderful against her face. As the minutes ticked by, she watched the steam rise from the wet fields, giving an otherworldliness to the normally dry environment.

Twenty minutes later, Tom arrived. "I spoke to Deputy Sims on the radio. Terri's weak and pretty shaken up," he said. "She hasn't had any food since the kidnapping, and the only water she had came from the sink. They destroyed her cell phone, which was why we couldn't reach her before. Terri's only contact was with the kidnappers, doing whatever they could think of to force her to talk. She says that they wanted to know where the money was and were sure she knew, though she claims she doesn't. But my gut tells me that Terri—rather Angie—knows a heck of a lot more than she ever admitted at the trial."

"And John Gutierrez? What about him?"

"Deputy Sims said he surrendered to you. Is that right?"

"He had us cold, Tom. Then he just put down his gun and gave up. He said he knew that I'd been following him."

"That heap of yours isn't exactly subtle."

"True. But here's something else. First he confessed to being a thief. Then he warned me about Terri, claiming she was the killer and that he was trying to get the evidence to prove it. He's Garza, right?"

"Yes, without a doubt. His scars are a combination of makeup and plastic surgery. But his fingers haven't been altered. The prints are a perfect match," he said, his gaze methodically taking in the crime scene. "His 'confession' may be just another attempt to con us, but it fits his behavior so far. I'm going to the hospital now to talk to Angie, but I intend on being very careful with what I tell her. Why don't you come along? One of my deputies can take Pax to the station."

Sister Agatha drove the Antichrysler to the hospital in Rio Rancho, the vehicle backfiring from time to time but moving forward at a decent pace. Once there, she waited with Tom in the ER lobby. Several long moments later a tall, thin nurse with short-cropped silver hair came down the long hallway.

"The doctor said that you can question her now."

Tom took a step, then turned to look at Sister Agatha. "I'm going to ask the doctor's permission to have you present, too. You might be a calming influence."

"Or not. Remember that she may blame me for leading John—Jimmy—to her."

"Good point. I'll see how this plays out first."

Sister Agatha watched him walk down the hall, weighing the events of the last few hours. There were still too many secrets being kept by the parties involved, and nothing was adding up right. After what had happened today, she still wasn't sure who else should be in jail.

A moment later, Tom appeared in the hall and motioned to her. She joined him inside one of the curtained partitions. Terri was lying down, her cuts now cleaned and her bruising even more pronounced under the harsh lights. An IV was hooked up to her arm, providing glucose, according to the labeled plastic bag.

"Terri, I'm so sorry this happened to you," Sister Agatha said softly.

"It was my own fault, Sister. I decided to go to the Siesta Inn and check things out on my own. When the maid was there the windows were open and, although I didn't see either man, I saw a bed filled with crossword puzzle magazines. That's when I knew. Jimmy Garza was addicted to those."

"So you decided to run?" Tom asked.

"Yeah. I wasn't about to stick around and take dumb chances. I drove back to my place, packed a couple of suitcases, and took off. But I think either Jimmy or Ralph must have seen me peeking in the window and then followed me home. I figured I was safe when I checked into the motel in Albuquerque, but again, I must have been followed. When I left my room to get something to eat, I got tasered and passed out. When I woke up, I was in that awful house."

"I'm missing something," Sister Agatha said. "If James Garza wanted revenge, why didn't he just kill you? What do you have that he wants?"

"*Nothing.* He just thinks I do—that's what kept me alive. I let him think that I knew where all that stolen money was— but I don't. I think Mark Rio took it, and since he's dead, we may never know," she said. "But don't kid yourself, Sister. Jimmy wanted revenge, too, so I doubt he would have ever killed me outright. He not only wanted the money, he wanted me to *suffer.* My testimony forced him to hide and change his entire life. He's hated me ever since the trial."

"We have both your kidnappers in custody," Tom said in a hard voice. "Ralph Simpson was heading out of town, but I was able to set up a roadblock and corner him. Simpson, who's now facing a kidnapping charge, has the most to gain by talking. We'll get the whole story soon enough. If you're holding back on me, lady, I'd advise you to reconsider before it's too late."

"I don't know how many lies they'll spin for your benefit, Sheriff, but Jimmy Garza is not only a killer, he's sick inside— a sadist. Just look at what he did to me," she said through busted, swollen lips. She started coughing and asked for a drink of water.

A nurse walked in then and shook her head at Tom and Sister Agatha. "I'm afraid I'm going to have to cut this short, Sheriff. Her room is ready and she needs to rest."

Tom remained silent as they stepped out of the curtained enclosure and walked down the hall. "She's lying to us," he said at last. "Or at least not telling us all of the story."

"I agree with you," Sister Agatha said. "There's something else that just doesn't add up. If Terri *does* know where the money is, why didn't she just take it once the heat was off?"

"It's got to be somewhere inaccessible to her. That's the only answer that makes sense."

"What does Garza have to say about all this?"

"He's insisting that Terri—Angie—is the killer, and that he was framed. He admits stealing the money, but claims that Rio was his partner and had the bulk of the cash in his possession. Garza's story is that Angie had to be the one who killed Rio. Her testimony during the trial revealed just how much she knew about what was going on. Garza says he didn't come back here for the stolen cash, only to make sure Angie was caught and made to pay for what she'd done to Rio. Turns out he really *is* rich. He bought himself a fake identity using the Gutierrez name when he relocated in Colorado. Under that name, Garza made a fortune in real estate."

"So I was right, but wrong as well. What about his illness? What's the story there?" Sister Agatha asked.

"He's in the last stages of cancer. He had a brief remission, but faked some of the more serious symptoms to get your sympathy. I checked with his doctors in Denver and they believe he'll be dead inside two months."

"Some of his story has checked out, so we'll have to see how it goes with Angie now," Sister Agatha said. "Will you be returning to the station?"

"Yeah. When you get there, why don't you stick around for a while. Unless I miss my guess, Simpson will crack soon. Then we'll see how close his story is to Garza's."

"Just put Pax in the room with him," Sister Agatha muttered. "That'll speed things up."

Tom laughed. "Why, Sister, what a positively diabolic—though admittedly satisfying—suggestion."

"I'm sorry. I shouldn't have said that," she said.

"Now you know how a cop feels . . . and how some brutality cases are born."

"It still doesn't excuse either of us," she answered with a sigh. She'd be doing penance over it later.

While Jimmy Garza and Ralph Simpson were being questioned, Sister Agatha sat alone with Pax in Tom's office. On his desk was an open file folder with Terri Montoya's name on the tab.

Sister Agatha debated the ethics of actually sneaking a peek, but then yielded to temptation. A stack of photos taken at the monastery was inside, along with a note explaining that they'd been downloaded from a disk found at Terri's home.

Spreading all of them out on the desk, she stared at the impressive array of photos taken of the monastery's garden, specifically the area adjacent to their cemetery. Although taken from many angles, they all had one thing in common—the statue of St. Francis.

Sister Agatha examined the photos for several long moments. She'd been under the impression that Terri had taken a few snapshots, but this selection looked more like a detailed survey of one portion of their grounds. Obviously there'd been a lot of photos Father Mahoney hadn't known about.

When Tom walked in thirty minutes later, he found her at his desk, still staring at the photos. He brushed off her apology and added, "I meant to tell you about those," he said. "We found the disk taped beneath a drawer. Interesting, don't you think?"

"Yeah," she said pensively, "and that just builds on a theory I've been developing. But first, did you get anything from Garza or Simpson?"

"Nothing that moves the investigation any further ahead. Garza claims to have had a small stash—his idea of small is $250,000—that he used to get his businesses going under the name of John Gutierrez—but still says that Rio had the rest of their cash. He admitted trying to force Terri to confess she'd killed Rio and reveal where she'd hidden the money."

"Come look at these," Sister Agatha said.

Sister Agatha left Tom's chair and he sat down, taking a closer look at the photos. "He may actually be telling the truth and has no idea where the money is," he said at last. "I think your theory is right on the money, Sister, if you'll excuse the wording."

"So the cash is probably hidden on our land, near or around the statue of St. Francis," Sister Agatha said. "It makes sense if you think about it, with the body being found just a few hundred yards west of the monastery. I remember that back then, we were still in the process of putting up the high wall around the monastery grounds. The chain-link fence had already been removed, and our grounds were totally unprotected. We all felt really vulnerable after hearing that there'd been a murder so close by. We didn't have Pax to watch over us during those days, either."

"So you're thinking that Angie buried the body down by the levee, then went to the monastery to hide the cash," he said.

"Exactly. It was the perfect place. The distance from the crime scene insured it wouldn't be uncovered by deputies searching the perimeter. But when Angie came back, she discovered that getting the money was going to be a lot tougher than she'd expected. We were locking up at night now, and we also had a very big dog. He'd set off an alarm for sure. But her stash was definitely safe, so she could bide her time."

Tom nodded pensively. "Then Garza, who didn't really know where Angie was, bought the winery, guessing the location of the stash was probably within walking distance of where the body was found. He may have had people keeping a watch out for her. That's what I would have done in his shoes. That would explain those people you all kept seeing in the area." Tom crossed his arms across his chest.

"Garza is the one who arranged the destruction of our gate, I'm sure of that now," Sister Agatha said. "He was hoping that our lack of funds would give me an incentive to take the job of locating Angie. And just to sweeten the deal, he even offered us a buffer zone."

He nodded. "It all fits, but if the money is on monastery property, that gives us a lot of ground to cover, even if we focus our search to the area around the statue. These photos don't narrow it down much."

"The statue was moved, too, when the wall went up, so it's not in the exact location it used to be. But a metal detector may help, providing she hid the cash in a metal box."

"I'll get a detector for you. If you do the preliminary search, it'll save me time and paperwork. But let me know immediately if you find anything. The murder weapon is still missing, too, so it may be with the cash. If you find anything, don't touch it. While you're off taking care of that, we'll work on Simpson."

"You've got it."

A half hour later, Sister Agatha was back at the monastery, sweeping the grounds around the statue of Saint Francis with the detector. She'd left Pax inside, knowing that he'd be tempted to dig in the wet earth, and his muddy paw prints would drive the sisters wild.

It was humid and the setting sun had gone behind the clouds again, but Sister Agatha ignored the penetrating cold and the ache in her hands—a constant reminder that she'd forgotten to take her pills. As the minutes ticked by, she started to shiver. The light was fading fast.

Concentrating on her duty, she never saw Sister Bernarda approach. "Your Charity, go inside and get warm," Sister Bernarda said, handing her a jacket and setting down the lantern she'd brought along. "I've used minesweepers and metal detectors before in a previous life. I've even probed the ground with a knife searching for booby traps. Just tell me what you're looking for."

Sister Agatha turned to explain, the long metal wand moving with her, when suddenly the beeping intensified. Sister Agatha froze, then moved the wand slowly toward the wooden bench, then beneath and behind it, until she pinpointed the source. It was somewhere beneath the flagstone that was now part of the walkway leading to the cemetery.

Though she tried to tell herself that it could be anything, even a lost gardening tool, Sister Agatha's heart began to hammer. "We need to remove a few flagstones and dig here."

"Okay, but let me do the digging. That's something else I learned to do well in the Corps," Sister Bernarda said.

Unwilling to call Tom prematurely, Sister Agatha worked with Sister Bernarda, first setting the stepping stones aside, then waiting as Sister Bernarda dug up the section below. Originally, the path to the cemetery had been nothing more than a dirt track with bricks lining the walk. Maybe one of those had been Terri's original marker, but the path had been altered after the wall had gone up.

Sister Bernarda worked energetically. After removing almost two feet of earth, she discovered the shredded remnants of a black plastic trash bag wrapped around a metal briefcase.

"I've got to call the sheriff, Sister Bernarda. Don't touch anything." She was now glad Sister Bernarda had brought a kerosene lantern for light. She had a feeling they'd be outside for quite a while, and the lantern would provide a little heat along with the illumination.

Sister Agatha reached the sheriff on the second ring. "Tom, we found what looks to be a metal briefcase. Should I pull it out to make sure? I could get the monastery's camera and shoot some photos first."

"Photos are okay, but don't touch anything. I'm on my way."

Sister Bernarda found their camera in the parlor, then took several shots, using a pair of gardening gloves to provide some scale in the photo. They'd also turned on the outside lights, which would help them get a better exposure than with a flash alone.

By the time they'd finished, Tom drove up. Using leather

gloves, he pulled the box out gently and set it on the ground. It was larger than they'd believed—more the size of a small suitcase. "It's locked," he said, "but I think I can force it open."

As they watched, Tom brought out an oversized pocketknife that had a screwdriver blade. He inserted the blade between the top and bottom halves and, with a twist of the handle, popped open the box. As the lid sprang back, exposing the contents, Sister Agatha gasped.

"I've never seen that much money in my life," Sister Bernarda said.

Sister Agatha stood beside Tom, leaning forward. "There's something else sandwiched in there. I can see it from this angle."

Tom followed her gaze then, using his pen, lifted a layer of cash. "It's a revolver—the missing murder weapon, no doubt."

"Not bad for a day's work," Sister Agatha said softly. "Not bad at all."

Thirty minutes later, in a dry habit, Sister Agatha sat in front of Tom's desk at the sheriff's office.

"Good news and bad," he said. "There are no prints on the briefcase or the gun. Terri's prints are on some of the bills, but that isn't damning of itself since she could have handled money at anytime in the office. Garza's are there as well, along with Mark Rio's and others that we haven't identified yet. The trash bag used to wrap the briefcase held together for quite a while, and the case was sealed tight, so the pistol is in pretty good shape—hardly any rust. One of our lab people is taking it apart to try and lift prints from the harder-to-reach areas. Afterward, they'll do a comparison between bullets fired from this weapon and the round that killed Rio."

"What if the pistol is no longer operable?"

"We can attach the barrel to the frame of another weapon of the same model and caliber. While the firing-pin mark will be different, it's really the barrel rifling that we're anxious to compare. We'll get what we need one way or another."

"Good. Has Terri been released from the hospital?"

"No, but I hear she's planning to sign herself out. I've managed to get her hospital paperwork put on the slow track, and I've also offered to have a deputy drive her home. I'll be notified when they leave the hospital."

"We can't let her slip away."

He nodded. "Simpson has backed up Garza's story one hundred percent. He admits to kidnapping Terri, but insists that it was the only hope they had of getting answers and evidence. He believes Garza's story that Terri's a killer."

"Could Simpson have been mixed up in Rio's murder, too?"

"No way. He was serving with the Army in South Korea when Rio got killed," Tom answered.

"You don't have anything you can use to hold Angie, so we'd better move fast. Fortunately," Sister Agatha said with a slow smile, "I've got an idea."

"Every time you say that, I get the urge to yell 'incoming,' and dive under my desk," he said with a grin.

"Praying offers better protection. But don't worry, my plan's really good. Call your deputy, and make sure Terri doesn't leave the hospital until I get there."

Sister Agatha drove to the hospital and, when she reached the nursing station, saw Terri signing some papers. The deputy standing nearby nodded to Sister Agatha in greeting.

"Hello, Terri," Sister Agatha said cheerfully, focusing her complete attention on the woman. "I'm so relieved that you're okay."

"Sister Agatha, I'm glad you're here. I was hoping I'd get the chance to thank you once more. If it hadn't been for you I might not have made it out alive."

"God was watching over you," she answered. "Are you going to spend a few days at home, recovering, before you go back to work?"

"I'm going home to spend the night, but after that, I'll be packing up my belongings and moving out of town. I'll sell the house. I'm never going to feel safe around here again."

"I understand completely. But, after what you've been through, you're going to need some downtime and a quiet, safe place to stay. If you don't mind a suggestion, we've set aside a room inside St. Francis' Pantry for overnight guests. Remember me telling you about that? Why don't you come and be our first guest?" Sister Agatha asked. "You'd be perfectly safe there."

"I'm not sure I want to be around anyone right now, Sister," Terri said slowly. "I need to sort things out in my own head."

Sister Agatha tried not to show surprise at her response. Maybe her theory about Terri had been wrong from the start—and Garza had lied once again. If Terri showed no interest in coming to the monastery—where she'd have access to the grounds—then they'd have to come up with a new theory to explain the presence of the money and the gun.

"Come to think of it, Sister, the pantry is well away from everyone, and your monastery is so peaceful! I've enjoyed visiting, even when it was just helping with deliveries. I can't think of a better place to go. I'll see you there in about an hour? I need to take my discharge papers by the front desk first, and then rent a car. Sheriff Green said my Toyota has to stay locked up in their impound yard for a few more days." She looked over at the deputy. "Can you take me to a car-rental place instead of my home, officer?"

As the deputy nodded, Sister Agatha smiled. "See you soon, Terri."

23

A HALF HOUR LATER EVERYTHING WAS SET UP AT THE monastery. With Sister Bernarda's and Sister de Lourdes' help, markers borrowed from the work site by the front gate had been hammered into the ground near the statue of Saint Francis as if construction work were pending there as well.

Sister Agatha wrapped a coat around herself. The clouds had dissipated, giving way to a bright full moon—and a really penetrating cold.

"What do you think of the markers. Too much?" she asked Tom, her hand resting on Pax's head.

"No, I don't think so," he answered, then checked his watch. "I better duck out of sight. I don't want her to see me hanging around. Just remember, if she's killed once, the second time will come a lot easier to her. Keep Pax with you whenever you're around Angie. I won't be far, but he'll be your first line of defense." He paused, then held her gaze. "Are you *sure* you want to do this?"

"Absolutely. And don't worry. I'll be careful."

He reached into his unit and retrieved a night-vision scope. "I'll be using a low-light camera, but you'll need this. Call me the moment you spot her outside. I'll do the same for you." He nodded to Sister Bernarda, then walked off.

Sister Agatha watched the sheriff drive away. She was determined to do all she could to put away a criminal who'd used their monastery as a shield to conceal stolen money and cover up a murder.

"Just so you know, I have no intention of leaving you alone with her," Sister Bernarda said firmly. "You have no idea how to handle yourself in a fight—I do."

Sister Agatha thought about the man who'd pulled a knife on her out on the road, and how she'd fought back. Anger had given her the strength then, but that wouldn't be the case now.

"I appreciate your offer, but we'll have to move quietly. Four footsteps are a lot noisier than two," Sister Agatha said as tactfully as possible. "And remember to act casual when Terri shows up. We don't want her to suspect what we're up to. She has to believe she's getting away with something."

"What cover story are you using for the markers?" Sister Bernarda asked.

Before Sister Agatha could answer, Terri drove through the open entrance and parked her rental car in the space closest to St. Francis's Pantry. Sister Agatha and Sister Bernarda went to greet her.

As Terri climbed out of the sedan, struggling against sore muscles, her gaze fell upon the markers ahead with their little orange flags flapping in the breeze. "You going to expand your driveway or something?"

Sister Agatha smiled blandly. "A friend of the monastery has volunteered to build a mausoleum for all our prioresses. Of course that means that our cemetery's borders will be expanded. The *banco*, the statue, and the flagstone walk will all have to be moved. They'll have to dig footings for the foundation walls. Work is supposed to begin tomorrow."

"It sounds like an ambitious plan," Terri said.

"It'll be a permanent memorial for all our abbesses," Sister Agatha answered, then glanced back at the monastery and noticed the outside lights being turned off. "Do you know about our horarium?"

"Your what?"

"I'll take that as a no," Sister Agatha answered with a smile. "We observe an old custom called the Great Silence after our last liturgical hour of prayer. Unless there's a real emergency, everyone inside the monastery will be silent until after morning prayers. That's when we'll be bringing breakfast out to you, at around eight thirty. Of course, you're welcome to attend our six-thirty Mass."

"I didn't bring an alarm clock, and I doubt I'll be up that early. I haven't slept in days."

"I'm sure you'll hear our bells. The first one rings at four thirty in the morning," Sister Bernarda said.

Terri cringed, then forced a smile. "Ooookay."

The two externs showed Terri the small guest room in the rear of the storage building. The bed was covered with a thick blue-and-yellow patchwork quilt Sister Maria Victoria had crafted. Curtains made out of yellow fabric covered the one window.

"It looks . . . homey and comfortable," Terri said as she looked around. "I expected it to be more austere, like just a cot and a crucifix."

"We wanted it to be more welcoming than that. This room is for our guests, after all," Sister Agatha said. "The other door leads to a small bathroom and shower. You'll find fresh towels there. Can you think of anything else you might need?" Sister Agatha asked.

"No, everything's perfect. Thanks."

"Then we'll see you tomorrow," Sister Agatha said.

Sister Agatha and Sister Bernarda made a show of walking back to the monastery, Pax at their side. Once they'd disappeared around the corner of the building and were out of sight of the pantry, they stopped behind the shelter of the two large cottonwoods.

Pax lay down at Sister Agatha's feet, his ears pricked forward as if he understood they were on duty. The only sound that disturbed the silence surrounding them was the nearly imperceptible click of beads as Sister Bernarda said her rosary.

Two hours passed with no signs of activity, and Sister Agatha began to wonder if they'd somehow given themselves away. She studied the grounds using the special binoculars Tom had given them, and wondered if he was growing impatient, too.

"Do you see the sheriff?" Sister Bernarda whispered.

"No, but he's out there," Sister Agatha answered, matching her soft tone. "He was going to park his unit out of sight from the road, then move in on foot. Tom was hoping to film Terri trying to dig up the loot before he arrests her."

As the temperature continued to drop, Sister Agatha wrapped her coat more tightly around herself and took the gloves out of her pockets. Sister Bernarda had slipped hers on already, but otherwise seemed oblivious to the frigid breeze as she surveyed the grounds.

"I just saw a flicker of light by the front of the pantry," Sister Bernarda said. "She must have found the flashlight."

Sister Agatha took the binoculars back from her and, focusing them, saw Terri closing the door behind herself. She took a long look at the monastery, then walked away in the direction of the flagstone walk, carrying a small shovel. Terri took special care to shield the flashlight beam with her body so it couldn't be seen from the monastery.

Sister Agatha had Tom's number preprogrammed, so all she had to do was press one number to call him. "She took the bait and is carrying a shovel."

"Hang back and give her enough slack to incriminate herself."

After an eternity, Terri looked toward the monastery again, pointed to a window, then turned and pointed to a nearby cottonwood tree.

"What's she doing?" Sister Bernarda asked.

"Getting her bearings, I think, looking for reference points that haven't moved."

Terri took two steps forward, and looked at the same places she'd studied before. Then she crouched and, with the aid of the flashlight, began studying the ground carefully around the spot where they'd found the case.

Suddenly Terri jumped to her feet, dropping the shovel at the same time, and raced away, heading for her car.

"She knows it's a trap," Sister Agatha told Tom, not bothering to lower her voice anymore.

"Let Pax go," Tom said.

"Pax, *voran, pass auf,*" she said, remembering the German commands he'd been taught. The dog immediately sprang forward.

"What'd you say?" Sister Bernarda asked quickly, jogging after the dog with her.

"Watch and you'll see," Sister Agatha replied, trying to keep up with her.

Pax caught up to Terri before she could reach the pantry, then backed her into a corner of the outside wall, barking and growling like he was about to eat her alive. When Terri swung the flashlight at him, he chomped down on it, yanking it from her grip and flipping it away like a toy. Then he lowered his head and gave an even deeper growl, inching forward. Terri froze, escape now clearly impossible.

"Better stay put," Sister Agatha yelled as she and Sister Bernarda caught up to them.

A heartbeat later Tom ran up. "It's over. This time *you're* going to prison," Tom said.

Sister Agatha waited until Tom had handcuffed her before she recalled Pax.

"What is going on? I'll sue! Your dog attacked me!" Terri said angrily. "I was going out for a walk and he just came at me!"

"Nice try, but we all saw what you were after," Tom shot back, "and I have it all on video. God bless telephoto lenses." He pointed to a lump in his jacket pocket. "There's more, too. I just got a call. Ballistics went over the gun we found buried inside that metal case—along with nearly eight hundred and fifty thousand dollars. We didn't find your prints anywhere on the box or the revolver, but you missed a spot. You forgot about the ammo. Your prints were found on three out of the six shell casings. The rifling marks on test bullets fired from this weapon match those taken from Mark Rio's body, too. This time, lady, you're going down."

When Terri turned around Sister Agatha saw the unbridled hatred mirrored in her eyes. "You have it *so* soft, Sisters," she spat out, looking from her to Sister Bernarda. "Neither one of you has the remotest idea what it's like to be truly alone. Even when you're out here you've got all of them behind you," she said, gesturing with her chin toward the candlelit chapel. "I bet the entire monastery is in there now, praying for you to come home safe. They *care* what happens to you. I've never had that in my life. My real uncle didn't give a rip about me. He kept me fed and I had a place to live, but he made it clear I was just a burden, someone he was saddled with. That's why I left."

"You'll always have God. He can't be taken from you—not ever," Sister Agatha said softly.

Terri laughed. "Easy for you to say. You live in your own universe. The monastery will never go away and it provides for all your needs. Companionship, family, it's all there in one neat little package."

As Tom led her away, Sister Bernarda stood rock still. "Though she doesn't see the whole picture, she's right, you know. Because we serve the Lord, we're part of something that's stronger and more permanent than any of us. The spirit of Our Lady of Hope Monastery beats inside our hearts. I may never know what it's like to have children, but I have a family," she said slowly, then added, "I'm exactly where He wants me to be—and where I belong."

"Let's head back inside, Sister Bernarda," Sister Agatha said, her hand on Pax. "It's time for us to go home."

The following morning, Sister Agatha took up her post as portress, giving Sister Bernarda a much deserved break from parlor duty.

At a half past eight she heard someone knock at the door.

"Deo Gratias," she said, softly thanking God according to their custom, then went to greet their visitor.

Seeing Tom, she smiled and waved him in. "I'm so glad you stopped by. I was just about to call you for an update."

The sheriff sat down in one of the parlor chairs. "A lot has been happening," he said. "Garza's murder conviction will be overturned, and he's already busy making a deal with the DA on the recent charges. My guess is that he'll end up spending the rest of his life in protective custody at a local hospice. Ralph Simpson admitted that he stole the SUV and grabbed the beer cans to make it look like it was a drunk crashing into the gate. It was like you'd guessed. Garza had wanted to make sure you'd need the money and agree to find Terri for him."

"Was Garza the one watching us from the vineyard?"

"No, that was Ralph keeping an eye out for Terri. He made sure he was spotted because it also served to heighten the monastery's concern about intruders and snoops. The idea of selling the vineyard to developers and offering you the buffer zone—again that was all part of Garza's plan to motivate you and smoke out Terri."

"Cold and logical."

"Yeah," he agreed. "Garza's told us a bit more about the original scam. When their victims started asking questions, he and Rio emptied the bank accounts and cashed out. Then Rio got cold feet and wanted to return the money."

"How did Angie play into that?" Sister Agatha asked.

"She found out about the money, killed Rio, and framed Garza for the crime. She testified against him, all the while planning to go back for the cash once Garza was in prison."

"Except Garza escaped," Sister Agatha added.

"With Garza after her, she had to get protection from the

Feds. They insisted she relocate, and that put her in Arizona, out of reach of the money. By then Garza had figured out that she'd stashed the money in the vicinity of the body, just not *too* close by—either the vineyard or the monastery."

"The rest is pretty much as we guessed, correct?"

Tom nodded. "Greed is the oldest of motives."

"Terri must have thought that fortune had smiled on her when Garza crashed through our gates. But she still had Pax to worry about. I remember how friendly she always was to him. She probably hoped he wouldn't give her away when she sneaked in to dig up the money. But after I found her and she identified Garza at the motel, fear trumped greed."

"Exactly." Tom shifted in his chair, then stood and walked to the window, staring at the workmen outside, who were applying a coat of plaster to the restored wall.

Sister Agatha remained at the desk. "We managed to get a donation for our wall, but it's a shame things got so fouled up. If John Gutierrez had been for real, we would have received another check. Heaven knows we could have used that money."

"You're going to be getting the money you need, and more," Tom turned, a smile on his face. "Didn't you know there was a reward—a finder's fee from a group of the investors Garza and Rio scammed?"

"Thank you, Lord," Sister Agatha said looking upward, then quickly glanced back at Tom. "Would it be uncharitable to ask how much?"

"Ten percent of whatever was recovered, which puts it at around eighty-five thousand dollars. That will give the monastery enough money to invest—perhaps in a vineyard?"

"Tom, that's a *great* idea. I wonder if Eric Barclay could use a partner? I know Garza owns the vineyard, but if there are no legal issues, do you think he might be willing to cut a deal? He asked me to help bring Angie to justice, and I have. I honored his last wishes."

"I can arrange for you to meet with him and his lawyers, of course. It would be difficult for anyone to prove that the money Garza stole years ago was the same money used to buy the winery, so a deal may be possible. I'd go for it if I were you."

"If you were me, you'd look awful silly in a nun's habit, Tom." She grinned.

Tom checked his watch and stood. "I've got to go now, but I'll stay in touch. Good luck."

Sister Agatha saw Tom out, then returned to her desk to answer the phone. The call was from their contractor, who was confirming that the gate would be up by tonight.

As she placed the phone down, another knock sounded at the door. Sister Agatha gave thanks to God and went to answer it.

Eric Barclay stood there, cap in hand. "I hate to bother you, Sister Agatha, but I've heard a rumor that the man who bought my property was a wanted criminal. I've been trying to catch up to the sheriff, and was told he might be here."

Sister Agatha ushered him inside. "You just missed him, but I can fill you in," she said, telling him about Jimmy Garza. "I haven't had the chance to discuss this with Reverend Mother yet, but I'm hoping we can come up with a way to save the winery. As it turns out, Jimmy Garza owes me a big favor, Eric. If things work out, it's possible we may join you as silent partners."

He grinned widely. "That's the best news I've heard so far!"

"There are still some rough spots that'll need to be smoothed over, but I'm very optimistic."

"Now I have some good news of my own. The leading

provider of altar and table wines in our area, Casa de Avila Winery, closed down a month ago. Our hope has been to take over the business they left behind. But we didn't have much of a chance—that is, until our San Miguel Rojo won a major competition. Word got around quickly, and the biggest distributor in our area wants to do business. Luz de Cielo Winery could pick up where Casa de Avila left off."

"That's wonderful!"

"May this be the beginning of a long association between Luz del Cielo and Our Lady of Hope Monastery, Sister."

As Eric left, Sister Bernarda came into the parlor. "How's everything going?" she asked.

"Our financial troubles may soon be behind us," she said and explained.

Sister Bernarda smiled broadly. "When we let go of our problems and put them in God's capable hands, wonderful things always happen!"

Sister Agatha smiled as the bells announcing Chapter rang. "Let's lock up the parlor and go join the community. It's time to share the news and give thanks for all our blessings."